RIGHT VISCOUNT

K. D. Miller

K. D. Miller
P.O. Box 14330
New Bern, NC 28561
www.kdmillerbooks.com

Book Layout ©2017 BookDesignTemplates.com
Cover art by @sennydoesarty on Instagram
Cover typography by Yall. That Graphic.

Wrong Place. Wrong Time. Right Viscount/ K. D. Miller. -- 1st ed.
ISBN 979-8-9887609-2-4

To Kayla, for always being one of my biggest cheerleaders and for being the only (mostly) sane person in the group chat most days...

And to anyone who was desperate to hear Anthony Bridgerton call you the bane of his existence and the object of all his desires – SAME. This one is for you.

"There's nowhere you can be that isn't where you're meant to be."

—THE BEATLES

Contents

Chapter 1

Eleanor Montgomery pinched the hip string of a black, silky thong between her thumb and forefinger. Elle had nothing against thongs, had gone through quite a thong phase herself just a few years ago and still rocked them on occasion. This one was cute—and expensive, based on the tag.

So, the problem wasn't that it was a thong. The problem was that this particular thong didn't belong to *her.*

And neither did the red, nearly identical one lying in the hallway a few feet away.

She could hear giggles and groans from the bedroom at the end of the hall and knew without a doubt what was going on. And still, she stood there in shock, unable to believe that this was actually happening. *This is what I get for surprising him,* she thought, almost laughing out loud at the fucking cliché of it all.

They weren't supposed to be able to see each other again for another few months, not until the wedding, but she'd decided to surprise him with a spur-of-the-moment, long-weekend trip. She had plenty of sky-miles to burn—a perk of being in a trans-continental relationship—and she'd just finished up a big commission and had a few days to relax before starting her next, so she figured why the hell not? She'd hopped on a red-eye and now here she was, bleary-eyed, in need of a shower, and exhausted.

And he's in there screwing the Thong Twins.

Elle tossed the offending garment aside and headed down the hall. She dimly registered that she should be feeling utter despair as she neared the door and heard those unmistakable sounds. Her fiancé was balls deep in someone—more than one someone—who wasn't her. She should be devastated and heartbroken. But she was just kind of...blah. Maybe that was normal. Maybe she was in some sort of shock and the hurt would come later, once she had time to process everything.

She gently nudged the door open with the toe of her shoe. She knew what she would find, at least a general idea, but still, the scene made her inhale sharply as she took it all in, her heart thundering. There he was, in bed with a redhead and a brunette. *Well, at least he likes variety.* Elle tucked a lock of her own honey blonde hair behind her ear as she stared. Brunette had her head in Ashton's crotch while his face was buried in Red's chest. It was like something straight off *The Hub* for crying out loud.

Again, she waited for the heartbreak, but it didn't come. Anger came though, swift and hot.

Elle cleared her throat loudly.

"Well, if I had known it was Threesome Thursday, I would have brought two of my own. Ya know, evened up the numbers."

Ashton reared back, tossing Red roughly to the side with a yelp, eyes wide in shock.

"Eleanor?" It took him a little longer than it should have for him to remove his cock from Brunette's mouth and leap from the bed. Elle curled her lip in disgust as he frantically searched for pants, and cast her gaze back to the women, oddly feeling no hostility towards them. It wasn't *their* fault after all. Ashton was the dirtbag in this scenario. Granted, if they knew he wasn't single and went along with it, they weren't exactly moral leaders of the world, but still—they didn't owe her a damn thing. Ashton did. They didn't move to cover themselves, clearly not modest by any stretch of the imagination, but they stared at each other, then shifted their gazes between Elle and Ashton, looks of confusion and then suspicion crossing their beautiful faces.

"He's all yours, ladies. Enjoy."

She turned and strode down the hallway towards the stairs. In that moment, she was beyond thankful that she hadn't agreed to move here yet, despite them having the conversation many times over the last few years. She'd always had reasons as to why it wasn't time yet, but she wasn't sure any of them had ever been particularly *good* reasons. Of course, she hadn't *loved* the long-distance aspect of their relationship, but it honestly hadn't bothered her all that much. At least, not nearly as much as it should have. This wasn't the first time she wondered why that might be, but just as she always did, she firmly shoved the question into a nice little box in the back of her mind to worry about later, not wanting to look at it too closely. Things with Ash were good. They were fine. They were...comfortable.

She shook herself as she reached the landing at the top of the stairs, ignoring the fact that she downgraded from *good* to *comfortable* in the span of a heartbeat.

"Norah, wait. Please, let me explain."

She whirled on Ashton, fire in her eyes, and he had the good sense to snap his mouth shut. His dark hair was tousled and his brown eyes were shining, the flecks of gold bright today. She wanted to sigh. He looked too handsome as usual, like the model he'd been for a time. Then she noticed the scratches down his chest, marring his creamy brown skin and rage flared. She wasn't even sure if the rage was because he'd cheated, or because he thought he could just sweet talk his way out of it.

"Explain? *Explain?!* What could you possibly explain about this, Ash? Did the brunette just trip and land mouth first on your cock? Or maybe the redhead fainted and you were just confused on where mouth-to-mouth should be performed? Little hint: nipples are surprisingly *not* involved."

"I...alright, you're right. I have no explanation other than that I'm a bastard." He at least had the decency to look contrite. "It didn't mean anything, it was only sex, I swear. I love you, Norah. Please believe me."

"I *hate* when you call me that," she grated. She'd told him how much she hated the nickname and yet he always used it, thinking it was cute or some little inside tease between the two of them. It wasn't. She *seriously* hated it. "And did you really just use the *it was purely physical so it's ok* line??"

"It's true," he said, coming closer. She glared but didn't retreat when he stepped up and gently cupped her face. He stared at her with those damn gorgeous eyes that had gotten him out of trouble time and time again. The eyes, and daddy's bank account, of course.

"Come on, babe. We can figure this out. It was just a stupid mistake. I just missed you so bloody much and I let the loneliness get the better of me. How could I not miss you?" He ran his fingers through her hair, brushing it back from her face and sliding one hand to her nape. She felt a small part of her crumbling. He must have seen it because he smiled, looking victorious. "There now. See, we'll fix this. It was all just a misunderstanding, yeah?"

A misunderstanding. Sure. She understood being lonely and the physical toll of that. She was by no means immune to it. *But I don't go out and bone random dudes. I read smutty books and buy a Rabbit like a normal person!*

"Everything will be better after the wedding when you're here full time. We'll extend the honeymoon, take as much time as we want to travel the world and spend every waking minute together." He smiled and gave her those puppy dog eyes. "We can reconnect. The distance has been tough on both of us."

He was right, wasn't he? They'd just been apart for too long, only seeing each other for a week or so here and there over the past two years, and the time difference didn't help anything...Maybe they *had* grown apart some and after they got married and moved in together, they'd get back to being them. Things would get better. Yes, it would all be fine.

Then a thought hit her: he hadn't once said that he was sorry for this little "misunderstanding." That would have been the first thing out of her mouth if she had done something like this. And yet, the words had never left his lips. *No. No crumbling. Fuck this.*

She pulled away from him, shoving him in the chest.

"No. I'm done. It's over."

"Elle, come on! You can't mean that. Five years just thrown away over one meaningless hook up?" If it was two people at once, does it still just count as one hook up? *Wait a second...*

She narrowed her eyes at him. "*Was* it just one, Ash? Can you honestly tell me this was the first time this has happened?"

"I..." He rubbed the back of his neck as he trailed off and that was answer enough. Ash had never been a good liar. He was a good omitter, but if he had to lie point blank about something, he could never quite pull it off. She'd always thought that was a good thing. Being bad at lying should be a good trait to have, right? Now, a part of her wished he was better at it, a very small part of her wished she could just believe him and maybe continue to live in blissful denial, to keep her comfortable existence and not rock the boat.

But thankfully the larger, smarter part shook her head with disgust.

"Goodbye, Ashton."

"Elle—"

"Ashton," the brunette said from the hallway just behind them. Ashton turned and Elle was glad to see that she'd managed to find her bra and thong. Her French accent was thick and annoyingly alluring. "What is this? Wedding? Five years? You said you were single, no?"

"Oui. *Free as a bird* you said," Red quipped, walking up beside the other woman. She crossed her arms over her extremely ample chest, giving Ashton a quelling look. Elle felt a little better knowing that neither of the women knew that Ashton wasn't single.

"Listen, I can explain all of this..." Ashton held his hands out and Elle turned and headed down the stairs while he was focused on his French girls.

Elle silently thanked the women for buying her some time. She needed a head start or she might just punch him right in his stupid perfectly perfect nose. She tore through the living room, snatching up her over-sized weekender bag and Ashton's keys on the way out.

She bolted out of the house and down the long drive, the white crushed marble crunching beneath her feet. She looked over her shoulder with a pang. She'd always loved this house, one of many that Ashton's family owned. It was supposed to have been *her* home in a matter of months, but right now she wanted to scream in frustration at its location. It was out in the countryside, truly idyllic, but the road between it and the nearest town wasn't exactly a main thoroughfare. All of this area had been huge manor houses once upon a time and most of them had been purchased by historical societies and the like over the years, so the land hadn't been subdivided off to make way for neighborhoods or strip malls like back home. The tracts of land were still ginormous which meant close-by neighbors were simply not a thing. She couldn't just run next door to see if someone might give her a lift. The driver that had dropped her off was already long gone, and she didn't have time to wait for another, so she started huffing it.

She only had the one bag, but she'd packed it for all it was worth and it already felt heavy on her shoulder. At least she had dressed comfortably for the plane in leggings, Converses, and a soft, slouchy sweatshirt—the perfect outfit for making a run for it.

"So, I got that going for me, which is nice," she muttered in her best Bill Murray impersonation.

She adjusted the strap on her shoulder and kept half walking-half jogging, the bag bumping against her hip in an annoying rhythm. She tossed Ashton's keys off into the manicured lawn—he'd find them eventually—and made it through the ornate gates at the end of the long drive. Thankfully, Ashton hadn't managed to escape his angry French girls yet.

Her engagement ring felt like a lead weight on her hand, becoming heavier with each step. *My relationship is over, just like that. Five years down the drain.* She squeezed her eyes shut and forced the thoughts away. She would deal with it all later, but for now, she just needed to get to town, get a ride back to London, and get a hotel for a few nights. Then she'd have a nice, old-fashioned breakdown. Lots of ice cream and crying and chick flicks.

Maybe even a post-break up haircut and makeover would be in order. Definitely some retail therapy. Then she'd deal with reality. Delaying it a few days wouldn't hurt anything.

"Just have to make it there," she huffed. She loathed cardio on a good day. Right now, she despised it to the depths of her soul. She neared the small-ish stone bridge ahead and groaned. "What now??" There was a line of cars backed up on either side, a four-car pile-up blocking the entire thing.

She jogged forward, hoping she could schooch past the wreckage. It looked dicey—two of the cars had broken through the stone barriers on either side of the bridge so there wasn't much wiggle room around them—but *maybe* she could manage it. If she was allowed through at all.

She caught a police officer's eye and waved.

"Any chance I can cross?" she panted when he approached. She gave him a smile and blew a blonde curl out of her eyes. She wasn't above a little harmless flirting if it got her over this bridge and further away from the lovely countryside brothel in her metaphorical rearview.

"I'm afraid not. Too dangerous, miss. It'll be a few hours before it's open again probably." He was young and cute, and blushed fiercely as he took Elle in.

Shit. She didn't have hours to wait. Elle nibbled her lip and glanced over her shoulder. No sign of Ashton yet, but she didn't want to just wait around. She turned back towards the bridge, squinting in the distance.

"The road curves back to the left up there, doesn't it? Around these trees?" She nodded to the stretch of thick forest bordering the road on the left. The officer looked a bit confused, but nodded. "So, one could potentially head that way through the woods and eventually meet up with the road again on the other side, right?" The creek that ran beneath the bridge was too wide to cross here, but surely it would narrow at some point. *And if not, I'll go swimming.*

"Yes, I suppose that's right, but..." He looked a little uneasy.

"But what?"

He rubbed the back of his neck, blushing once more. "Well, there are stories about that forest. Tales. My mum used to say there were fairies there, that they would snatch people away and they'd never be heard from again." He gave her a shy smile and hiked one shoulder, trying to seem as if he thought they were just silly stories, but she could tell that part of him believed them. She didn't blame him. Elle had always been a big believer in the unexplainable and the unknown. Superstitions, magic, legends, myths—she would even swear on anything that she'd seen the Mothman once in West Virginia. So, Elle had a healthy respect for all of that stuff.

But she also had a healthy respect for getting away from Ashton as soon as possible.

"Well, I think I'll take my chances with the fairies. I've got an uber to catch and a cheating ex to avoid," she said with a smile and a nod over her shoulder.

"Do you need help?" he asked, straightening and pulling himself up to his full height, which was only about an inch taller than Elle's five foot seven.

"No, no, I'm fine. He isn't dangerous, but *I* might be a danger to his balls if he catches up to me." She grinned at him and he chuckled a bit.

"Well, I'd say he deserves that and more for cheating on you, Miss."

Elle shot him another grin. "Thanks, Officer..." She raised her brows, waiting for him to fill in the blank.

"Charlie. Er, I mean, Slack. Officer Slack. Charlie Slack." His cheeks heated again and she found it utterly adorable. He looked like he couldn't have been more than twenty-one, maybe twenty-two. Or maybe he just looked young. Elle was always mistaken for being younger than she was too, and though she was twenty-six, she was constantly getting carded when everyone else at the table was given their drinks without a second glance.

"Well, thank you, Officer Charlie Slack. I owe you one."

She winked, hoisted her bag further up on her shoulder, and jogged through the thick grass that led to the tree line. She paused for second before stepping into the forest, trying to remember if London wildlife included snakes. She bit her lip and glanced back to the road. In the distance, she saw the familiar black Jag making its way along the winding road towards the bridge. *Shit. Guess Ash had a spare key handy.* She decided to take her chances with the nope ropes and darted between the two thick trees closest to her.

She kept to the edge of the creek, following its path deeper into the woods, trying to find a good spot to cross. She really didn't feel like having wet shoes for the rest of the afternoon on top of everything else, so she decided to give it a little longer before finally giving in and wading across. She let her mind wander as she walked, desperate to figure out how her entire life had just derailed so quickly. One minute, she was engaged to a man who was practically perfect (at least on paper), and the next, she was single and not quite sure how she felt about it. She should be more...*broken* about all of this, shouldn't she? Sure, she was pissed as hell, but she didn't feel the devastation and betrayal she should feel, the kind she saw on TV dramas or romance movies. Would it just take time before it all hit her? Or was she not feeling it because deep down, she was...relieved? No, that couldn't be right.

Sure, she'd dragged her feet on picking a date for the wedding until she finally relented and agreed to the first date Ashton's mom had thrown out as an option, but that was normal, wasn't it? To be nervous about cementing such an important, life-altering decision? And she admittedly hadn't been excited to start the actual wedding planning. In fact, she'd dreaded it and had let Ash's family handle basically every decision. But again, it was normal for planning something so monumental to be stressful. Probably. Elle sighed.

Maybe it was, maybe it wasn't. She honestly wasn't sure and she didn't have any close friends to talk to about this kind of stuff. She had plenty of friends, was very much a never met a stranger kind of person, but they were *go-to-concerts-or-brunch* friends, not *have-deep-meaningful-help-me-figure-out-my-life-conversations* friends. She cared about them, but she could admit that she was mostly a loner, and she was mostly ok with that. And no, she didn't need a psychology degree to know that her lack of close relationships stemmed from her parents' deaths and her fear of letting anyone else in only to lose them too—her therapist had already told her that more than once.

So, yes, she'd been hesitant about the wedding, stressed about its fast-approaching date, but things had been...fine. That was the problem. They were fine. Not good. Not great. Not I-can't-live-without-you-for-another-second. Just *fine.* And that was the reason she'd decided on the impromptu trip to see him. It was like she needed to prove to herself that she *was* happy with him, that she *did* love him, that things were still *right* with them.

"That backfired in the most epic of ways," she muttered to a squirrel as it chittered at her from a branch.

Elle felt as if she'd been walking for hours already, but it had only been about thirty-five minutes. She sighed, deciding walking farther and farther into the deep, dark woods was probably not a good idea, and accepting the fact that she was going for a little dip. She screamed as she slid down the steep bank, nearly losing her balance and face planting in the water, but she managed to right herself at the last second. She stepped into the water and gasped at the chill.

"Fuck, fuck, fuckity fuck," she complained through gritted teeth as she made her way across the creek that suddenly seemed more like a small river. She slipped on the rocks and the current pressed heavily against her shins, trying desperately to take her down. "Not today, Satan. Not fucking today."

She was soaked up to her knees when she finally climbed up the other side and headed back the direction she'd come, figuring going back towards the bridge, just on the other side of the creek was the best bet. She pulled out her phone—*already six missed calls and fourteen texts from Ashton*—and quickly booked a suite at the Savoy for the next few days. She sighed in contentment, already imagining ordering room service and wrapping up in the exquisitely soft robes.

Many people assumed Elle was a gold digger and with Ashton because he was obscenely rich, old money kind of rich, but what they never seemed to realize was that she had plenty of her *own* money. Elle had inherited a large fortune when her parents had passed. Montgomery Hotels was one of the largest chains in the

U.S. Her grandfather had started it, her father had joined the family business and her mother had helped him grow it to epic proportions. So, not only did she get a hefty inheritance from their estate, she owned a majority of the company when they died as well. She sold her shares to her uncle, and he was happy to carry on the family name and legacy in her stead while she quietly faded into the shadows. Her father had always told her that she had a knack for business, and she admittedly had always been good with numbers, but none of it had ever interested her. He'd always encouraged her to follow her own path, though, whatever it might be.

So, she had always had family money, but she also worked her ass off to start her own business for her digital art. She had big name authors commissioning her work almost daily, big publishing houses coming to her for character renderings and book covers, and her waitlist was almost a year out at this point.

Bottom line: Ashton's money could go suck a nut and she would be pampering herself up right in the next few days—on her *own* dime. Despite wanting to castrate him, she couldn't stop herself from scanning Ashton's texts.

Please come back... We need to talk about this... Where are you staying tonight? The Ritz? I'll meet you there in a few hours and I'll make this right... Come on, don't ignore me. I love you... What am I supposed to tell people?... What about the wedding?... What do I tell my mother?... Baby, talk to me.

"Unbelievable! Still no fucking apology!" Elle shook her head in disbelief and almost threw her phone into the nearest tree. She thought better of it at the last minute and instead shoved it back in the side pocket of her leggings and trudged on, stopping every so often to switch her bag from one shoulder to the other. She vaguely remembered a marine she'd hooked up with for a while in college talking about trench foot, and she wondered how long one might have to walk around with cold, soaked feet before they were afflicted. Probably a lot longer than she'd been hiking, but still. She was beginning to feel bone-wary and verging on dramatic.

It was then that she realized she'd been walking too long. She should definitely be out of the woods by now, shouldn't she? She glanced to her right and her stomach plummeted into her soggy Chucks: she'd somehow managed to wander away from the creek. There was no sign of it anywhere. How in the hell had that happened? She'd been lost in thought, but there was no way she wouldn't have noticed that...right?

"So not good." She pulled up her navigation app on her phone—only to find that she had no service. The app couldn't show her how to get back to the road if it couldn't even find her. Her heart began to pound but she willed herself to remain calm. "Breathe. Just breathe. It's ok." She shifted her course walking back to her right in hopes of finding the creek again.

Just as scenes from *The Blair Witch Project* started to play in her mind, she heard what she thought was a car. She nearly sagged with relief. *Almost there.*

She picked up the pace but paused before two large trees, their branches having grown together about fifteen feet up, creating a kind of natural archway. The trunks were covered in vines, dotted with small white flowers, and beneath them, a strange symbol had been carved into each one. An elegant knot of intersecting lines, and she assumed this must have something to do with the fairy stories that Officer Slack had mentioned.

"Please take me away," she muttered. "Anywhere but here." She reached out and ran her finger over one of the symbols and frowned as a surge of static settled around her, like the sizzle before lightning strikes. She cast her eyes upward. It was a bit overcast, but nothing crazy, definitely not a brewing storm. She shook it off, even as unease skittered up her spine.

"Ok, I'm done with the woods," she whispered as she stepped between the trees. The static grew stronger, pressing in uncomfortably on her from all sides. The hairs on her arms and the back of her neck stood on end. A wave of nausea crashed into her, and she alternated between hot and cold too quickly to keep track. She heard wind rushing through her ears, circling all around her, but felt nothing on her skin.

"Wh-what the hell..." she whispered through numb lips, trailing off as she fell to her knees, darkness rearing up and taking her under in an instant.

Chapter 2

Elle jolted upright, panting. Sweat beaded on her forehead and trickled down the back of her neck uncomfortably. She glanced around, trying to figure out what the hell had just happened. She was sitting on the ground, still in the fucking woods, her bag sprawled beside her.

"Did I just pass out?" *What the hell?* She might hate cardio, but she *did* do it five days a week, plus she taught pole dancing classes at her friend Shreya's studio on Tuesdays and Thursdays—and those were much more of a workout than people might think. So, she was in pretty decent shape and she hadn't even been walking that long. There was no reason she should have blacked out like that. Maybe it was just everything that had happened? It had all just hit her and she couldn't deal, so her brain took a little T.O.?

She pushed to her feet and took stock: no injuries that she could feel, that weird static feeling was gone, and her temperature felt normal.

"Ok, weird, but whatever. I just need a bed ASAP," she muttered.

She eyed the sky warily as thunder rumbled ominously overhead. Thick clouds had rolled in while she'd been passed out and were now completely blocking the sun. The woods shifted from semi-foreboding to straight up fucking creepy without the light shining down through the branches. She needed to get out of them, and she needed to do it now. Wandering around in the woods in the dark was not a good idea.

Without any other choice, Elle decided on what she hoped was the right direction and started walking. She tried not to panic, but it was seeping into her bones, a cold trickle of unease slowly working its way up her spine. She walked faster, ignoring the annoying squeak of her wet shoes. She should have found the road again by now. She'd heard a car just before she passed out, hadn't she? The road had to be close. She walked faster and cursed when the sky opened up and cold rain began to pelt her relentlessly. She began to run, desperate to get out of the rain and hating Ashton with renewed fury, letting her anger at him overshadow the fear rising inside her chest.

"That fucking bastard, this is all his fault!"

She ran as fast as she could without twisting an ankle, slipping on the slick leaves twice, landing hard on her knees once, before the end was finally in sight. Her feet and knees were throbbing, and her entire body was shuddering from cold when she finally made it through the last line of trees—and froze.

"Fuck," she breathed. There was no road. Instead, before her lay an expansive, perfectly manicured lawn that eventually led to a mansion in the distance. She must have chosen the wrong direction...but at least she was out of the woods, so it was a win.

She pulled out her phone and groaned: no service, of course. She glanced towards the house again. At least she could get out of the rain and call an Uber. She just hoped that the owners of the house were one: home, and two: not serial killers.

The lawn stretched for at least two hundred yards, and as she sprinted through the rain, she developed a newfound respect for football players. Closer to the house, a wide stone path lined with rectangular fountains and large topiaries led to a back patio with elegantly carved stone railings. She could make out the shadows of what looked to be climbing ivy sprawled along the back of the house, giving it a refined and classic look. Even in her miserable state, Elle could appreciate how gorgeous it would be when it wasn't in the middle of a freezing downpour.

She hastened around the side of the house and up the wide front steps. She saw no cars in the long, circular drive, but hoped someone was home. A house this big and fancy, they probably drove luxury cars that were kept in heated garages.

The house looked dark, but Elle knocked on the ornate front door, thankful for the reprieve from the pounding rain as she stood under the portico. Her teeth chattered so hard she thought she might bite clear through her tongue, her sodden clothes so heavy they felt as if they weighed a ton. There was something...off, but she couldn't figure out what. She told herself that it was just everything that had happened that day all coming to a head. Of course she felt like something wasn't right: her entire life had been turned upside down and she'd been walking through the woods for hours soaking wet. Even as she rationalized it, the feeling intensified.

Elle knocked again, but the knocking quickly transformed into panicked banging.

"Hello!? Hello is anyone home? I'm sorry to assault your door here, but I'm a bit lost and need some help. Hello?" She stepped back out into the rain, squinting at the windows along the second and third floors. Elle saw muted light from several windows, but no other signs of life. She ducked back out of the rain and pounded again. "Hello! Please open up! Please! I promise I'm not crazy I just...I just...I need help," she finished, nearly sobbing and leaning her forehead against the cold wood. It had been the longest day in the history of days, and a shitty one to boot. She was exhausted. She was freezing. She was very close to having a complete mental breakdown.

It was hard to tell over the rain, but she was pretty sure she finally heard someone inside. Her eyes flew open and she stepped hastily back from the door. Elle wasn't in the states anymore, but she kept her hands where whoever came to the door could see them easily, just to be safe. Unwanted banging on doors by strangers back home wasn't always greeted with open arms. Sometimes it was greeted with the barrel of a shotgun, especially out in the country.

The door opened and a young woman peeked out, nineteen or twenty maybe. She had glossy black hair pulled back into a tight bun and beautiful brown doe eyes.

"Can I help you, miss?" she asked, polite, but apprehensive. Elle didn't blame her. She wouldn't be too keen on a crazy person banging on her door, either.

"I'm so sorry, but I got turned around out in the woods, and then caught in this downpour, and I don't have any service. I just need to call an Uber." The girl looked at her like she had two heads. "*Please,*" Elle begged, wondering if she sounded as pathetic as she felt. The girl pursed her lips but finally nodded, stepping back and opening the door wide.

"You best come inside. You'll catch your death out there."

"Thank you," Elle breathed as she hurried inside. She was escorted through a large foyer and down a wide hallway, and she was struck by how beautiful but...old fashioned everything was. And by old fashioned, she meant *old* fashioned. Like period-piece-Mr.-Darcy-should-be-asking-for-my-hand-soon kind of old.

"Is this like a museum or something?" Elle asked as the girl led her into a formal living room with a roaring fire going in the large stone hearth. Elle quickly rushed towards it, dropping her bag to the floor with a wet *thud.* She held her hands out to the flames, nearly moaning at the pleasure-pain sensation as the heat chased away the chill.

"A museum, miss?" the girl asked, confused. Elle turned to look at the girl over her shoulder. Her clothes were...strange. That unease flared again and Elle swallowed hard.

"Or maybe one of those like live action role playing type places?" She looked around the room and didn't see *any* hints of the modern age. No TV, no phone chargers, not even a floor lamp. The light in the room came from the fire, candles, and lamps—but the kind with flames dancing inside them, not glowing light-bulbs. Even the thick curtains over the windows were clearly an-tique, not mass produced in a factory somewhere.

This definitely had to be a Colonial Williamsburg type place where everything was as it was back then, no hints of the modern world anywhere, and everyone played the part like it was real.

"I, um...better go get Lady MacTavish. Wait here." The girl handed Elle a blanket, eyeing her warily before hastening out of the room. *Lady MacTavish?*

Elle pulled out her phone again and wiped the screen with the blanket. She was glad she had the Lifeproof case. Her bag was made of water-resistant material too. She'd been caught in a tor-rential downpour once a few years ago waiting for a cab in New York. After being stuck with soaking wet clothes and having her laptop ruined, she'd gone waterproof all the way.

Still no bars, but forty-seven texts and twenty-two missed calls from Ashton. Elle rolled her eyes. *Deal with it later.*

After a few more minutes, the door flew open and a woman stared at Elle from the threshold in utter disbelief. Elle studied her back and she too was in the strange clothing: a simple but beautiful empire waist dress made of deep blue silk. The woman's chestnut brown curls were piled high on top of her head and she looked to be in her early thirties maybe.

"It's true," the woman whispered.

"What's true?" Elle asked, confused. Instead of answering, the woman turned to the younger girl.

"Lottie, bring some food and wine. And more blankets. Quickly." The girl inclined her head and set off.

Turning back to Elle, the woman said, "I'm Jocelyn Mac-Tavish. This is my home." She eased forward, holding her hands out in front of her, and speaking in soft, soothing tones. It reminded Elle of how you might approach a trapped animal to avoid being attacked. *Wrong, wrong, wrong,* Elle's instincts warned. "What's your name?"

"Elle. I'm Elle. Look, I...I just need to borrow your phone. Mine's not working and I just need to get to town and catch a ride back to London. I'll get out of your hair as soon as I can make that call, I promise."

Jocelyn's lips parted on a quick inhale. "A *call,*" she whispered to herself, her lips curling upwards into an almost wistful smile. She shook herself, her smile fading. "Why don't you sit?"

"I'm good, I just...I just need a phone. Please." Elle didn't know what was going on, if this woman meant to hurt her or hold her hostage, but a cold pit formed in her stomach, icy tendrils of unease spreading through every inch of her. Something was very,

very wrong. "Or I can just go, actually. I'll just leave and walk the rest of the way to town, no big deal, really. The rain is starting to let up, I think." Elle made to move towards the door, but Jocelyn stepped in her path.

"I'm afraid I can't let you make a call or leave, dear."

What the hell?? Elle backtracked and lunged for the fire poker near the hearth, her fight-or-flight response settling firmly on *fight*. She brandished it in front of her like a sword. She'd taken self-defense classes at the local college about a year ago and felt confident she could take Jocelyn down if she needed to.

"Look lady, I don't know what you're trying to do, but I'm leaving. *Now.* I've had a shit day and I refuse to let being kidnapped be the cherry on the top of this fucked up sundae. So back the hell off!" The poker shook wildly in her hands, but she kept it raised in front of her, letting Jocelyn know that the threat was real.

Jocelyn held up her hands. "I'm not going to hurt you, I promise. I'm trying to help you. There's a reason I can't let you make a call or walk to town. If you'll just sit down—"

"I don't want to sit!" Elle screeched. "I want to know what the fuck is going on!" Jocelyn pressed her lips into a hard line, a pitying look in her eyes. It was the look that people had when they're about to deliver bad news. *Like the look a police officer has standing on your doorstep, about to tell you that your parents were killed by a drunk driver.* Her heart beat wildly in her chest and she waited for the shoe to drop. There was more to this than her walking the wrong direction in the woods. She knew it, but her mind couldn't come up with any plausible answers, so she just stared at Jocelyn, gripping the poker like a lifeline, her entire body starting to tremble.

"Alright, just calm down. First and foremost, I need you to know that you're safe. Everything will be alright, I promise you. It's hard to explain, even harder to believe..." Jocelyn took a deep breath. "But..."

"But what?" Elle demanded through clenched teeth.

"What year do you think it is?" Jocelyn asked, surprising her. Elle's brows drew down.

"Huh? What do you mean? It's 2020." *Is this woman alright in the head??*

"2020," Jocelyn breathed in...awe? She swallowed hard and then said in a soft voice, "This is going to sound crazy and there's no easy way to say it, but...you've come back through time. You're in the year 1813."

Elle stared for a long moment and then burst out laughing. Jocelyn obviously had a few screws loose. More than a few. A whole fucking hardware store's worth. She continued to laugh, harder and harder, bending over and clutching her stomach. Tears sprung to her eyes, but the laughter began to turn a bit hysterical as her instincts tried to tell her that maybe Jocelyn *wasn't* actually crazy. *The old house, the lack of cars or lights or electronics, the strange clothes...*Elle's laughter faded as, against all odds, reality sank in. She met Jocelyn's gaze.

"Well...that sucks." Elle giggled once more before her knees buckled.

She blacked out before she hit the floor.

Chapter 3

Elle slowly came to in a soft, warm bed. She stretched and flopped over, burying herself deep into the pillows. She inhaled deeply, the sheets smelling pleasantly of lavender. *The Savoy?* Had she made it there? She couldn't remember getting a car, or the drive back to the city, or checking in, couldn't remember making her way out of the—

She jolted upright as the memories came flooding back: running through the woods, the strange house and stranger occupants...

"And being told I...time traveled?" She pressed the heels of her hands into her eyes, rubbing hard until she saw stars. "This can't be real. This cannot be fucking real."

"I'm afraid it is."

Elle gasped and snapped her eyes to the doorway. The woman from the night before—Jocelyn—quietly closed the door behind her.

"No. No, you're crazy. This is insanity," Elle said, throwing her legs over the side of the bed. She frowned when she realized she'd been dressed in a plain, white nightgown that reached her ankles. *Am I six years old?* While this would give further credence to the fact that she was, in fact, in a different time, she refused to accept it. *No, this woman is just some psycho who has a weird fixation with Jane Austen. That's all.* She leapt off the bed and began searching the room for her clothes, keeping Jocelyn in her sights from the corner of her eye.

"I know it sounds that way."

"Where are my clothes?" Elle demanded.

"Believe me, I couldn't accept it at first either," Jocelyn said loud enough to force Elle to listen. Elle froze as the words sank in, and straightened from searching under the bed for her clothes or bag. She turned to face the woman.

"What, *exactly,* does that mean?" she asked slowly.

"It means," Jocelyn exhaled roughly, "that I'm the same as you. I'm not from...*here.*" Jocelyn eased forward towards the small fireplace on the other side of the room, slowly again, as if Elle were a wolf snared in a trap, as if she expected an attack at any moment. The room was large, with a big four-poster bed, a desk, a standing wardrobe, a small table with a basin of what Elle would assume was water, and a nice sitting area in front of the fire. Elle studied the room, the furnishings, and was again struck by how not-of-this-century everything was. *No, no, no. This cannot be real. NO.*

Elle eyed Jocelyn warily. Jocelyn sat in one of the chairs before the fire and gestured for Elle to take the other. Her entire body was tense, her heart thundering, but she crossed the space and slowly lowered herself into the second chair. She needed more information, or at the very least, to figure out if this woman was *put-the-lotion-on-the-skin* kind of crazy or just harmlessly eccentric. So, she squared her shoulders and took a deep breath.

"Let's pretend for five seconds that I believe you...Explain exactly what the hell is going on."

Just then, there was a soft knock on the door and the young woman from last night entered with a tray of what looked like tea.

The British version of course, not the sweet, iced version that Elle would kill for right about then. She sat the tray down and turned to Jocelyn.

"Anything else, mam?"

"No, that'll be all. Thank you, Lottie." Lottie inclined her head, gave Elle a brief, quizzical look, and left the room. After the door closed, Jocelyn filled their cups. "Tea?" she asked with a gentle smile.

Elle figured why the hell not and took a cup. She took a sip and scrunched her nose. It wasn't bad, exactly, but it wasn't her, well, cup of tea.

Jocelyn smiled. "You're American, aren't you?"

"What gave me away? The accent or the lack of love for British tea?"

Jocelyn chuckled. "Bit of both. I lived in Oklahoma until I was sixteen. Then moved to England when my mother got remarried." She took a sip of her own tea and then let out a long breath. "Believe me when I say that I understand how ridiculous this all sounds. It took me weeks to even begin to accept it. I can't explain it all, save the very unsatisfying answer of *magic* or *fate*, but I assure you that it's all true."

"How...how did you come to be here then?"

"The same way as you, I would imagine. You were in the woods, weren't you?" Elle nodded, her pulse jumping. "And suddenly it felt like energy pressing in on you from all sides, and you got too hot and too cold at once and felt like you might vomit?" Elle sat her tea back down, the cup clanging loudly on the saucer, her palms sweating. There was no way Jocelyn could know exactly how Elle had felt unless...

Elle licked her lips, her mouth feeling dry as sandpaper.

Unless it was...true.

"But how...?" Elle stopped herself from finishing the question, knowing Jocelyn didn't have the answer. She shook her head, trying to keep her breathing even. *Open mind, open mind, open mind,* she chanted to herself. She believed in aliens and ghosts and Nessie—time travel wasn't completely outside the realm of possibilities...but shit, this was harder to swallow than the idea of Big Foot running around or vampires existing.

"Why were you in the woods alone?" Jocelyn asked gently.

Elle blew out a long breath. "Bastard cheating fiancé and a traffic jam blocking the road to escape. I thought I could cut through the trees to the road on the other side. Apparently, I was very much mistaken." Jocelyn gave her a sympathetic smile.

"I'm sorry to hear about your fiancé."

Elle shrugged. She was still feeling weirdly fine about it. Still pissed, but not broken. *And that's probably a huge red flag.* Not wanting to talk about Ashton, Elle asked, "What about you? Why were you in the woods?"

Jocelyn's expression turned bleak for a moment, as if the memory wasn't a good one, and Elle tensed.

"I was running too," she said, her voice quiet but strong. She absently ran her fingers over a faint scar at her throat and Elle's stomach clenched. *Had someone cut her there?* "I was eighteen. I managed to get away and the only place to run was those woods. I ran and ran until that strange feeling settled over me. When I came to, it was storming like mad, the rain coming down so hard I could barely see and the lightning striking so close I could smell the burnt air. I screamed when a tree limb came down not ten feet from me. And he heard it."

"He?"

Jocelyn's face lit up as she smiled. "My husband, Callum. One of his stallions had broken free from their stable, and he was out rounding him up, despite the storm. He heard my screams over the din somehow, and came riding in to rescue me. It was like a romance novel, I swear, the kind with Fabio on the cover that I used to hide from my mother. Do they still make those?" she asked with a smile, scrunching her nose a bit.

Despite everything, Elle huffed out a laugh, thinking of her own collection of books with shirtless men on the covers. "Oh, you have *no* idea."

"Anyway, Callum saved me, in so many ways. He helped me come to terms with what had happened."

"You told him the truth?" Elle asked, shocked. "He...didn't think you were a witch or something? Try to burn you at the stake or shove you in an asylum?"

Jocelyn smiled. "Callum's family has always had a healthy appreciation for folklore and superstition. This was his mother's ancestral home and there had long been stories associated with those woods. Stories of people *appearing out of thin air.* I was hesitant to tell him the truth at first, but I couldn't stop myself. I fell in love with him the second I saw him, as ridiculous as that sounds, so I had to tell him. It took me a little while, but eventually I told him everything, and by some miracle, he believed me. He helped me hide the truth, construct believable lies about my past and adjust to this life."

Elle tried to imagine showing up in the past with no one to help her, trying to navigate everything without Jocelyn here explaining things. She could handle almost anything, but that? She wasn't so sure.

"How long have you been here?"

"Almost twenty years."

"And," Elle couldn't believe she was about to ask this, "*when* did you come from? Do the years work the same here as they do there—er, *then*?" Her head hurt trying to figure out what she was trying to say and she rubbed her temples. "I mean, if 20 years pass here, did 20 years pass there? Or then?"

"Based on you coming from 2020, I believe so. I left in 2000, so that seems to track."

Elle nodded slowly and let out a long exhale.

"I know it's a lot to take in and I'm sure you'll need time to deal with it all, but we're here to help you. It's why I insisted we remain in this house, so we could be here should anyone else ever come through like I did."

"Have there been others? Before me?"

Jocelyn nodded. "Two. A young man, not long after I arrived, and an older woman just a few years back."

"And what happened to them?" *Did they believe you? How long did it take them? Did they go crazy?*

"The young man, Renaldo, he's a ship captain now. He adjusted exceptionally well—this life was much better than his other one. He thought it was a gift from God, a new start."

"And the woman?"

She gazed away, shaking her head. "She was injured when she came through. She'd gotten lost in the woods and taken a bad fall. Some kind of internal bleeding, I think. There was nothing we could have done, not in this time. Probably not even then, either." Elle felt a pang for the woman. She couldn't imagine being scared and hurt and alone, wandering in those woods and then suddenly finding herself back in time. Not that she fully believed any of this yet, that she had actually traveled back in time, but...

"We made her as comfortable as we could. She said she didn't have any family back home, that she'd always been afraid of dying alone, so at the very least we made sure that didn't happen." Jocelyn gave her a sad smile and Elle knew immediately that Jocelyn was one of those rare, actually *good* people.

Elle rubbed her neck, trying to wade through everything, balking at the thought of having to figure out life in another time...She froze. *Wait.*

"Why did you stay here? Why did this Renaldo guy? I know you found your husband and this life was apparently better than Renaldo's other one, but still..." At Jocelyn's look, Elle's blood went cold. *No. Don't say what you're about to say.*

"I'm afraid it's a one way ticket."

Chapter 4

Elle rose from her chair and began to pace, her blood rushing loudly in her ears.

"No. No, I can't believe that. If there was a way here...which I'm not a thousand percent saying there is because this could still be all some kind of weird dream or hallucination or something...but if there was a way here, there has to be a way back."

"We've scoured those woods. We've gone back to the twisted trees time and time again and found nothing. Whatever magic is there in the future, it's simply...gone here."

"Twisted trees?" Elle asked, jerking her head up and stopping her pacing for a moment.

Jocelyn nodded. "When I was brought back, I felt a wave of energy just before I stepped between two trees that had grown and twisted together, like a doorway. Some ancient people carved symbols into the trunks. We think it has something to do with the magic that brings people back, but we can't find much written in the histories—well, anything accurate, anyway. There are plenty of stories, but they are full of tales of fairies and bargains and cautioning children not to disobey their parents or leave their beds at night."

Elle remembered the trees now, trailing her fingers over the symbols and muttering—*oh fuck.*

Please take me away. Anywhere but here.

That's what she'd said, right? *Jesus, it had been a joke! Not a fucking request!* She pinched her forehead, a fierce pounding behind her temples and her chest feeling tight. She rubbed at the knot there, the one making it impossible for her to breathe.

"I...I just...I need a minute."

"Of course, dear. Take as much time as you need, but just remember that you're not in this alone." Elle gave her a jerky nod, barely even hearing her, and Jocelyn quietly left the room. She stood motionless for endless moments, her heart pounding and her pulse racing.

"Breathe, breathe, breathe," she whispered to herself. She had to breathe. She had to think. She couldn't have a breakdown, not right now. Eventually she calmed herself enough to start searching the room. Elle explored every last inch of it, looking for any sign that Jocelyn was nuts, that this was all some strange set up. Wires, outlets, hell, even hidden cameras—there had to be *something*.

She found nothing.

She ran to the window, looking for cars, lawnmowers, cell towers in the distance. Nothing. She stared at the sky for what felt like hours, just waiting for a plane to fly overhead and, again, nothing. Despite all odds, despite part of her mind screaming that this was utter insanity, the evidence all pointed to the fact that this was...real.

She finally sighed, admitting defeat. She had gone full Marty McFly and was truly in the past.

"Except Marty had at least gone to a time when electricity and indoor plumbing were still a thing," she muttered as she climbed back into bed and pulled the covers high over her head. She eventually fell into a deep sleep as the tears began to fall.

It was a full three days later that Elle finally accepted her fate—to an extent. She accepted that she had indeed somehow traveled to the past, but she refused to believe that there was no way back again. She would explore every inch of that forest herself before she gave up hope, but in the meantime, she decided that she couldn't just sit around in bed. She decided to try and have a positive outlook—it was how she approached everything else in her life, so why not this? How many people got to see Regency England with their own eyes? She was going to look at this as the coolest, most epic vacation of all time.

Or try to, anyway. She'd always had the *adapt and overcome* mentality about most things in her life. Things happened, she took a minute to digest them, then rage or cry or whatever the situation called for, but then she figured out how to deal with it. This was far beyond anything she'd ever been faced with before, but she was going to do her level best to stick with the plan. She'd had her minute to digest, this situation called for both raging and crying and she'd done a lot of both, and now it was time to deal with it.

Right on time, Lottie knocked lightly on the door before entering with a tray of food and tea.

"Oh!" she gasped to find Elle out of bed and waiting for her. The items on the tray slid and nearly toppled off the edge. "You scared me, Miss Montgomery."

"I'm sorry! Here, let me help." Elle rushed forward to take the tray and set it on the table, leaving Lottie looking a little flustered. "I'm sorry, I've been a little, uh, tired for the last few days," she hedged. Elle knew that Jocelyn's husband knew the truth and wouldn't be phased by Elle's predicament, but she wasn't sure if anyone else in the house did.

"You've had quite a journey, I understand. It is quite understandable that you would need to rest."

"Journey?"

"From America. Your aunt said you'd been traveling for weeks on end." *Aunt.* Well, she supposed that was as good a cover as any. "I can't imagine being on a ship out on the seas for such a long time." She shuddered, her fair skin turning a bit green at the thought.

"Oh, yes. Long journey indeed." *About four thousand miles...and two hundred years.* "Um, could you help me draw a bath by chance?"

"Of course, Miss Montgomery." Elle devoured the food, ravenous after not eating anything for days, as several other maids filled the tub with steaming water. Elle felt a twinge of guilt for their hard work on her behalf, but knew that it was just how things were done here and she'd have to deal with it. "I'll fetch you some clothes as well. Lady MacTavish said that all of your things were lost on the voyage." She'd ask Jocelyn about that later, but for now, Elle just nodded.

"Thank you. Will you ask my aunt if she can meet with me once I've finished my bath?"

"Yes, of course. I'll be back to help you dress."

"Oh," Elle said, blinking. "Um, that's alright, I think I can manage." Hopefully. Was this time period big on corsets? Elle was admittedly not a history buff by any means and her only real knowledge of this era came from movies like *Pride and Prejudice.* Elle frowned inwardly as she realized that she wasn't even sure if that was the correct time period, wishing desperately that she'd paid more attention or been more of a fan of classic literature. Lottie let it go, promising to wait for Elle outside whenever she was ready to be escorted to the drawing room.

The bath was quite possibly the most amazing one Elle had ever taken. It wasn't particularly special or glamorous in the strictest sense of the word—just a simple copper tub, no fancy bath oils or bubbles—but it soothed and warmed her to her soul, and the soap smelled like roses. As she soaked, she tried to wrap her mind around time travel and recall everything she knew about it, which admittedly wasn't much and mostly came from eighties movies. *Probably not great.*

She had heard of wormholes and tachyons, but didn't know (or understand) nearly enough about those to be at all helpful. Would her remaining here tear a hole in the space-time continuum and destroy the world somehow? Or had she created an entirely new, alternate timeline now, the other one still existing as-is? If she stepped on a butterfly, would it lead to the apocalypse?

"Ugh, my brain hurts," she whined, throwing her hands over her face. Since there was really nothing she could do about being here and about her path forward, she decided there was no use worrying about it. If the future was altered, then it was altered. If she ended up destroying the universe, well...oops. *My bad.* Not like she did it on purpose.

Once she decided not to worry about that part of this exceedingly complex problem, she felt a tiny bit better. She soaked until the water grew chilly, finally reluctantly dragging herself out. She dressed quickly in a sky-blue gown of soft silk. A corset-type garment was left too, and though it thankfully didn't fit with what Elle had always understood a corset to be (corsets in her mind were synonymous to Elizabeth Swann getting squeezed into one and fainting in *Pirates of the Caribbean*), she instead donned her own black push-up bra again. The dress was a bit tight in the chest, but other than that, fit great. Though she longed for her Chucks, Elle put on the soft slippers that had been left for her and headed out into the hallway where, as promised, Lottie was waiting to guide her through the mansion. *Manor? Castle?*

The drawing room was large and boasted two separate seating areas, a beautiful piano and harp at one end, and an ornate fireplace at the other. Jocelyn stood when Elle entered, giving her a cautiously bright smile.

"I'm feeling much better, *Aunt* Jocelyn," Elle said with an arch of her brow and a small curl of her own lips.

"Well, I thought you being our niece was a bit more plausible than you being a random stranger we found wandering the woods," she replied with a smirk. "We've told the staff that you're my estranged sister's daughter, come to live with us from America."

"A good a cover story as any, I guess. And it at least explains the accent—it would be a disaster if I was expected to put on a British one at all times."

Jocelyn laughed. "I was lucky in that regard, having lived in England long enough before I...made the trip, that I was already picking up bits of it here and there anyway." They sat down on one of the sofas. "How are you doing?" Jocelyn asked.

"I'm...alright. I've decided to just go with the flow."

"Go with the flow? Just that easy. Seriously?"

Elle shrugged. "There's not much I can do about the situation. Being angry or upset about it won't help, so I might as well just soak in the experience, right?"

"You're handling it much better than I did, that's for sure." Jocelyn shook her head with a laugh. "So, I'm sure you have more questions now that you've had a bit of time to digest things."

"Only about a thousand," Elle said with a laugh. "I don't really know much about this time, so I guess I'll need a bit of a crash course so I don't say or do the wrong thing."

"We're happy tae assist with that, lass," a rumbling Scottish brogue sounded from the doorway. Elle's eyes flew wide as she took in who must be Callum. He was just over six feet tall with broad shoulders and laugh lines fanning out from his sky-blue eyes. His deep red hair was a bit on the longer side, his jaw square with a scar running across the length of it, and he had an intense, rugged handsomeness about him, though he held himself like a nobleman. He looked like he would fit in just fine entertaining royalty or roaming the highlands in a kilt.

Elle leaned towards Jocelyn and muttered, "And where can I pick up my Hot Scot Welcome Package, please?"

Jocelyn snorted into her tea as Callum came closer. He leaned down to kiss her on the forehead before nodding to Elle and taking a seat across from them.

"I'm Callum MacTavish."

"Eleanor. Elle," she amended, finding that it was nearly impossible not to smile at him.

"So, Jocy tells me that you are...no' from *here*," he said with a pointed look.

"Not even close," she said with a laugh.

"I cannae imagine what that must be like, but know that we are here tae help you, however you may need."

"Thank you, I...I don't know what I would do if I were trying to deal with all of this alone." Jocelyn reached over and placed a hand on Elle's forearm, giving her a reassuring squeeze.

"Well, the good news is that we're fairly isolated out here. There's one estate that borders ours, but Lord Kentworth rarely ventures out these days. Other than that, there's no one, so you won't have to worry about getting all the ins and outs of society correct very often, at least not right away," Jocelyn said, Callum nodding in agreement.

"Oh, that's a relief then."

"You are welcome tae stay here as long as you'd like. We've told everyone that you are Jocy's niece and our home is your home for as long as you want it tae be." Elle nodded, a knot in her throat at their kindness.

They talked for hours more, Elle telling them a bit about her life and what the world looked like in 2020, and Callum and Jocelyn trying to explain this new—or old?—world to her.

"Do you think I'm a missing person?" Elle asked later that afternoon. "That they're combing the woods for me now? Or for my body?" She thought about Officer Slack, about her telling him how she needed to get away from Ashton. If Ashton did report her missing, surely Officer Slack would learn of it and tell everyone how she'd been trying to get away from him. "God, I bet Ashton is suspect number one in my probable murder." Elle rubbed her head. Sure, she was mad at him and things were most definitely over between them, even without the time-traveling factor, but she didn't want his life ruined. She sighed heavily. Not much she could do about it now. She took solace in the fact that his family had really great lawyers on retainer, so if Ash *were* somehow arrested in connection with her disappearance, he wouldn't stay that way for long.

Elle tried her best to update Jocelyn on everything she'd missed in the last nearly two decades, but she'd barely touched the surface of the status of boy bands when a soft knock drew their attention to the door. After a moment, a young girl entered. She was tall and lithe, with the same deep red hair as Callum and greenish-gold eyes. A small smattering of freckles covered her nose and she was graceful as she moved, like a dancer. She was absolutely stunning.

"Come in, dear, come in. I'd like you to meet your...uh, cousin, Eleanor—Elle. Elle, this is our daughter, Rose." Elle quirked a brow in Jocelyn's direction. Rose wasn't a popular name choice in this day and age, was it? Jocy muttered under her breath, "I was very, *very* into Titanic, alright?" Elle stifled a giggle and looked back at Rose.

Rose inclined her head and Elle gave her a smile and a wave in return.

"It is so nice to meet you, cousin." Her accent was British, but with a hint of her father's brogue, though not as thick.

"You too. You are *gorgeous*, by the way. My God, I would kill for your hair." As Elle studied it, she found that there were subtle streaks of gold woven into the red, most likely from days spent in the sun. Her skin was more tanned, like Callum's—despite Cullen-level pasty being all the rage apparently—and Elle imagined the two of them riding the countryside together. *Like I used to do with my dad.*

Rose blushed but smiled shyly, absently running a hand over the locks. Was she self-conscious of her hair? People paid good money to have their hair look like that back home. Elle herself had shelled out a pretty penny to give red a try for a few months sophomore year of college, but she couldn't pull it off like Rose.

Rose looked to be about sixteen, maybe seventeen, so she'd been born not too long after Jocy's time traveling adventure.

It seemed to Elle that Jocelyn's life had fallen perfectly into place when she got sucked back to this time—meeting the love of her life, having a child, living in this beautiful home. Elle didn't see herself being so lucky.

The next couple of weeks flew by as Elle tried to adjust to her new life. She still hadn't accepted that it was going to be her life *forever*, but she was trying her best to settle in and enjoy it as best she could for now. The food was a bit strange to her seriously unrefined palate, but she could tell that it was all very five-star-restaurant quality for the eighteen hundreds. The clothes were both frustrating and amazing. She longed for the ease of leggings and a comfy t-shirt, but she couldn't deny the fun of dressing up in the beautiful dresses. Jocelyn had several of her old gowns altered to fit Elle since her chest was admittedly a bit bigger, and they were planning a shopping trip soon to get Elle some things of her own. Life without electricity or modern plumbing was...different to say the least. It showed Elle just how spoiled she was, and she vowed to never take hot water from the tap or a flushing toilet for granted if she were ever given the chance to have them again.

But despite all the difficulties, she was slowly managing, learning something new each day. Jocelyn had thankfully kept all of her belongings, but warned her to keep them hidden.

"I still have the clothes I was wearing when I arrived and everything from my purse, even after all these years. It's like my little piece of home, a tiny reminder of who I used to be," Jocelyn said as she handed Elle's things to her. "I couldn't take that same comfort from you. All of the clothes have been cleaned and dried—I did it myself, don't worry. Most of the staff have come to...expect the unexpected here. Most of them come from families who believe in magic and folklore, so they're a bit more understanding about anything strange than most. Plus, we've got you being American on our side. You're a bit of a mystery to everyone anyway." She smiled. "Still, try to keep most of this hidden away, especially the electronics."

As she handed the tablet over to Elle, she shook her head. "I still can't believe that is a *computer* of sorts. When I left, everyone had those candy-colored Macs that looked like bubbles. Or wanted them anyway."

Elle chuckled. "I know. Even I'm still shocked by how slim they're making them these days. Or those days," she said, scrunching her nose. "You know what I mean. But here, I can show you some of my work if you want. No internet needed for that."

"Oh yes, please. I'd love that."

Elle powered the tablet on and pulled up some of her pieces. Jocy gasped.

"You...*drew* these? On the *computer*?" Elle nodded, smiling proudly. "But...my goodness, they look like photographs almost." She reached out and actually stroked her finger across the screen. "Oh!" she laughed when the picture changed, before doing it again, fascinated by the touch screen. Elle found it endearing.

"What are they for?"

"They're mostly characters from books. I started out just doing them for me, just for fun, but the more I shared them, the more I had people requesting that I do this character or that, or if I could create things for them from scratch." Elle shrugged. "It just became a thing. So, I started a company and now I literally get paid to do what I love. Or, I did. Not much call for digital artists in this century, I suppose." Elle tried to ignore the pang in her chest as she stowed the tablet in her bag and put it with everything else into the oversized trunk at the end of the bed. She piled a few blankets on top, just to be safe, and closed the lid.

"See, nothing," Jocelyn said as Elle walked around the twisted trees, studying them like a detective on crime shows studied bodies. "The magic or energy or whatever you want to call it, it's gone."

Elle willed herself to feel it, opening her mind and trying to keep her body relaxed, welcoming whatever the hell had found her before. *Take me back. Take me home. Please...*She sighed in frustration. Jocy was right: there was nothing here.

"But how could it just be gone? How is it here one day and gone the next?" Elle kicked the trunk of one of the trees, hopping up and down as pain radiated up her leg. Callum laughed but attempted to cover it with a cough.

"I think that the magic finds those who need it, when they need it," he said thoughtfully after a few moments, eyeing the symbol on the trunk that Elle hadn't assaulted.

"What do you mean?"

"Jocelyn was fleeing for her life," his fist seemed to clench unconsciously at the idea of anyone threatening his wife, even almost twenty-years ago, "Carol was injured and needed help. Renaldo was desperate tae find a way out of a terrible situation." He didn't mention Elle, but he obviously thought that she fell into the same category. "Tae me, it seems as if the magic gave each of you what you needed at the time. You all needed an escape in one form or another. Maybe...maybe the magic not only takes you from where you don't want tae be, but takes you where you're meant tae go, tae what you need tae find."

Elle thought it over and supposed it made a sort of sense. Jocelyn was obviously meant to be here, Renaldo was off being a captain of the high seas and living his best life, Carol had died, but she hadn't died alone...

But Elle didn't belong here. She had a great life back in 2020. A good life. She was happy...mostly. She scowled inwardly. Ok, so she could admit that she'd been in a bit of a rut lately, not feeling quite...right no matter how hard she tried, but that didn't mean that she needed to be rescued by a meddling, magical fucking time machine!

"I still think there has to be a way back. I'm not giving up hope," Elle said determinately, walking away from the trees and back to the waiting horses.

A few days later, Jocy bounded into the garden where Elle was enjoying a rare, cloudless day.

"I have a surprise for you," she said, the excitement in her eyes making her look younger. It was easy in moments like this for Elle to see the eighteen-year-old who had traveled through the twisted trees, the one who had had dreams and a family and an unhealthy obsession with *Titanic*.

"A surprise?" Elle asked, intrigued. Jocy nodded eagerly and dragged her from the garden and towards the stables.

One of the (surprisingly) many things Elle was loving about this strange little vacation was riding again. She'd forgotten how much she loved the freedom of it, the wind in her face, the connection she had with the beautiful animals, the respect for their strength and beauty. She rode nearly every day, often with Rose and Callum, and the three of them usually ended up galloping through the gates laughing so hard their stomachs ached by the end of it. It was strange that Elle wasn't having her typical reaction to letting people get close to her. The walls weren't going up, she didn't feel the need to distance herself or pull away. It was the opposite. She leaned in, wanting to be around them as often as possible, feeling a sense of family again in a way she hadn't had since her parents had died.

She decided not to read anything into that at all, especially after Callum's little declaration in the woods about travelers finding what they were meant to and blah blah blah. She didn't belong in the 1800s, she just *didn't*. End of story.

But she would enjoy it for the time she was here, and if that meant her heart breaking a little when she left Jocelyn and Callum and Rosie, then she would deal with it. The thought sent an unnerving pang through her chest, the idea of leaving them feeling so wrong that it made her eyes sting with tears. She blinked rapidly, forcing the thoughts away with the tears, and focused on happier things.

She and Jocelyn rode through the grounds towards the small lake on the opposite side of the property from the cursed forest, and Elle was struck all over again by the sheer size of the place. It had to be at least a hundred acres, maybe more. The lake was surrounded by trees, and tucked within them, just on the side of the water, was what looked like an enclosed gazebo in a small clearing. A miniature barn sat just off to the side and they tied their horses up inside. Elle's brow furrowed in confusion.

"Callum built this for me ages ago so I'd have a place to come and...be myself when it all became a bit much. I used to come out here and listen to my CD player. I couldn't afford an iPod, so I was still in the Discman days. I must have listened to that burned mix at least a thousand times at the beginning, until the batteries finally died." She smiled a bit sadly, but fondly, and Elle wished so badly that she had spare batteries in her bag somewhere. She did have plenty of 90s and early 2000s music on her phone though and, thankfully, had solar-powered chargers for all of her devices tucked away in her trunk. She'd bring them out here to charge them in secret and make Jocy her own playlist.

"Anyway, I came out here so much that I insisted he build the barn for my horse so he didn't have to stand out in the sun or rain."

"I would have done the same thing," Elle said, stroking Joey's nose lovingly—Jocelyn's horse was Pacey. Elle had grinned at the names, having done a binge of *Dawson's Creek* herself not that long ago. Elle had been delighted to break the news to Jocy that Pacey and Joey did, in fact, end up together. She'd been brought back before the finale had aired and she'd wondered for nearly twenty years what happened in the end.

"Come on," Jocelyn said enthusiastically, tugging Elle up the stairs. She gripped the handles of the double glass doors. Elle couldn't see inside as the glass panels were covered in light curtains, but she was dying to know what was within. "Drumroll please..."

Elle laughed and obediently did a horrible drumroll sound with her tongue. Jocelyn threw open the doors with a wide smile and Elle's mouth popped open.

"It's...it's beautiful," she breathed as she stepped inside and spun in place, taking in the room. It wasn't huge, but it was big enough that there was a sofa, a desk, some shelves, and a large easel with a blank canvas sitting on it. A pillowed stool sat before it and a thick fur rug covered the middle of the space. More blankets and a few pillows were stacked in one corner. The curtains were a soft blue and a large chandelier hung in the middle of the ceiling, candles in the tapers with thick rivers of hardened wax down their sides. Several small lanterns were mounted to the walls on either side of each set of two tall windows.

"I thought you could use a space to be yourself, too." She gestured at the easel. "I know it's not the same as drawing on your computer—or tablet, you called it—but I thought maybe this would be close? You've got pencils and charcoal and paint. If there are other things you'd like, I'm sure we can track them down. Or you said you like to do yoga, so you could do that here as well. I'd like to try that too maybe. I thought it was only for old hippies before, but apparently that's not the case." Elle huffed out a laugh as she turned back to Jocelyn. Elle was already completely in platonic love with Jocelyn. She was a friend-slash-big-sister-slash-mother figure, one that Elle could admit she desperately needed.

"I thought the blue was beautiful, but we can change anything you want, it won't hurt my feelings, I promise." Jocelyn continued, biting her lip, looking nervous. "Do you like it?"

"Like it?" Elle shook her head, at a loss for words for a second. "I more than like it, but it's too much, Jocy. You didn't have to do all this." Elle trailed her fingers along the canvas, then across the charcoal and paints and brushes lining the desk. "Why are you doing all this for me? This," she said gesturing to the gazebo around them, "letting me stay with you, pretending I'm family—all of it."

Jocelyn held Elle's gaze. "I was lucky enough to find Callum when I got here. I'll be damned if someone goes through this alone. We may not be blood, but we *are* bonded. We are family now, for as long as you want us to be."

Elle lunged forward and threw her arms around Jocy, tears stinging her eyes.

"Thank you," Elle whispered, squeezing her fiercely. Jocy stroked her hair with one hand and hugged her tightly with the other.

"You're welcome. I'm sorry that this happened to you, but I won't deny that it's so damned nice having someone here who understands. *Really* understands. Who I can talk about home with."

And, so they began talking almost every night, often into the wee hours. Sometimes in the drawing room, sometimes out in the gazebo as Elle drew or they listened to music. It took a little bit of practice to get back into sketching again with actual pencils instead of on the tablet, but she realized how much she'd missed it. It was almost like therapy, letting her emotions come out through lead and charcoal and paint.

Sometimes the conversations were full of laughter, like when Elle explained fashion trends and lamented the return of the mullet; sometimes they were full of wonder, like when she explained smartphones and streaming services; others, they were somber, like when Elle told her about September 11 and the myriad tragedies that had shaken the world since.

Sometimes Callum joined them, just as fascinated by the future as he seemed to be by his wife. The way he stared at Jocy when she wasn't looking, so much adoration in his eyes it made

Elle look away, the way he instinctively moved towards her without even seeming to realize it, the way he would absently stroke her cheek or touch her shoulder as he walked by...*God, I want that. I don't think I ever had that with Ashton.*

On one such evening, with Callum settled on the sofa beside Jocy, Elle announced, "I'd like to contribute something, uh, monetarily."

"You will do no such thing," Callum scoffed. "You may no' truly be my niece by blood, but I've already come tae think of you as such. You are family, it is as simple as that."

"We're happy to do it, Elle," Jocelyn added. "Truly. We have more than enough."

"I know, and I appreciate it, but please. I need to do this. Where I'm from, *when* I'm from...well, I ran my own business, made my own money, took care of myself. I miss that. I know that the actual money I have with me is useless, but what about jewels?" Jocy studied her for a long minute but seemed to completely understand.

"If you're insistent on it, then yes, Callum can get coin in exchange for jewels."

"And if they aren't the typical pieces you'd find in this time?..."

"No' tae worry," Callum assured her, knowing where her thoughts were headed, "my cousin is a jeweler and does no' ask questions of anything I need of him."

Elle rubbed her fingers over the diamond on her left hand. Things with Ash were over on so many levels, but still, she had to take a deep, settling breath before she slid it off her finger. She held the rock out to Callum, pinching the band between her thumb and forefinger. It was four-carats, pear cut, flawless. Worth a small fortune. Well, at least back home it was, she wasn't sure what it might fetch here, but it had to be worth something, right?

"Well, you can start with this."

"Are...are you sure, Elle?" Jocy asked softly as she eyed the diamond with both appreciation and concern. Elle had told her all the gory details about Ashton and the epic end to their relationship, and she appreciated her new friend's concern about this big step.

Elle nodded. "I am, and I've got more upstairs." Ashton had a thing for showering her with gifts that almost exclusively consisted of jewelry. The kicker was that Elle didn't even particularly *like* jewelry. She barely even wore earrings unless it was a special occasion, but Ashton kept it coming. Every holiday, every special occasion, every make up after a fight, jewelry was his answer. She probably should have just come out and told him that she would have preferred something that was more personal, something that showed that he actually knew her or cared about what she liked versus what was just the go-to gift, but she hadn't wanted to hurt his feelings or seem ungrateful.

It probably didn't help that she always made sure to bring a handful of things with her when she visited, so he could see her wearing them. Even on this short surprise visit she'd been sure to bring the diamond tennis bracelet he'd gotten her for their anniversary the year before, the birthday necklace that had a ruby pendant the size of a grape dangling from a cluster of smaller ones, an emerald ring that was honestly so big it looked fake (though she was certain it wasn't), and two sets of diamond studs, two carats each.

She really didn't mean to sound ungrateful, and she knew part of it was her own fault, but being away from it all was letting her step back and really analyze her relationship with Ash.

And hindsight was indeed 20/20.

A week later, Elle was getting her first real taste of civilization in the 1800s: they were traveling to a nearby town to purchase some new dresses. Though a bit nervous, Elle was beyond excited. She'd decided to embrace this strange trip and by God, she was ready to embrace it with open arms. Though she loved Chestwick Hall, and had already come to think of it as her home away from home, she was dying to see, well, *anything* else. And now that she truly had her "own" money again, she was excited to finally do some retail therapy.

They traveled by carriage, an honest to God horse-drawn carriage, and though it was a bit bumpy, the ride was overall pleasant. She could tell the carriage was expensive and well made, with thick, cushioned benches covered in soft, embroidered velvet, and luxurious curtains lining the walls and covering the windows. She couldn't help but feel a little like Cinderella.

The town was quaint and Elle wanted to go into every single shop she saw, regardless of what they were selling—pastries, cloth, weapons. Didn't matter to Elle, she was enthralled by every single thing she saw. Jocy laughed but indulged her.

"Have you never been shopping before, Elle?" Rose asked with an amused smile.

"Not like this," Elle told her honestly. The clothes, the sights, the smells. It was all a bit overwhelming, but Elle was loving the adventure of it all.

They eventually made their way to the dress shop—or modiste, as Jocy called it—and Elle roamed around, admiring all the beautiful gowns while Rose tried something on and Jocy spoke with the seamstress in the back. They'd already made several selections for Elle and, to her surprise, she was told that the dresses would be made for her within the next few days. *Made.* By hand and from scratch specifically for her. It was wild.

"Hello there," a high-pitched, falsely sweet voice said from behind her. Elle whirled to find a short, stout woman eyeing her oddly, almost like a cat eyeing a tasty-looking mouse. Her eyes were the color of mud, her hair only a shade lighter and piled high on her head in the same style that Jocelyn often wore, but this woman didn't look nearly as elegant.

"Um, hello," Elle said, inclining her head slightly to the older woman.

"Are you a relation to Lady MacTavish, dear?"

"Oh, yes," Elle said with a bright smile. "She's my aunt. I've come from America to live with her and my uncle." Elle had memorized their cover story, but this was the first time she was really trying it out. She felt like an undercover cop or something, pretending to be someone completely new and different. It was a little fun, actually.

The woman eyed her, raking her eyes down Elle's body and back up again, her attention snagging on her hand.

"Are you unmarried?"

Elle blinked at her. Was that a normal question to ask someone you met exactly thirty-seven seconds ago? Maybe in this time it was.

"Yes," Elle answered, a bit uncertainly. "I'm...unattached."

"And how old are you, dear?"

"I'm twenty-six," Elle said defensively, though she wasn't really sure why. Something in the woman's tone when she'd asked the question had Elle's hackles rising. She didn't like this woman at all.

"How very *interesting*," the woman said with a strange smile. *And what the hell was so* interesting *about it?*

Jocelyn hurried forward then and looped her arm through Elle's.

"Eleanor, dear, there you are. Lady Wilshire," Jocy said to the short woman in greeting. It was polite enough, but it was clipped and there was a coolness beneath the words that she'd never heard from Jocy before. Elle looked between the two women and could practically see the tension and agitation between them. *Cause baby now we got bad blood*, Elle sang silently to herself.

"Lady MacTavish, your lovely niece here was just telling me that she is unwed. She is well of age, but I haven't seen her announced for the season. Surely now that she's under your care..." The Wilshire woman arched a bushy brow in some strange challenge. Elle looked between the two women again, obviously missing something important.

"Of course she'll be presented," Jocy all but snapped, annoyance clear in her voice. "She only just arrived, but we are announcing it later this week, in fact."

"Wonderful. It would look *so* dreadful on the great MacTavish family if she didn't..." There was some kind of strange threat in her words that Elle didn't quite get but didn't like. She balled her hands into fists at her sides.

"Don't worry your pretty little head about the MacTavish family, *Matilda*," Jocy said with the most venom Elle had ever heard her use, throwing etiquette out the window, apparently. "Now, we must be going if you'll excuse us." Matilda looked like she wanted to do something very unladylike, but Jocy was already turning away.

Rose had trailed up at the end of the conversation and Elle met her gaze, giving her a *what gives* look. Rose gave her a small shake of her head in an *I'll tell you later* gesture. The three of them quickly headed out of the shop and back to the carriage, handing off packages to the driver to stow away somewhere. Once they were safely inside, Jocy collapsed back against the bench seat.

"Ok, who was that? And what is the deal with you two? And what the hell was she talking about?" Thankfully, Rose had grown used to Elle's "strange way of speaking," so she'd allowed herself to be a little more lax around the girl.

"She shouldn't have even been here," Jocy muttered to herself. "They must be visiting her husband's family." She met Elle's gaze and sighed. "That is the dreadful woman who is convinced that I stole Callum from her. It was almost twenty years ago, you would think she'd have moved on by now. Especially since she's married and has four children of her own." She rolled her eyes. "And I never *stole* him. She fancied him and had begged her father to offer up their entire fortune to Callum in an effort to get him to marry her, but he had never even considered it. Since then, she's been hellbent on tarnishing the MacTavish name one way or another, just itching for our place in the Ton to be tainted."

Elle had come to understand that *The Ton* was the elite of British society, and the MacTavishs were very much a part of it, though they didn't necessarily seem to enjoy it.

"Ok, well, I officially don't like her, but what was all that *season* and *presented* talk? Why did she care so much that I'm not married? Which by the way, I almost was, so it's not like I'm some spinster cat lady or something—which, also, what is so wrong with being a spinster cat lady?" she added in a huff, not sure why she was defending herself against a woman who wasn't even there.

"Cat lady?" Rose asked a little ruefully.

"Oh, uh, in America unwed women often acquire a number of cats for companionship. Or, that's the stereotype anyway," she added under her breath. "Anyway, Aunt Jocy—answer the question. What was she talking about?"

Jocy sighed heavily. "Congratulations, Eleanor Montgomery. It appears that you will be coming out to London society this social season."

Chapter 5

"What?" Elle sputtered. "No. No way! I am not participating in this!"

Jocelyn exhaled warily. "Matilda will have already started spreading the news. If you don't come out, it will look...suspicious. People will talk and the MacTavish name will be...not tarnished, exactly, but it would be a blemish and Matilda would be sure that the blemish became a scandal, and scandal never bodes well, even on the wealthiest of families. Really, that wouldn't matter to me or to Callum, we've never much cared about all of that, and generally stay out of London altogether with the exception of Callum's business endeavors, but..." she cut her eyes to Rose, "well, if you don't, it might reflect badly on Rose this season."

Elle blinked several times. Jocy couldn't be serious, could she?

"I was going to tell you later this week actually, about the plans for the upcoming months. We were going to travel to London for the season—Rose is being presented this year," she added with a warm smile at the girl, who was beaming, "But we were going to let you remain at Chestwick so that you needn't involve yourself with all of this. But now..."

Elle ground her teeth. She would have been perfectly content to be the secret hiding back at Chestwick, but she couldn't have anything messing with Rose's big debutante shebang. She already adored the girl and felt fiercely protective of her, like the little sister she'd never had but had always wanted.

But to be paraded around like cattle? To be *courted* by potential husbands? Reminded of her last potential husband, Elle clenched her fists. *Ugh.* Jocy seemed to read her mind.

"You won't have to actually marry, I promise you. You just need to go through the motions. Attend the balls and entertain suitors when they come to call. Callum will refuse any offers for your hand—unless you don't want him to, of course," she added, almost hopefully.

"Of course he should refuse them," Elle snapped, getting more irritable by the second. She had zero plans to hitch her wagon to anyone, let alone someone in the wrong century. Jocy held up her hands in surrender.

"But why?" Rose asked curiously. "Don't you want to be married?"

"Oh, yes, of course, but it's just...we don't really have this in America," Elle hedged. "The whole coming out and high society and all of that. And I wasn't prepared to even think about being married so soon after arriving here is all." Elle glanced at Jocy before looking back to Rose again. The girl was silently pleading with her with those big beautiful eyes, more green than gold today. Though Elle wasn't looking to bag a man right now, she understood how important it would be to Rose. This was all she knew. Coming out, being courted, finding a suitable husband. This was all vital to her life.

Elle let out a long, semi-annoyed sigh, knowing that she couldn't stand in the way of Rosie's life.

"Alright, fine," Elle said, rolling her eyes. "I'll do it."

Rose squealed and threw herself at Elle, hugging her tightly.

"Thank you, Elle. Thank you, thank you, thank you."

"I better at least get to wear some bomb-ass...er, I mean, some amazing dresses," she hissed at Jocy over Rose's shoulder.

Jocy laughed. "Of course. We'll do some proper shopping the second we get to London, I promise. In the meantime, we've got six weeks to get you prepared for the height of London society."

Well, fuck.

The weeks came and went in a blur. Elle had been taught how to dance—which had actually been really fun and came to her easily enough—how to speak, how to walk, all the ins and outs of being a proper lady. Jocy had been thrilled to find out that Elle already played the piano because apparently playing an instrument really determined if you were wifey material or not. Elle's mother had been a magnificent player and had taught Elle growing up. She'd never gotten to the skill level of her mom, but she was fairly decent and had always kept it up as a hobby, especially after her parents had died. Whenever she missed her mom, she'd play and feel closer to her. It didn't erase the ache, but it did ease it a bit.

"One less thing to worry about," Jocelyn had said with a nod and a smile.

"You remember I'm not actually trying to get any of them to propose, right? So, it doesn't really matter if I can do any of this crap. I just need to not disgrace the family name. Oh and not fall on my face in front of the Queen, of course."

"I remember," Jocy had muttered with a roll of her eyes, but there was a glint of something there, something that was somewhere between mischief and hope. "And I'm sure you'll do just fine with the Queen."

Elle had narrowed her eyes. "I can see you plotting, Jocelyn MacTavish," she said, pointing an accusatory finger. "You are not sneaky. And I will *not* be changing my mind on the husband front."

Jocy only grinned and was the picture of innocence when she said, "I haven't the slightest idea what you're talking about, Eleanor."

Elle's lips had quirked and she let it slide for the time being. "This is so ridiculous, by the way. Why should men care if I can play piano or sing or paint? Shouldn't they be more worried about whether I can carry on a conversation or tie my own shoes or am a decent human being?" She held up her hand to stop Jocy from replying. "I know, I know. It was rhetorical. I'm just missing the post-nineteenth amendment world right now."

"I understand, I really, really do. The first time some well-to-do old jackass told me to essentially stand there and look pretty while the men talked, I think steam came out of my ears." Elle had laughed at that. "I won't say that it gets easier to deal with, but you learn to live with it."

Elle made no promises, but agreed to do her best.

The next morning, they left for London. Despite her initial irritation, Elle had grown more and more excited as their departure grew closer. Who didn't want to put on gorgeous gowns and go to fancy balls? Get to play pretend for a little while on the grandest of scales? She could do that for a time, especially if it meant helping Rose. The girl was beyond ecstatic to finally come out and experience the whole dog and pony show, and, touching Elle's heart, she said she was even more excited that she got to experience it with her cousin.

Elle could hardly believe her eyes as she took in London. It was so different, yet so familiar at the same time. It was a bit of a mind-fuck actually. Trying to reconcile the past with the future, trying to see beyond what was there to what it would one day become. It made her head hurt. She vaguely recognized Hyde Park and Savile Row—where Jocy promised they would be shopping the second they arrived and Elle was practically foaming at the mouth—but many of the buildings were new to her, only their ghosts remaining in the London she knew.

The carriage finally pulled into a large courtyard in front of an absolutely massive house. It was three stories and made of beautiful light brown stone. Ivy climbed up the walls and sculpted topiaries lined the front of the house on either side of the wide front stairs.

"It's beautiful," Elle breathed as she exited the carriage, twisting to stretch her back out after sitting for so long.

"It is," Jocelyn agreed, "but I much prefer the country."

"Aye. Chestwick is where I found you, mo grá. It will always be my favorite place as well," Callum said as he kissed Jocy quickly but fiercely on the lips before staring into her eyes in a way that made Elle flush. Callum looked at Jocy like she hung the moon, like she was his reason for living. Elle didn't think she'd ever had that before. She knew that Ashton had loved her, at least in the beginning, and she knew that he thought she was beautiful, but he'd never looked at her like *that*.

As promised, they'd shopped til they'd nearly dropped, buying Elle almost an entirely new wardrobe, complete with enough of the most beautiful gowns she'd ever seen to wear a different one practically every night for months. Elle tried to say that it was overkill, that she really didn't need *so* many...but only half-heartedly. *Talk about retail therapy.*

Other than the assault on her nostrils, London in 1813 was thrilling to experience, and Elle actually found herself a bit excited at the prospect of going to dances and ballets and who knew what else. She'd deal with the rest. It would be fine.

When the day finally came to be presented to the Queen—*the Queen of freaking England*—she found herself nervous as hell. Her gown was ivory silk with a row of silvery beads lining the empire waist. More beading wound around the edges of the short sleeves, the bottom hem, and along the small train. Lottie had done her hair, pinning half of it up with combs of the same silvery beads that had been sewn into the dress, and letting the rest flow down her back in soft curls. After Lottie left, Elle pulled out her makeup stash that she'd brought from Chestwick Hall. She kept it soft, going for a more natural look, and with one last swipe of mascara, she sat back to take in the whole package.

"Well, I guess you're ready to see the Queen, Elle Montgomery," she whispered to her reflection.

The presentation to the Queen hadn't been as bad or daunting as Elle had imagined. She was still a bit nervous when they first arrived, but once she realized that the Queen that was sitting at the end of the room wasn't the one that she'd grown up seeing on tabloids at the supermarket, it made the whole thing a little easier to deal with. It was less like meeting a celebrity and more like meeting dignitaries and diplomats, which she'd actually done on occasion with Ash's family. Still very important and powerful people, but not ones that you'd watched on television or followed on social media.

So, Elle had made it through the whole ordeal without making a fool of herself or shaming the MacTavish name, feeling relatively calm as she walked down the long aisle to stand before the Queen. She made sure to give that toad Matilda a saccharine smile on the way and the woman glowered at her in return. Elle heard whispers swirling about her as she walked the length of the room. Jocelyn had warned her that gossip would abound, but Elle had never cared much about gossip. She held her head high, did as she was instructed, and the Queen eyed her with intrigue. She honestly wasn't sure if that was a good thing or a bad thing. One girl fainted, but Jocy told Elle later that she suspected it was a ruse to get attention. Elle felt almost as if she were on some reality show like *The Bachelor* or *America's Next Top Model* or something, like none of this was quite real.

Now came time for the fun part: the first ball of the season. Elle had chosen a sapphire blue silk gown, almost the color of her eyes, that was cut a bit lower than the gown she'd worn to the presentation. It wasn't exactly scandalous, but it was a bit more...fashion-forward than a lot of the gowns she'd seen while they'd shopped. Her cleavage wasn't looking too shabby between the cut of the dress and the way the stays she was wearing beneath pressed her breasts upward. The cap sleeves were made of looped blue crystals and matching ones cascaded down the center of the bodice and the flowing skirt.

Her hair was swept up into a slightly messy up-do with a thick French braid snaking down one side. She gave herself a subtly smoky eye, winged her liner out slightly, and took her time to contour and highlight. She may not be looking for a husband, but she could still dress to impress. It was a real *ball* for crying out loud! She applied a second coat of mascara just as Rose entered.

"Oh my," she breathed. "Elle, you look...beautiful doesn't seem to be adequate."

"Back at you. You look stunning, Rosie!" The girl blushed, as she always did when Elle complimented her, but smiled warmly. She wore a sage green gown of satin with a lace overlay that looked gorgeous with her red hair and green-gold eyes. Rose eyed the tube in Elle's hand questioningly, and Elle waved the girl over. She swiped the brush over Rose's thick lashes and smiled at the lovely effect it had. She added just a touch of eye shadow and a bit of blush to complete the look.

She turned Rose to look in the mirror and her eyes widened just as her smile did.

"Heavens," she whispered, turning her face this way and that to admire herself. "I don't mean to sound overly prideful, but...I think I look quite pretty."

"You look more than *quite pretty*, Rosie," Elle promised, squeezing her shoulders gently.

She met Elle's gaze in the mirror. "Are you ready?"

Elle let out a long exhale. "As I'll ever be."

They hooked arms and headed downstairs. Jocelyn teared up at the sight of them and Callum cleared his throat roughly, his own eyes glassy.

"You both look quite bonny," he said gruffly, kissing each of them on the cheek.

They took the carriage to some Duke's house—Elle couldn't remember his name. It could be the Duke of Buckingham for all she knew—and she tried to remember everything she'd learned over the last six weeks. The dance steps, the etiquette. The biggest rule was apparently *do not be caught alone with a man*, but Elle was pretty sure she could handle that one.

Elle stared in wonder at the house that was one small step below a castle in her opinion, and the wonder only grew as they entered. It was absolutely gorgeous, the absolute definition of opulence with its grand staircases and soaring ceilings painted with heavenly scenes, and the ballroom was no exception. Huge mirrors in gilded frames hung on almost every wall making the room bright and lively, with candles and overflowing bundles of flowers and crystal accents on every available surface. The floors were painted with an intricate pattern of leaves and flowers, all in shades of gold, and a band—or hell, maybe it would be considered a small orchestra—played softly from a large balcony on the far end of the room. Elle had been to plenty of high-class events over the years with Ashton, but this was on a whole different level.

The girls were all in beautifully elegant dresses and the men wore striking suits, the jackets having long tails. Elle felt like she was in a movie, or a dream. As they walked down the grand staircase into the ballroom, almost every head turned in their direction, admiring glances falling heavily upon them. *Don't fall, don't fall, don't fall.* Before Elle could even blink, she and Rose were bombarded by men, all asking for dances.

The night became a blur of swirling skirts and casual conversation, mostly revolving around her accent, how she was enjoying London, and complimenting how she looked. It was fun. Really fun, actually. Many of the other girls looked stressed and tense beneath their beaming smiles and Elle felt a twinge of guilt. They were all here in the honest hopes of finding a husband and starting a life. She was just here to have a good time in a pretty dress. Many of the girls looked at Elle with clear challenge, seeing her as competition. Though Elle completely understood the situation from their point of view, she did her best to diffuse the hostility.

She'd been on the bitchy end of a *Mean Girls*-esque clique once upon a time and she never wanted to be that person again. She gave genuine compliments to the other women, fixed a shy girl named Emma's hair when her pins had been knocked loose, and though some seemed taken aback or even suspicious, many thawed towards her.

After a bit, Rose and Elle took a much-needed break and found drinks.

"This is amazing," Rose beamed. "Everything I dreamed!"

"It is pretty amazing," Elle agreed with a smile as she took a sip of the punch. Her eyes flew wide as she barely stifled a cough. "Woooo," she whispered, "that is some punch." When she'd heard the word *punch,* she'd imagined something light and fruity with sorbet in it, like she had at the engagement brunch Ashton's mother had thrown for her, but this was more like the punch she'd made in a trash can in college that led to bad decisions and fantastically hazy memories.

"Mmm," Rosie hummed, taking another sip, "I like it."

Elle laughed but then whispered, "Oh, incoming," from the corner of her mouth as a young man approached.

He inclined his head. "Miss Montgomery, I wonder if I might fill a spot on your dance card?"

Rose was eyeing the man with extreme interest from her spot semi-hidden behind a pillar, a flush creeping up her cheeks. Rose had been happy with all of the men she'd danced with so far, but she hadn't looked at any of them like *that.* Elle took another look at the boy. He was very cute, with curly brown hair, light brown eyes, and dimples. *Elle Montgomery, Matchmaker Extraordinaire, at your service.*

"Mister...?"

"Delvington. Percival Delvington."

"Mister Delvington," Elle said, nodding. "I'm afraid all the dancing has made me feel a bit faint. I believe I need some air, but I'm sure my cousin, Miss Rose MacTavish, would love to dance with you."

Elle yanked Rose forward and Percival's eyes widened in appreciation.

"Rose speaks three languages, is well read, and plays the harp beautifully," Elle added, laying it on a little thick, but who cared? Rose blushed again but couldn't hide her smile.

"I-I would be most honored, Miss MacTavish," Percival said, giving her a bow and extending his hand.

Rose took it, letting him lead her onto the floor. She looked over her shoulder, and Elle winked at her. Another man approached, but Elle pretended not to notice, walking the other direction. She really did need a break, so she tried to make her way through the throng of people and to the doors leading outside. She smiled and gave small nods of acknowledgment as she wound her way through the crowd along the side of the room. She turned back to watch Rose and Percival and her lips curled upward. They were staring at each other as they danced and Elle thought that there were most definitely sparks flying.

Elle turned forward again just in time to run right into someone. The man's drink sloshed out of his glass on the impact, liquid splashing over her chest.

"Oh!" she gasped.

She glanced up to find deep green eyes staring down at her quizzically. Tall, with light brown, tousled hair, an aristocratic nose, chiseled cheekbones, and though it certainly wasn't the norm here, he had a bit of a five-o'clock shadow that instantly intrigued her. He could have stepped right out of an ad for high-end cologne. Handsome. *Beyond* handsome. There were plenty of attractive men here tonight, but not a single one had caught her attention like this one.

His eyes flickered over her and he tilted his head slightly, studying her. She finally recovered from her initial shock and began furtively wiping at her chest to clear away his drink—whisky from the smell of it. She was probably ruining her gloves, but whatever. She didn't particularly like them anyway, but she'd resigned to wearing them. Stockings on the other hand had been a hard pass for her.

"My drink," he finally said.

"I'm sorry?"

"Ah, good, so you *do* know how to apologize."

"What?" She stopped wiping her chest and yanked her gaze up to meet his again.

"Well, you did spill my drink. It is only polite to apologize." His voice was smooth, his accent swoonworthy. "Are proper manners not taught to ladies in the Ton these days?" She narrowed her eyes at him.

"You have got to be kidding."

"Oh, I never kid about choice alcohol. This is a lovely vintage and you wasted half of it."

"*You* spilled your drink on *me*. I thought the men *in the Ton*"—*eye roll*—"were supposed to be gentlemen," she shot back, knowing she shouldn't but not able to stop herself.

"I never claimed to be a gentleman."

Elle glanced around, casting a smile to a few other men who were waiting in the wings for her to finish her conversation. She knew better, but she didn't care. She would blame the punch. She shifted her gaze back to Captain Jackoff.

"And *I* never claimed to be a lady," she said quietly before knocking the bottom of his glass, spilling what remained of his drink. He leapt backwards, blinking in surprise as he watched the contents splash to the floor. He quickly cut his eyes back to hers. The look was a mix of annoyance and surprise.

"Clumsy me," she said sweetly before storming off.

Chapter 6

"Well, I never thought I would see the day that Alexander Kentworth willingly attended a ball during the season."

Alec turned from investigating an honestly horrendous painting of Duke Rallings in one of the smaller parlors just off the ballroom to find Daniel Harrington grinning from ear to ear, arms stretched out in welcome. Alec smiled back at his old friend.

"Oh believe me, I'm not here by choice. My father insisted I return this year and participate in this carnival." He rolled his eyes as he gestured to the ballroom. Alec had never understood the draw of the season, of the balls and the courting and the nonsense. He was glad that he'd been away all these years, avoiding the entire thing, and, more importantly, avoiding marriage. He was here because his father bade it, and, really, his father asked very little of him, let him live the life he'd chosen when many others in his position wouldn't have. Alec could give him this.

"Well, it is about time, is it not?" Daniel held out his glass and Alec tapped it with his own. "It's good to see you. How long has it been? Three years?"

"About that, I believe. At...at mother's funeral." A pang echoed through Alec's chest at the thought of his mother.

"That's right," Daniel said, looking down into his glass. A heavy silence lay between them for a long moment before Daniel cleared his throat. "Well, I for one am glad you're back. I don't think I could stomach another of these dreadful things alone."

"Didn't land a wife last season, eh?"

"Courted a few prospects, but they didn't accept. We aren't all future viscounts after all," he said with a grin.

"Don't remind me," Alec grumbled, taking a deep sip. Another thing he had no interest in? His title, being the true Lord Kentworth, running a house, joining his father's various business ventures. He wanted none of it. Until recently, he'd had an entirely different life planned. Now, he supposed he'd be resigned to accepting the life he'd tried so hard to avoid.

"Not to worry though, I have no plans to take any of these lovely ladies off the market and out of your grasp." Daniel arched a dark brow. "Father bid me come and show my face at these events. He did not demand that I actually take a wife. So," he gestured to himself, "here I am."

"And I'm sure everyone is much appreciative of that," Daniel laughed, "though you probably could have at least shaved?" Alec smirked and Daniel laughed harder, shaking his head ruefully. Daniel had learned long ago that though Alec was technically high born, he much preferred to act otherwise.

"So, have you got your eye on anyone in particular?" Alec asked, swirling his drink around his glass.

"Well, it's early yet, but the Wilshire twins are both high on the list this year." He gestured towards two raven-haired girls across the way, a few men surrounding them. They weren't exactly *un*attractive, but they wouldn't be called beautiful by any means. And when one let out a high-pitched peel of laughter, both Alec and Daniel winced. "Their father recently came into a large inheritance from some long-forgotten uncle from what I understand. A much larger dowry than before is anticipated."

"I don't think any dowry is worth being saddled to that for the rest of my life," Alec said as the second girl snorted with laughter, knocked over an entire tray of drinks as she threw her arms wide, and then began to berate the maid as if it were *her* fault. It was people like this that had made Alec want to leave London in the first place.

"Hmm, I see your point," Daniel said, huffing out a laugh and pursing his lips. "The MacTavish girl is a prize, of course." He nodded towards Rose, dancing with who Alec believed was one of the Delvington boys. Rose was like a younger sister to him, and it was hard to see her as a young lady ready to be courted. She would always be the girl in braids who pushed him into the creek when he told her that girls shouldn't ride or hunt—she'd only been eight or nine at the time but had knocked him neatly on his arse. He smiled into his glass at the memory. God, he'd missed her. The whole MacTavish family, really.

"And her cousin? *My God* man. You have never seen anyone so beautiful. She's like Aphrodite come to life." Alec raised his brows at that. Daniel glanced through the crowd. "I can't seem to find her now, but when you see her, you will know it. Don't know much about her though. She's come from America if you can believe it. There's gossip a plenty about her sudden appearance, but I haven't the foggiest idea what of it might be true."

"I shall keep my eyes peeled," Alec said dryly, though he couldn't deny he was intrigued. He'd known the MacTavishs all his life and he'd never heard mention of this cousin or any family in America.

Daniel slapped Alec on the shoulder. "I suppose I should continue to make the rounds." They parted ways, promising to meet at one of the gentleman's clubs later that week. Alec began to wander through the crowd, keeping to the edge of the room and trying to avoid detection as much as possible. He'd entered the ball late and quietly enough that most hadn't noticed him yet, but he was arguably the most sought-after suitor here and mothers would soon be throwing their daughters at him bodily. He would go through the motions to appease his father, but the longer he could go without having extra attention, the better.

A moment later, someone ran headlong into him, his drink sloshing over the side of his glass. He glanced down and was...awestruck. She was the most beautiful woman Alec had ever seen. Her hair was the color of morning sunlight and though it was piled atop her head, tendrils had pulled free around her face. The imperfectness of it made her even more attractive, though he couldn't quite explain why. Perhaps it was because the women at these things were so hellbent on being so perfect that it was suffocating. Alec didn't blame them—the importance of these events, of being perfect at all times and finding a proper husband had been ingrained in them since birth—but it made him feel like nothing was *real*.

The girl's skin looked as if she spent her days in the sun, and though that typically denoted someone of low birth, he admittedly found it exceedingly attractive. She had high cheekbones, flushed with color from dancing, he supposed, a slender nose that upturned ever so slightly, and her lips bowed in an obscenely alluring way. A swift and unwelcome desire to press his lips to hers rushed through him, and he quickly forced the thought away. Then it hit him: this must be the cousin.

"Oh!" she gasped, glancing up. He could only stare back for several long moments. *Alexander Kentworth left speechless?* She had the most beautiful blue eyes, like sapphires, almost the exact shade of her shimmering dress. They were rimmed with kohl and her lids were dusted with some kind of dark, shimmering powder, giving her an intensely sultry look. He couldn't stop his gaze from skating down the length of her again. Thin but not frail, her arms having the slight curvature of muscles, as if she did *actual* labor? *How odd*, he thought, but then again, America was a very different place for ladies from what he understood. His eyes slid downward. *My* God *her curves...*He had to stop himself from rubbing his hand across his mouth. Her chest was still wet from his drink and the sight made him long to wipe it away.

Perhaps using his tongue.

He tilted his head, his brow furrowing ever so slightly. *Where had that thought come from? What in heavens is wrong with me tonight?* He shook himself and made sure that his mask of indifferent boredom was firmly in place.

She began to wipe the mess away with her hands, ruining her gloves. *Interesting.* Most women he knew would be in a tizzy over a spill like this, would never absently wipe it away like it was nothing. He realized then that he was still staring like an oaf and he needed to speak.

"My drink," he said simply, because it was honestly all he could think to say in that moment.

"I'm sorry?" she said, sounding confused. Her accent was very strange, though not unpleasant. He had to remind himself again that she was from America. Perhaps that explained her behavior and her overall demeanor. She wouldn't have been brought up with high society London in mind, though he knew that Jocelyn

MacTavish would have prepared her as much as possible since her arrival.

"Ah, good, so you do know how to apologize," he said in a cool voice.

"What?" She stopped wiping her chest and yanked her gaze up to meet his. He was again struck by the vibrant blue.

"Well, you did spill my drink. It is only polite to apologize." He frowned. "Are proper manners not taught to ladies in the Ton these days?" She narrowed her eyes at him and it made him want to smile. She obviously had no idea who he was and he liked that very much. If she did, she would never react this way. She'd be fawning and apologizing and being insufferable.

"You have got to be kidding."

"Oh, I never kid about choice alcohol. This is a lovely vintage and you wasted half of it." Her eyes went wide and incredulous, and he fought a smile.

"*You* spilled your drink on *me*. I thought the men in *the Ton*," she sneered with thick sarcasm, "were supposed to be gentlemen."

"I never claimed to be a gentleman." It was true. He was one by birth, but he was a rake and almost as far from a gentleman as one could get.

The girl glanced around, casting an easy smile to a few other men. Her teeth were straight and brilliantly white and he knew that smile could open any door for her, make any man drop to his knees. *She'll have suitors lined up down the street tomorrow morning.* She cut her eyes back to him, the smile disappearing almost instantly and calculation glinting in her eyes.

"And I never claimed to be a lady," she said quietly before knocking the bottom of his glass, spilling what was left within it.

He leapt backwards, watching the contents hit the floor in shock before looking back to her, torn between amusement, astonishment, and annoyance. *Had she really just done that?* She smiled again, this time a cunning curl of her lips, like a cat who had just caught a mouse. "Clumsy me," she said sweetly before turning to storm off.

In shock, he watched her leave, admittedly enjoying the sensual sway of her hips as she walked. He'd never seen a lady in the Ton walk like *that.* She had an effortless grace about her, a confidence that drew every eye in the room. And her *backside...*He shook himself and clenched his jaw. He watched as Lady MacTavish beckoned her over, quickly pulling the girl into one of the many adjoining rooms. Alec waited a moment and then followed, standing just outside and leaning in close. Eavesdropping wasn't gentlemanly, but, as he'd told the girl, he'd never claimed to be one.

"Do you have any idea who that was, Elle?" Jocelyn asked. Alec had known the MacTavish family his entire life and was quite fond of them, had spent many summers playing in their lake with Rose, going on hunts with his father and Callum MacTavish. In all that time, he'd never heard of Jocelyn having siblings or of this niece, this Elle. *And what kind of name is Elle?* Of course, he really didn't know much about Jocelyn's family prior to her marriage to Callum, so it wasn't completely unreasonable that he hadn't heard of this girl before. Shaking off the errant thoughts, he continued to listen.

"Lord Bastard, of the Cambridge Bastards?" the girl responded dryly. He huffed out a quiet laugh, despite himself.

"That was Alexander Kentworth."

"Bee-Eff-Dee." *What on Earth does that mean?* "I don't care who he is. He was a jackass and I don't like jackasses." The way she spoke was very strange, but he couldn't deny that he...liked it. It was refreshing. *She* was refreshing.

"He is a future viscount and the most eligible man here. He also happens to be a friend to our family."

"I'm now *seriously* questioning your judgment..." Elle muttered, but Jocelyn continued as if she hadn't heard, though he knew she had.

"And you just *threw his drink on him*?"

"Ok, *he* spilled his drink on me first! I just...finished the job." *Quiet pause.* He envisioned Lady MacTavish giving the girl that look she had, the one that made a young lad nearly relieve himself in fear when he *accidentally* ate all of the tarts that were meant for a party she was having...

"Ok, ok, fine. I'm sorry," Elle said, sounding a tad petulant. "I mean, I'm not sorry I tossed his drink because he deserved that, but I'm sorry that I acted so...unbecoming." He could practically hear her rolling her eyes and his lips curled up in amusement. "Anyway, Rosie sure seems smitten with Percival something or another out there."

"Oh I saw," Jocelyn said, a smile in her voice. "He comes from a good family. It could be a good match if that's what makes her happy." Alec was again reminded how different the MacTavish family was from most of the others in the Ton. Most other mothers wouldn't care if her daughter was happy, only if the match was advantageous, if it brought riches or glory or both to the family names.

"Are you having fun?" Jocelyn asked.

"I am actually, minus the drink incident. I hope I'm not screwing up too badly."

"Oh, dear, not to worry. With what I'm hearing, you are the absolute talk of the night."

"I don't know if that's a good thing or not," Elle sighed. "Alright, I guess I should get back out there."

Alec walked away quickly so as not to be caught and was almost immediately accosted by Matilda Wilshire. He barely stifled a groan. She was a vile woman who looked very much like a toad. In fact, he and Daniel used to *ribbit* behind her back when they were children, though she could never prove it had been them. The Wilshires were a relatively affluent family, but they had always been on the fringes of the Ton. Matilda had been trying desperately for years to change that fact. Apparently, the sudden inheritance had now helped her achieve that dream and she was practically vibrating with smugness and joy.

"Lord Kentworth, it is so lovely to see you. I didn't know you were here for the season this year."

He bowed. "Lady Wilshire."

She beckoned and her daughters tittered over. "May I present my daughters? Harrietta and Wilhelmina."

They fell over each other trying to get closer to him as they curtseyed. They looked at him expectantly and he sighed inwardly. *Duty calls.*

"Would you do me the honor of a dance?"

"Um, which one of us?" Harrietta asked in a nasally voice. Or possibly Wilhelmina. He'd already forgotten which was which.

It really couldn't matter less, he thought, but he smiled thinly and extended his hand towards the one on the right. She was slightly taller with a wider nose and she squealed in excitement as they made their way onto the floor.

And so the hell began. Word quickly spread of his presence—largely due to Matilda telling anyone who would listen that *her* daughter had secured his first dance of the evening—and he quickly became bombarded. He danced as was expected and tried to have conversations with the women, but it was all so...stiff. Rehearsed. As if they were parroting answers they'd practiced a hundred times. *Unlike the beauty who called me a bastard and a jackass.* They'd found each other several times throughout the evening, their eyes locking across the ballroom as they each danced with their partners. Each time, Elle—whose name was actually Eleanor, come to find out—quickly pulled her gaze away, but his always lingered for an extra moment, watching the way she moved, the way she smiled and laughed.

He couldn't stop himself from searching for her again now as he somehow managed to get a break from dancing. She was a mystery to him and he had always been interested in mysteries. His gaze roamed the room, finally spotting her dancing with Henry Astley. Alec scowled. He and Henry Astley had hated each other since they were boys and had gotten in more than one row over the years. Astley was a bastard, truth be told. While Alec pretended to be a haughty, arrogant prick, Astley really was one. He'd always been jealous of Alec, always tried to prove he was smarter or faster or stronger—usually to no avail. Alec wasn't even sure when or why the rivalry had started, and as happy as he would be to just forget Astley existed completely (which he usually did), being back here for the season meant that that wasn't an option.

Alec watched them through narrowed eyes and realized that Elle didn't seem to be enjoying herself at all. Her body was tense and rigid, her smile tight and brittle. When she'd danced with other men, she had been relaxed and genuinely looked to be having fun. Now, it looked like she wanted to be anywhere but with Astley.

Before he even realized he was doing it, he strode forward, interrupting the dance. It wasn't exactly polite, but really, he could pretty much do as he pleased. Astley scowled but nodded in greeting.

"Kentworth."

"Astley. I hate to interrupt—well, that's a lie, isn't it? I'm more than happy to interrupt," he said with a thin smile. Henry looked as if his blood was beginning to boil, his face turning a deep shade of red. "But I believe that Miss Montgomery actually promised me this dance."

Elle's eyes flew wide, darting between the two men. She was clearly relieved for the interruption from Astley, but wasn't exactly fond of Alec either. Alec arched a brow and extended his hand. She debated for a moment more and then gave Astley a stiff smile that didn't reach her eyes.

"He's right, I'm afraid. Apologies, Mister Astley." She quickly took Alec's hand and they began to dance as Astley stormed off, hands clenched and face blotchy with rage and embarrassment.

"I'm not going to thank you," she said stonily as they began to dance. He chuckled low, unable to stop himself. They danced in silence for a few moments. She was an excellent dancer, but there was something different about the way she moved, unlike anyone else in the room. An extra roll of her hips, a sensual fluidity as she transitioned from one movement to the next that Alec had never seen before.

"You know, I don't think anyone has ever thrown a drink on me before."

"I find that extremely hard to believe."

"Do you know who I am?" he asked, amused. This was oddly the most fun he'd had in...well, too long, really.

"I'm aware," she replied coolly. "Am I to act impressed? Fawn? Maybe worship at your feet?"

"If the mood takes you, I shall not stand in your way. I am rather impressive and do enjoy a good worshipping." She clenched her jaw, clearly fighting not to respond, and he smirked. He enjoyed ruffling her feathers, and, even more so, he enjoyed that she *allowed* her feathers to be ruffled. Most women in her position wouldn't deviate from the perfect puppet-like persona no matter what he said or did. He could put his clothes on backwards and run screaming through the room that the sky was a lovely shade of green, and they would simply agree with his assessment and compliment his impeccable style.

But Eleanor had no reservations about pushing back against him. She didn't seem as if she were at all concerned with trying to impress him, and he wondered why that was. Jocelyn had explained who he was, but perhaps the girl didn't truly understand what that meant? Or perhaps she already had another man in mind for her hand?

They continued to dance, but a strange heaviness seemed to settle in the air around them as their bodies drew closer and then apart, over and over. He was suddenly very aware of her body, of every sinful curve and the delicious fragrance gently wafting from her. It was slightly floral, but not cloying, and brought to mind sunny mornings in his mother's garden.

When they stood palm to palm and began to spin slowly, their gazes locked and held for an endless moment. For those few heartbeats, the tense animosity fell away and something else took its place. Something that made his pulse quicken and his mind race. Her lips parted on a soft inhale and her pupils expanded. He shook himself, clenching his jaw and she scowled, pressing her lips into a thin line as the strange spell broke around them.

"This is the longest song in the history of songs," she grumbled.

"So anxious to be rid of me?"

She gave him a mocking smile. "Pretty *and* smart. You really are quite the catch."

"Ah, so you think I'm pretty then?" She ran her tongue over her teeth in irritation and he actually grinned. Finally, the music ebbed and the dance ended. They quickly stepped away from each other and Alec's hands clenched into fists at his sides.

"Thank you for the dance, Miss Montgomery."

"My favorite part was the end," she responded with a smile and quick curtsey, before turning on her heel and rushing from the floor. He stood for long moments, staring after her, perplexed by this strange woman.

Perplexed, but admittedly intrigued.

Chapter 7

Elle grumbled as someone gently shook her awake, rolling over and burying her head under the pillow. She was exhausted from the night before and not nearly ready to be up and at 'em.

"Miss Montgomery, I'm afraid it's time to wake." Lottie. Elle liked the girl very much, but right now she wanted to throw something heavy at her.

"Five more minutes," she groaned, blindly shooing Lottie's hands away when the girl gently shook her shoulder again.

"I'm sorry, miss, but Lady MacTavish says you need to be getting dressed now. Suitors will surely be coming to call soon."

Elle groggily eased up, rubbing her eyes hard. She'd had fun at the ball—mostly anyway—but she wasn't exactly looking forward to this *coming to call* business. She knew it was part of the deal though, so she dressed, ate some breakfast, lamented her lack of Starbucks, and headed to the drawing room, only slightly less cranky than she'd been when she'd first woken up.

It was set up very similarly to the one at Chestwick Hall, with various sitting areas, two grand fireplaces, a piano, and Rose's harp. It was decorated in whites and pale blues and golds, the large windows along two of the walls letting in the morning light and giving the space a nice, airy feel.

Elle threw herself down on one of the couches across from Jocelyn, moaning loudly and tossing an arm over her eyes.

"Dramatic much?"

"I'm not a morning person," she grumbled before hoisting herself up into a seated position. "I would literally chop my left foot off for an iced shaken espresso with hazelnut mocha, oat milk, and sweet cream cold foam right now. Ok maybe not my whole foot, but a toe at least."

"Coffee seems to have gotten extremely complicated since I've been away," Jocy mused.

"At least the way I drink it." Elle shrugged and rolled her head on her shoulders. "Ok, so what exactly happens now?"

"Well, any interested suitors will come to call. They'll sit here with you—chaperoned of course."

"Oh *of course.*" Elle rolled her eyes. "God forbid I be in a room alone with a man, lest I fall immediately upon his penis and sully myself and my good name."

"Elle!" Jocelyn scolded with a laugh, glancing to the door to be sure no one had overheard the conversion. "You'll talk with the men. Get to know each other. You'll be *courted.*"

"Can't wait," Elle said with a false smile and two thumbs up.

Apparently, Elle and Rose were both highly sought after prizes. A stream of men continually flowed through the room as the morning wore on. Elle was polite to each of them, trying to keep an open mind and think of it as speed dating or something, but by the fourth or fifth one, she'd lost interest in the game. Rose was being the perfect lady, smiling demurely and obviously enjoying the fact that she had so many suitors interested. Elle couldn't imagine the stress of waiting to see if anyone would come—and the sense of utter disappointment and failure if no one did.

When Percival arrived, Rose beamed, nearly leaping off of the sofa to greet him. Elle and Jocelyn shared a look, both trying to hide their knowing smiles. Elle tried and failed to pay attention to whatever Baron Whats-His-Face was rambling about. He'd gone on for forty-five minutes straight about the pedigree of his Great Danes. Elle was a dog lover, but *come on.* Now he'd moved on to listing all the different vessels in his shipping fleet. He thought himself *extremely* clever for naming them all after Greek and Roman goddesses, as if no one else had ever thought of such a thing. She was very close to stabbing herself in the eye just to change the topic of conversation, but Jocelyn thankfully intervened before that step.

"Eleanor is a very talented pianist, Baron Carroway. Perhaps she can play for us."

"Oh indeed, indeed. Please," he said in his booming voice, throwing his arm wide towards the piano in the corner. She made her way across the room, mouthing *thank you* to Jocelyn as she went. She settled onto the bench and began to play Moonlight Sonata. She tried to focus on the music and ignore the way Baron Carroway slurped his tea loudly behind her, but it was a Herculean effort. When she finished, a familiar smooth voice sounded from somewhere behind her.

"That was quite lovely."

Elle's shoulders bunched with tension and she ground her teeth before turning slowly on the bench. Alexander Kentworth stood in the doorway beside a blushing Lottie. He wore a deep blue coat over a lighter blue vest, and she hated him for looking so good in it. His hair was a bit windblown but he looked all the better for it, a bit more devil-may-care than most of the men that had come to call on them, and in the natural light streaming in from the windows, Elle could see streaks of auburn within the brown strands.

"Is that Alec Kentworth?" *Alec?* Jocelyn smiled and rushed forward to wrap him in a hug before pressing a palm to his cheek. It was a motherly gesture and Elle narrowed her eyes at her *Aunt.* She knew that the Kentworth douchebag was a friend of the family, but Elle hadn't realized that Jocelyn was obviously very fond of him.

"Hello, Lady MacTavish," he said, a genuine smile creeping across his face rather than the sarcastic turn of his lips she'd seen at the ball. It was nice. Ok, it was better than nice. It was damn near perfect, which only made Elle more annoyed with him.

"It's been too long, dear. I had no idea you were going to be here for the season, not until I saw you last night."

"It wasn't planned. Father requested my presence without much warning, I'm afraid. I only arrived in the city just before the ball began."

"Well, we are all very glad that you're here." Elle snorted in utter disagreement, but quickly covered it with a delicate cough when all eyes shifted to her. Jocy gave her an admonishing look and Elle bobbed her head in a reluctant apology. She didn't have warm and fuzzies for Alexander Kentworth, but Elle knew that she owed Jocy and Callum more than she could ever repay. The least she could do was behave and be civil to someone who Jocy was obviously cared about. Not just Jocy—Rose flew across the room and threw herself at Alec, hugging him fiercely.

"I've missed you. You haven't written for ages," Rose scolded him with an almost-scowl, but she couldn't keep the smile off of her face.

"I'm sorry, Rosie. Truly. Forgive me?"

"Only if you've brought chocolates back with you from Marseilles again." The two laughed as Elle watched in fascination. Was this really the same pompous ass she met the night before?

"Have you come to speak to Callum, then?" Jocy asked as Rose made her way back to the couch and sat beside Percival. "I'm not certain if he's returned from a meeting with Lord Bambridge as of yet."

"I've actually come to call on Miss Montgomery."

Elle's eyes flew wide and Baron Carroway coughed violently into his tea before standing so quickly you would have thought the sofa was on fire. "I'll just be going then, shall I?" He hustled away with a quick bow to everyone in the room as Elle watched in shock. Was Lord Dickhead really *that* big of a deal? And did he seriously come to call on her? Was this a sick joke?

Jocelyn's brows flew upward and she looked between Alec and Elle, clearly surprised, but she quickly stepped aside and ushered him in.

"Of course, of course. Come in. Eleanor, come speak with Lord Kentworth."

"I'd rather eat glass," she gritted quietly. Alec arched a brow and Elle cleared her throat, adding hastily, "I'd prefer to keep playing actually, if it pleases you, Lord Kentworth." She didn't quite manage to keep the sarcasm out of her voice, though she tried. Sort of. Maybe.

"Elle," Jocelyn warned.

"No, that's quite alright. I would love to hear her play another." There was an amused challenge in his voice and Elle ground her teeth. Jocy had Lottie bring new refreshments for Alec, Rose and Percival looking on in interest.

Elle shot him a venomous smile and then played the opening bars of *Piano Man*. Jocy hissed her name and she pulled her lips in to hide her grin. She quickly morphed the song into *River Flows in You*. She probably should have played another classical piece, but this one just kind of came out. It had been one of her mom's favorites and Elle had learned to play it not long after she died. It was a comfort piece, so she wasn't quite sure why it was the first place her mind went now. She usually played it when she was sad, not when she was trying not to chuck furniture at stupid dukes or princes or whatever the hell Alexander Kentworth was.

When the song ended, she turned to find everyone in the room—including Lottie and Callum from the doorway—staring at her with odd expressions on their faces.

"That was beautiful, Elle," Rose breathed.

"What was that?" Alec asked, staring at her intently, his arrogant, cocky demeanor forgotten for a brief moment.

"Oh, um, it's...nothing. You wouldn't have heard of it. Something I learned in America." Elle quickly stood from the bench and made her way to the sofa. Jocelyn eyed her, silently telling her to behave, and began reading in a chair on the far side of the room.

Elle perched on the edge of the sofa next to Alec and hissed quietly, "Why are you here?"

"To call on you," he said slowly, looking at her like she was an idiot. "I thought that I made that perfectly clear by announcing it to the entire room only moments ago..."

Eleanor—Elle—looked like she was fighting the urge to hit him, her hands balled into tight fists resting on her lap, and he found it entirely amusing. He hadn't planned to call on anyone during this season, but he hadn't stopped thinking about this girl all night. He decided to give in to his curiosity and come to call. Plus, he adored the MacTavish family and hadn't seen them in far too long. So: two birds, one stone, as it were.

Her nostrils flared and she seemed to be struggling for calm before she said in a clipped tone, "Yes, I heard. My question is *why*? I wouldn't exactly call our meeting last night a pleasant one. And from what I've been told far too many times, you are quite the catch."

"I am that," he confirmed with a smirk.

"My point is that surely there are other ladies who caught your attention at the ball, ones who were far less...*clumsy* than I." Her lips curled at the corners in a smug smile, clearly remembering the way she'd tossed his drink on him.

"You were rather uncouth. I am happy to see that you can admit to your faults." The smile faded and that ire was back in her stunning eyes.

"If I'm so uncouth," she mocked, "then again I ask: *why are you here?*" If he didn't know any better, he would have sworn that she barely stopped herself from cursing.

He said simply, "Because I can be." Her lips parted and then pressed into a hard line. Why did he enjoy provoking this woman so much? She glanced past him to Jocelyn, who he could imagine was giving her a warning look. Elle snatched her tea cup off of the table and drank deeply, grimacing slightly. *Not a fan of tea?*

"So, get on with it then. Call on me."

Eleanor was tight-lipped for the remainder of their conversation, only giving him the briefest of answers to each of his questions, though he could tell that she was holding her tongue too many times to count. He didn't help matters by being intentionally condescending and less-than-gentlemanly on several occasions, he could admit. Something about this girl had him off-balance though he couldn't fathom why.

Alec was torn between being completely intrigued by the fact that she didn't seem to care at all who he was, the title he would one day acquire, the wealth a marriage to him would mean for her—and being utterly annoyed by it. *Why* didn't she care? As she'd said, he was the prize to be won. So, why didn't she want to win him? He couldn't quite explain why, but jealousy flared at all of the unnamed suitors that might come to call on her. What did any of them have that he didn't? What could any of them offer her that he couldn't?

Not that he was offering her anything, of course. Not that he ever would. His head was beginning to ache with the ridiculous train of thought going in endless circles. So, he continued to ask her the expected questions and she continued to give him the most succinct, clipped answers she could. With each one, his intrigue faded and his irritation grew.

In the end, his annoyance at her lack of interest and her annoyance with his apparent existence became too much. They were very close to outright bickering in front of everyone in the room, though they were both trying to keep their voices down. Jocelyn didn't seem to be fooled, looking wary, and Alec didn't want that, so he finally stood. Jocelyn did as well, moving towards him.

He bowed. "I must be going, Miss Montgomery. I thank you for the...scintillating conversation," he said in a stiff voice.

She stopped grinding her teeth and staring daggers at him long enough to stand and curtsey.

"It was a pleasure, Lord Kentworth," she said, though it was clearly anything but.

"You must join us for dinner soon, Alec," Jocelyn said, cupping his cheek again in that motherly way that made his chest twist painfully. Jocelyn had always been a bit of a second mother to him, but even more so since his own had passed on. He immediately felt shame for how he'd behaved towards her niece. She had been nothing but good to him—she and Callum both—and he owed them better. *But this girl drives me mad...*

"Of course," he said, giving her a kiss on the cheek. He glanced over his shoulder for one last look at Eleanor as he left the room. She was staring towards the windows on the far side of the room, a strange look on her face. The anger was gone, replaced with a sort of melancholy that he suddenly longed to understand and erase. Was she missing her home? Her family? Or had he truly upset her?

Shaking himself, he smiled at Jocy and Callum, nodded a goodbye to Rosie and Percival, and hastily made his exit.

Chapter 8

Elle surveyed the park. It was beautiful, to be sure. Lightly rolling hills of green, large trees lining the wide path that wound its way through the grounds like a lazy snake. A small stream ran through the center, several stone bridges crossing it at intervals, and eventually emptied into the large pond on the far side near a thick copse of trees. She wished she'd been able to bring her drawing supplies along. It had been years since she'd done any landscapes, but she had the urge to try and capture the beauty of this place.

The park was full of people: ladies in beautiful dresses, many carrying delicate parasols; men in coats that made Elle sweat just looking at them, some even wearing top hats that made her want to laugh.

"So, we literally just...walk?"

"Well, it *is* called the promenade," Jocelyn said wryly. Elle gave her a dry look and she chuckled. "Yes, you literally just walk around—usually with a gentleman." She nodded towards Percival who was bee-lining in their direction, Rose already beaming at his approach.

The two lovebirds walked close enough to hold a low conversation, Rose giggling demurely every so often and Percival grinning ear to ear. Jocy and Elle trailed behind them, far enough to give the two a bit of privacy.

"Is it weird? Thinking about your seventeen-year-old getting married?"

Jocy nodded and smiled to another group walking the other direction, exchanging quick pleasantries before turning her attention back to Elle.

"It is and it isn't. The part of me from *then* is appalled at the idea, but the part that has been living this life for almost twenty years accepts it and is happy for her to find a good husband who makes her happy and can give her a good life." She hiked a shoulder as if to say *I know it's weird, but it is what it is.*

Elle mulled that over. She supposed she understood, and as Percival swooped down to pick a handful of yellow daisies and present them to Rose, she shared in Jocy's joy at the idea of Rose being happy. She just had to constantly remind herself that this wasn't 2020 and things were very, very different here.

"So, what is that Alec guy's deal? Is he always an ass to everyone, or am I just special?"

"He's a good boy—man," Jocy corrected, shaking her head. "I've known him since he was just a boy. Their family estate abuts ours," she explained. "He's about ten years older than Rose, but the two of them practically grew up together—used to fight like brother and sister, that's for sure. She was heartbroken when he left to study to become a doctor and chose to stay away to practice instead of coming home."

Elle tried to imagine Alec as a boy, pulling Rose's pigtails or making mud pies, but she couldn't quite manage it.

"And the whole being an ass thing?"

"He isn't really, not deep down. He's..." She pursed her lips, seemingly trying to figure out the best way to explain. "He's complicated," she finished lamely. Elle snorted and shook her head.

"Of course he is."

"You have to remember that he isn't actually being an ass—not in the way you think," she added quickly as Elle began to object. "Here, in this time," she said quietly, "he has every reason to act the way he does. Haughty. Entitled. Because he *is* those things. In this society, it is just...how it is. I know that isn't an excuse, at least not for you, but you have to think of things as they *are*, not the way they *will be* two hundred years from now."

"So, he's an ass, but here, asses are just the norm."

Jocy huffed out a laugh. "I suppose, but he really isn't like that at all. He puts on a front for most people...and he's also walking up right now."

Elle's eyes snapped up from where she'd been watching a bee flitting from flower to flower. She saw the turd in question approaching and cursed beneath her breath, wishing the bee would fly up and sting her in the eye just to have an excuse to run away.

"What did I do to deserve this?" she hissed at Jocy just as Alec reached them. Elle plastered on a fake smile and said louder, "Speak of the devil and he shall appear."

"Ah, so you were speaking of me, Miss Montgomery? I'm flattered. Truly."

Choosing to ignore him, she turned to Jocy.

"I'd love to go see the pond. I'll leave you two to chat about the dinner plans you mentioned yesterday. If you'll excuse me." She inclined her head and didn't wait for a response before turning and striding off as quickly as she could without drawing attention or looking crazy.

Her escape attempt was short-lived.

"If I didn't know any better, I would think you were trying to get away from me, Miss Montgomery." She balled her hands into fists but didn't stop as he moved to walk beside her. She was already annoyed by his existence. Now she was equally annoyed that she was all but jogging and he was just taking a leisurely stroll. *Damn his stupid long strides. Why does he have to be so tall?*

"And I was led to believe you were smart," she said with feigned politeness. He didn't respond and she couldn't stop herself from glancing sidelong at him. He was staring at her with a strange expression, the same one she'd seen several times in their short acquaintance: curiosity, amusement, and annoyance. His eyes were a shade lighter here in the sun, rings of gold around his irises that she hadn't noticed before sparking to life. His hair was tousled, as it had been the day before, and Elle got the feeling that he simply liked it that way, not caring if he looked perfectly coiffed or not. Again, he wasn't clean shaven as most of the men were either. So, he was Mister Fancypants, but he didn't seem to care about keeping up the image. She admittedly liked that aspect of his personality, but quickly mentally kicked herself. The bastard had insulted her over and over during their conversation yesterday, and when he wasn't insinuating that she was basically just a poor, dumb American, he was being a condescending ass. There was nothing to like.

"Have I done something to offend you?" he finally asked, seeing the change in her expression.

Elle stopped and whirled on him, incredulous.

"You spent the better part of the afternoon yesterday insulting my family, education, and social status."

"I did no such thing," he countered, looking truly affronted, brow furrowing.

Elle's mouth popped open, her blood boiling. She tried to speak but couldn't even get a full word out, she was so annoyed, just random syllables making their way past her lips. He held up a hand to halt her.

"I asked if your family held any titles. You confirmed they did not. Was that incorrect?"

"Well, no. But—"

"I asked if you had tutors and you said you did not. Was *that* incorrect?"

I didn't have tutors, I went to school like a normal person and have my fucking Bachelor's! She wanted to scream.

"No," she said through gritted teeth.

"I asked—"

"Ok, ok, you made your point. It wasn't what you asked but *how* you asked it." He arched a brow and she rubbed her temples, not wanting to have this conversation. She tried to remember what Jocy had said, about it being a different time. Maybe he really wasn't trying to be a dick, he was just asking the questions that any man of his position might ask a woman in hers. *Different time, Elle*, she reminded herself, *Different time, different time, different fucking time.*

She shook her head, expelled an annoyed breath, and turned to continue walking. She decided to go with the silent treatment from that point forward, merely nodding or giving him non-committal grunts in response to the few questions he did ask before he understood what she was doing. Instead of taking the hint and leaving her alone, he continued to walk beside her in silence, hands clasped behind his back and his shoulders tight with tension. They both stopped in the middle of one of the arched stone bridges, and she leaned her arms on the edge, watching the gentle bubble of the water as it flowed beneath them.

He stood beside her, enough space between them to still be proper though they were far from alone in a park filled with people, and stared into the water as well.

Without looking at him, she finally asked, "Why do you continue to speak with me? I am clearly beneath whatever standards you envision for someone you'd like to court—no titles, no tutors, no great family legacy to my name." *At least not in this century.*

He turned to look at her, but she kept her gaze on the water, only seeing him in her peripheral. He seemed to study her, as if the answer to the question were written on her face.

Why *did* he continue to put himself in her path? She was beautiful, that much was obvious, but as she'd said, she wasn't a woman someone of his station should be courting. Though, he reminded himself, he wasn't *actually* courting anyone. So, part of the blame could be placed squarely on his mind taking orders from his cock. The rest? He had no idea.

She clearly didn't enjoy being around him and he himself was conflicted on if he enjoyed being around her. Part of him was amused and intrigued by the girl. The way she spoke was refreshing, the way she held herself so differently than any woman he'd ever encountered was fascinating and admittedly alluring. But the other part of him was thoroughly vexed by her, annoyance skittering up his spine each time she smirked or didn't show the respect due to him. He'd never *wanted* what was due to him, but when this particular woman refused to give it, it...bothered him. He scrubbed a hand down his face, knowing it made no sense at all.

"I don't know," he finally answered honestly.

It was the wrong answer.

She bristled and turned to glower at him. She clenched her jaw, the muscle there ticking in tight pulses. Her eyes were blazing, like there were twin flames behind the sapphires. He suspected she might be thinking of slapping him...or *punching* him? He quirked a brow at her balled fist at her side. He didn't think any lady in the Ton even knew how to form a proper fist, let alone would think of actually swinging one at anyone, least of all a future viscount. *This,* he thought. *This is why I continue to put myself in your path. You surprise me and I...like it.*

In the end, she didn't try to assault him, merely blew out a long breath and said in a clipped tone, "I am feeling a bit faint, I think I need to sit down. Excuse me." She strode off quickly, looking like she wanted nothing more than to run away from him as fast as possible. He let her go, remaining on the bridge, but watched her as she reached Jocelyn, gave her a swift kiss on the cheek, and walked towards the line of carriages waiting on the road lining the park. Henry Astley watched with an annoyed expression on his face, obviously having been planning to ask Eleanor to walk with him before she raced away. *Silver lining.*

"Did you insult the girl's mother, Alec?"

Daniel met him atop the bridge, grinning widely.

"What do you mean?" Alec asked innocently.

Daniel huffed out a laugh. "I don't think I've ever seen someone so eager to get away from you, especially not a woman. Normally they must be pried off of you with the force of ten men."

Alec laughed at that. It was almost true.

"She was feeling faint is all. Being in my presence can be quite overwhelming, as you can imagine," he said with a rakish grin. "How goes your hunt, my friend?"

Daniel exhaled roughly. "It goes, I suppose. I've got my eye on Emily Rushing and it looks hopeful. She's quite shy, but seems very amenable and it would be a good match. Her father owns a textile factory and a partnership with my father's shipping fleet would be advantageous."

It had always seemed so odd to Alec that marriage was looked at as a business arrangement, at least for most. A simple partnership that was beneficial, financially or socially or both, to the parties and families involved, but the actual companionability between the bride and groom meant very little. Perhaps that was why he'd been so against the idea of it, against participating in the seasons before now. Alec's father and mother, and Jocelyn and Callum MacTavish for that matter, were the exceptions to the rule. They'd loved in a way that Alec couldn't even accurately explain or describe, as if they were truly one soul split into two bodies. After growing up with that as his example of what marriage was, how could he possibly stand to merely choose a woman whose family may be of good stock or aid in his family's business affairs in some way?

Daniel pulled him back from his thoughts, asking, "So, you've got your eye on the Montgomery girl then? Truly?"

"Ah, you know me, I have my eye on every girl within my proximity."

They both laughed, but Alec's mind unwittingly drifted back to Eleanor. Before he could think more on her, however, the Wilshire sisters and their mother made their way onto the bridge.

"Stab me, stab me now and toss me into the creek," Alec said quietly to Daniel, who had to hide his laugh with a cough. Clearing his throat, Daniel greeted them politely, ever the gentleman.

The girls tittered as they inclined their heads. Their mother looked at Alec expectantly and he reluctantly gave in, asking one of the sisters—no idea which—if she would care to walk with him. Daniel dutifully took the other, giving Alec a look that said *you owe me.*

"Father, what are you doing up?!" Alec demanded as he rushed forward. His father had decided to make the trip into London from their country estate, despite his ill health, and the journey had been hard on him. "Where is Bennett?"

Jonathan Kentworth rolled his eyes but allowed Alec to help him across the drawing room and into one of the large chairs by the empty fireplace.

"I am perfectly capable of walking around on my own without supervision, or did you forget that this is my house, Alexander?"

"Bennett isn't there to supervise, he is there to assist you," Alec corrected. His father gave him a dry look. "And maybe to supervise, just a bit," he amended with a small grin.

His father's lips curled upward, eyes crinkling at the corners. He chuckled, but it quickly turned into a coughing fit. Alec's chest constricted, the evidence his father was indeed getting worse was here before his eyes and hitting him like a battering ram to the heart. Alec knew this was the reason his father had requested he come home for the season: he knew he didn't have much longer and wanted Alec settled with a wife when he became the viscount.

A part of him knew he was resisting for more than just the reluctance to stop cavorting and settle down. In his mind, if he didn't take a wife, didn't prepare for becoming the head of the Kentworth house, then his father couldn't leave. Of course, he knew logically that wouldn't keep his father from dying, but matters of the heart, especially between a son and his father, rarely followed logic. To Alec, he was still a boy, looking up to his father as if the man had hung the moon. Despite the gray streaking his black hair now and the deep lines in his skin that came with age, Alec still saw him as the stalwart, larger-than-life man he'd been in Alec's youth. It was strange, seeing the present and the past so clearly together at once.

Alec quickly brought his father some water, and the coughing eased.

"Stop looking at me like that," his father scolded.

"Like what?" Alec asked, taking the cup from his father and setting it on the table.

"Like a doctor looking at a patient." His father arched a brow and gave Alec a pointed look. Alec chuckled.

"Apologies, father. Old habits and all of that."

Bennett burst into the room then, and both men turned to look at him expectantly. Bennett had been with them longer than Alec had been alive and was far more than a butler, he was truly a part of the family. He looked at Jonathan with thinned lips and accusation sparking in his deep brown eyes.

"You didn't hear Margaret screaming for help at all, did you?"

Jonathan's lips curled upward and he hiked a shoulder, not at all sorry for the ruse. Alec couldn't help but laugh and though he was still clearly frustrated and worried, Bennett shook his head and smiled.

"I know you both mean well, but all of this fussing is too much." Jonathan held up his hand when both of them began to speak at once. "I am ill and on my way to the grave. We all know it to be true." Alec winced, the words hitting him like a physical blow, slicing into his core like a blade. "But," his father added, leaning forward to make Alec meet his eyes, "I am not there yet. So, can we stop tiptoeing around and treating me like I'm a frail duckling?"

After a few moments, Alec sat heavily in the other chair. "A duckling?" he asked wryly.

"It was the first animal that came to mind."

"I would have gone with mule. A stubborn ass," Bennett said quietly, though loud enough that he knew he could be heard. Alec and his father both laughed loudly and Bennet exhaled roughly. "I'll fetch some food then, shall I?"

When the two of them were alone once more, Jonathan turned to Alec. "And how is the season going for the most eligible gentleman?"

"Father, really," Alec groaned, leaning his head against the back of the chair.

"Come on, Alec. Humor a dying old man." Alec shot him a dark look and his father laughed, but thankfully the coughing didn't follow. Alec ran a hand through his hair, his mind immediately gravitating back to Eleanor.

"Have you ever heard of this MacTavish cousin from America?"

"Can't say that I have. Jocelyn's niece?" When Alec nodded, his father looked thoughtful. "I recall Callum saying that Jocelyn was mostly estranged from her family, but he never gave the details. The girl's mother must be Jocelyn's sister?"

"I guess the girl had no other family then if she wound up here. Jocelyn seems to adore her, so whatever animosity may have been between her and the sister, it does not appear to have tainted any relationship with Eleanor."

"Eleanor. Hmm. Pretty name."

"Pretty girl," Alec responded before he could stop himself. He cleared his throat. "She's lovely enough, though being from America you can imagine how...out of place she is at times in the Ton."

"And yet, you've called on her?"

Alec cut his eyes at his father. He had been gossiping with the staff, it seemed.

"Yes, but mostly because I thought it might look rude if I didn't come to call since we are so close to the MacTavishs of course. Rose is taking to coming out like a fowl to water," he said, quickly changing the subject.

Jonathan smiled at that. "I had no doubts." Silence fell between them, comfortable at first, but then becoming thick with unspoken words. "Alec, you need to take this seriously," his father finally said, though not ungently.

"Father, I don't need a wife. You said it yourself, you aren't dying yet. There is no need for me to marry this season. Besides, there is no law that says a viscount *must* have a wife."

"Is that truly why you think I called you home this season? Because I think you need a wife simply because you will soon be the viscount? Alec, I called you here because I am worried about you. I feel like you are...floundering."

"Floundering?" Alec said with a quirk of his brow.

"Yes, ever since...well, ever since it happened, you haven't been the same. You've been restless with no direction. I hear the rumors, I know the types of places you spend your time in and the type of women with whom you keep company. And that is all fine and good, I was quite the rake myself before I met your mother and became the man you know and adore." Jonathan waggled his eyebrows and gave Alec a mischievous grin, making Alec huff out a laugh. "But I'm afraid that you are using those things to fill a hole inside yourself."

Alec ran his fingers along the arm of the chair, picking at a loose thread in the embroidery. His father was right of course, but that didn't mean he wanted to admit it. Admitting to his father that he *did* feel like something was missing inside him, that he had no idea what he was doing or where he was going, or that he sometimes felt as if his life had no real meaning anymore...that he was *lost*, well it made him feel like a failure, a disappointment as a man and a son.

"And there's something wrong with that?" he asked quietly.

"Son, I don't want you to find a wife because you will be the viscount, I want you to find a wife because I think it will make you *happy*. I want you to be happy, Alec, and I don't think that you are."

Alec's throat felt thick. His father had always somehow seen to the heart of him, known the deepest secrets and truths Alec kept hidden from the world, hidden even from himself sometimes.

"I...don't know how to be happy," he admitted quietly.

"Well, the answer is simple: you find a woman who can teach you."

As if it were that easy. Again, his mind drifted to Eleanor. She seemed to despise him, and he wasn't convinced he cared much for her either, but...he felt drawn to her, for whatever reason, and he supposed that was something? Despite his father's words, Alec still had no plans to actually marry anyone any time soon. But he would keep up the charade, for his father's sake.

"I shall try," he lied.

Chapter 9

Elle was over being a part of high society London in a big way. The dances and beautiful gowns and spectacle of it all had lost its novelty after the first month. Now, all she wanted was to return to Chestwick Hall, to spend time in the gazebo that Jocelyn had given her, to just have a minute to be *her* again. She needed to get away from all of the suffocating teas and promenades and dances and etiquette and tradition and—*ugh!* She wanted to scream. It was just too much.

She couldn't stop thinking about her home, about the fact that she may never return there. Could this really be her life now? Being something pretty for a man to gawk at? What the fuck was she supposed to do if she really was stuck here? Maybe she could go back to America, though the thought of being on a boat for weeks on end crossing the Atlantic before things like GPS and the Coast Guard made that a less than appealing option. But she couldn't just stay here, the spinster niece of Jocelyn MacTavish who lurked around their house like a ghost, could she? Surely that would cause people to talk, and if there was one thing she'd learned about these people, it was that they *loved* to fucking talk. It was a non-stop gossip factory and Elle loathed the idea of being in the center of it. Or well, she would hate if she was the reason that Jocy and Callum were. She didn't really care what people thought or said about her, personally.

Alexander Kentworth hadn't come to call on her again—though too many others had and she was seriously contemplating throwing herself down the stairs just to get a break from them—but their paths did continue to cross. He came to dinner at the MacTavish manor several times, and the two of them had mostly ignored each other, only having the scantiest of conversations which mostly consisted of the necessary pleasantries—*How are you faring, Miss Montgomery? Well, thank you for asking*—all said in polite but clipped tones. Jocy and Callum had seemed both curious and amused by the obvious animosity between them.

As much as Elle hated the dinners, she couldn't deny that she loved the way Rose lit up whenever Alec was around, and, to her surprise, Alec let his mask fall away whenever he was around Rose. Sometimes he'd laugh or share in some secretive joke with her from their childhood, an easy smile on his face that made Elle's pulse race, and she wondered if this could really be the same guy who looked down his nose at everyone. Sometimes he'd catch her watching them and clear his throat, stiffening and pulling the mask back into place. Rose would just roll her eyes, as if she were used to him acting like someone else around other people, but she knew the true Alec and was alright keeping his secret.

At each ball, their eyes would inevitably meet across the room throughout the night, him usually staring at her with some mixture of irritation and interest that she didn't understand, but always got under her skin. He would ask her to dance and she would agree, sometimes because she knew it was expected of her to, and others to simply get away from other men like Henry Astley. Henry had taken a keen interest in her, coming to call almost every day and constantly asking her to walk with him in the park. He was handsome and cordial enough, but he just gave off that vibe, the one that said *I am better than everyone else and you are a stupid, insignificant woman who should do nothing but worship at my feet and live in my bed and give me babies and be grateful for it.*

And with the way he always seemed to make sure they danced close to Alec, walked past him as they strolled through the park, it was as if he were trying to flaunt her in Alec's face. Why, she had no idea, but who was she to understand an obvious dick-measuring contest between two nineteenth-century gentlemen. Either way, when it came to Henry, she was glad that unmarried women and men couldn't be alone together. He seemed mostly harmless, but he wasn't necessarily one of those guys you'd want to be the last girl at the bar with.

Each dance with Alec was...interesting. They both held themselves stiffly, clearly annoyed to be near each other, but there was also an attraction there that she couldn't deny. The air seemed to thicken all around them when they danced, the tension nearly suffocating in its intensity. Their bodies so close together, electricity thrumming in the small space between them, the promise of something dark and carnal waiting in the shadows if they would just let it out. If she'd been at home, she knew without a doubt that they would have anger banged a time or twelve, and it would be the best sex of her life.

But here, she simply had to dance with him and clench her teeth as her body betrayed her mind. Afterwards, they'd part ways, both flushed and irritated, until the next time when they did it all over again. *Lather, rinse, repeat.*

She didn't think she could deal with him tonight, though, and hoped this was an evening that he decided to go to a brothel or whatever the hell it was that men did in these times, instead of attending the ball. She was quiet as they rode to Lord Yorkshire's mansion. The day had been a hard one for her: it was supposed to have been her wedding day. Though she knew that not being with Ashton was the best thing, it still all hit her hard that morning as she lay in her four-poster bed, staring at the ceiling. It wasn't so much that she missed him, exactly, it was more just a gut-punch reminder that her life had been completely uprooted. *Everything* had changed so quickly, even before being sucked back through time. She'd caught her fiancé cheating on her, mere months before their wedding, and despite the fact that she knew without a doubt that they really weren't meant to be together, thinking about how they'd been at the beginning and how they'd slowly drifted apart without even seeming to notice, or care, hit her doubly hard today. If she hadn't caught him, if she hadn't been brought back in time, would she have gone through with the wedding, even knowing deep down it wasn't right? She honestly wasn't sure, and that was a scary thought.

She'd been flip-flopping all day between crying and being so pissed she wanted to punch something. She didn't want to be stuck in the 1800s. She wanted to be back in her own house, in her own bed, binge watching Netflix and playing *The Last of Us*. She wanted a double bacon cheeseburger and a beer. She wanted to go out dancing with her friends and maybe find a random stranger to make her forget how shitty her stupid ex-fiancé was. She wanted a hot shower for fuck's sake! She just wanted her life back, even if it was a life that looked different than she planned.

"Are you alright?" Jocy asked her quietly as they gently swayed with the movement of the carriage.

"Fine," Elle said, trying her best not to snap. "Fine...enough," she amended.

Jocy looked concerned, but nodded, knowing Elle well enough already to realize that talking it through was not going to help matters right now. Elle had always been one of those people who just needed time to process things on her own. Constantly being nettled to talk about it or asked what was wrong only made things worse—and usually ended with Elle lashing out on a big scale. She'd regret it later, not even really understanding why she'd gotten quite *so* mad, and wasn't too proud to apologize when she needed to, but it was just how she was wired. She would talk with Jocelyn about it later, would appreciate her ear and her insight and the hugs she would inevitably give, but right now, Elle just needed to *not* talk about her life. She needed to not think about it either, but that part wasn't coming so easily.

She had debated all day if she was going to attend the ball that evening, and Jocy said she'd be more than happy to tell everyone that she was ill, but eventually Elle decided being alone with her thoughts would be worse than dealing with people all night.

She'd been wrong.

As soon as they arrived and she'd been bombarded by men eager for conversation and dancing, she realized her mistake. It was just too much. Too many in-her-face reminders of how very off-course her life had veered in the past months. She saw Alec across the room and knew she couldn't escape a conversation with him tonight without it ending in a fight. That would be most unbecoming of a lady, so she grabbed a glass of something off of a table, gathered her heavy skirt, and quickly made her way outside, hoping to hide for a while.

The large stone patio off the back of the house was dotted here and there with people admiring the grounds illuminated in the distance by what seemed like hundreds of lanterns held on iron posts. A wide expanse of perfectly trimmed grass sat just off of the patio, and a grand hedge maze and gardens lay beyond that.

Elle wandered to the left side of the patio, thankfully empty of other party-goers. There were torches burning brightly at intervals around the space, but much of it was still in shadow. She wished she could just disappear within them. She closed her eyes and tried to breathe around all of the emotions knotting in her throat: despair, betrayal, pain, sorrow, anger, longing. She knew she wasn't meant to be with Ash, but it still hurt to think about how their relationship had ended, it still hurt to think about the fact that right now, if things hadn't gotten so fucked, she would be someone's wife, mistake or not.

She closed her eyes and fought back tears, honestly not even sure what she was crying about.

"Escaping so early in the evening?" Alec's voice drawled from just behind her.

She gritted her teeth and clenched her fingers around the glass in her hand. She hadn't even taken a sip yet, she realized, and wondered how long she'd been out there, staring into the distance but not seeing much of anything, lost in her thoughts. She opened her eyes just as he came to stand near her at the stone railing that ran along the right and left sides of the porch, the back open to the grass just beyond.

"What do you want?" she snapped in a low voice. She knew she shouldn't speak to him this way, but with no one else near enough to hear them, she figured it didn't matter. She didn't care what *he* thought, after all. She was still keeping up appearances in general for Rose's sake, but Elle didn't really give a fuck about Alexander Kentworth's opinion of her at this point.

He arched a brown brow, his lips thinning in irritation. *Good. Be irritated. Give me a reason to lash out.* She was practically itching for a fight.

"A bit of air," he replied, eyeing her. The fire light flickered across his face, throwing shadows across his cheeks and making his eyes look nearly black.

"Get your air elsewhere," she hissed through clenched teeth.

"And who are you, exactly, to tell me where I can and cannot go to *breathe*?" he said in that haughty tone she hated.

Eleanor looked absolutely breathtaking that evening, wearing a silk gown of deep crimson, almost the color of wine, that flowed over her body like a river. Her hair was pulled into an elegant knot at the back of her head, drawing his attention to the delicate column of her throat, making him wonder what it might be like to press his lips there, to feel her pulse race beneath his tongue...

But she seemed off tonight, stiff and distant in a way he hadn't seen in all these weeks. Sure, she was never thrilled to see him, annoyance radiating from the lines of her body whenever she spied him, but this was different. Was something wrong? He didn't know why he cared. He *shouldn't* care. But here he was, making his way towards her in the soft torch light. She didn't even notice his approach, seemingly completely lost in thought. Her eyes were shut and her shoulders slumped, as if she were upset. *No, not just upset, she looks...defeated.* He ached to know why, and part of him wanted to help, to clear that look from her beautiful face, to make her smile.

He told himself it was just curiosity, nothing more, but even that irritated him. *Why* was he constantly drawn to this girl despite her clear lack of interest in him? Perhaps that was precisely why. No other woman had ever so obviously disliked him before. It was novel, but also grated on his pride.

She was clearly in a mood, her defeated look disappearing as soon as he'd spoken to her, anger taking its place. She usually at least attempted to maintain a semi-civil tone, but not tonight.

"And who are you, exactly, to tell me where I can and cannot go to *breathe*?" he asked in a peevish tone when she told him to get air elsewhere. He knew the moment the words left his mouth that he'd made a mistake, and guilt flared in his chest. She was obviously upset and he was provoking her, just because he could, because he found amusement in it. Usually, anyway. Now, he wished he could take the words back. To his surprise, when she whirled on him, instead of tears, her eyes blazed with something very close to *rage*. He reared back slightly, not expecting this intense of a reaction.

"You arrogant, pompous, pretentious prick!" she hissed. Alec blinked, not sure he was hearing her correctly. Had she...had she truly just called him a *prick*?

He stared at her, clenching and unclenching his jaw, nostrils flaring. The guilt had dissolved like sugar in water the instant she turned that burning hatred on him. He was constantly torn between intrigue and irritation with this girl, between wanting to be near her and to stay as far away as possible.

"Why won't you just *leave me alone*?" Her voice was raised, but still low enough that she wasn't drawing too much attention from the other people milling about.

His temper flared. Who was she to speak to him this way?...And why *couldn't* he leave her alone?

"I find you...vexing," he finally ground out.

"Then I suggest you stop finding me *at all*," she snapped before tossing the contents of her cup down in one large swallow and shoving the empty glass into his chest. His hands flew up in surprise, gripping the glass as she let go. She gathered her skirt in her hands and strode away from him, determined to go where, he had no idea—she was walking off of the stone patio, out into the night. He followed on her heels, catching up to her in a few long strides and giving a reassuring smile to the older couple admiring the ironwork over the doors leading back inside.

"Where do you think you're going?" he demanded just as she stepped off of the stone and out into the grass. She whirled, seemingly burning with a rage he didn't understand, practically shaking with it. He knew she disliked him, but this seemed like an overreaction, even if he had been a bit of an ass.

"I know that everyone in this ti—" She pressed her lips into a hard line, shaking herself, and his brows drew down in confusion. "—in this *place* thinks that a woman couldn't possibly have a single thought without the assistance of a man, but I assure you I am perfectly capable of storming off in a huff on my own!"

If looks could kill a man, he would have been slain on the spot ten times over. He held up one palm in surrender, still holding her glass in the other, and she turned on her heel to *storm off in a huff,* as she'd put it. Alec watched her go, not taking his eyes from her until a butler approached. He gave the man a wry smile and handed him Eleanor's empty glass.

"Ladies," Alec breathed ruefully, as if that explained Eleanor's outburst fully, and the butler inclined his head with a knowing smile.

"Yes, sir."

The two shared an amused moment, but it was interrupted by a scream piercing the night. *Eleanor?* Alec and the butler exchanged worried glances before Alec ran in the direction of the sound, the other man not far behind. Others from the patio followed, though Alec quickly left them behind as he raced forward. His heart thundered in his chest as he ran across the grass, slightly damp with evening dew.

He skidded to a stop at the edge of a small drop in the lawn and saw Eleanor in a heap on the ground, clutching at her ankle. She was muttering curses under her breath—some he knew quite well and was surprised to find *she* did, as not many ladies would have heard such things; others he didn't understand and assumed were American terms. *What on earth was a "fucking fuckity fuck"?*

The others arrived and she glanced up. She stared at them standing above her, face pinched in pain and flushed with what he believed to be embarrassment. He felt a tiny flare of pity for the girl: no one had warned her of the Yorkshire's famed "stepping lawn"—it dropped off at intervals, like an expansive staircase made of earth.

Alec hopped down and knelt beside her.

"Are you alright?"

She pressed her lips into a thin line and glared at him, looking like she was prepared to ignore him completely, but when he gave her a stern look, she sighed in defeat. A lock of golden hair fell across her temple as she nodded.

"I'm fine, it's just my ankle."

She shooed him away and stood, only to gasp in pain and nearly topple. She clutched at his arm to steady herself, and without thought, Alec scooped her up, one arm beneath her knees, the other wrapped around her back. She inhaled sharply in surprise, but quickly snaked one arm around the back of his neck to steady herself. He ignored the way her body felt in his arms, the warmth of her skin burning through his coat and shirt. Despite their shared irritation of one another, he'd felt the pull between them when they danced, but this was something entirely different. It was intense and addictive and dangerous. It felt...combustible, like gunpowder just waiting for a single spark. Did she feel it as well? He swallowed hard and kept his thoughts from spiraling.

He knew he'd never be able to hold her like this under normal circumstances and he felt himself grip her tighter against him. *Enjoy it while I can.* Her breath hitched, and though he could feel her eyes on him, he didn't allow himself to meet her gaze. If he did, he wasn't entirely sure that he wouldn't do something incredibly horrid and unrefined, like kissing her in front of God and everyone in the Ton. *But my God, it might be worth it,* he thought as he inhaled deeply. Her floral, sunny smell enveloping him as it always did when they were near each other.

The others were in tizzy as the small caravan made its way back towards the house, chittering loudly about the hows and whys and how many broken bones she might have. Alec rolled his eyes, already imagining the way gossip would spread through the ballroom.

"This way, sir," the butler said, leading them to a study down the hall from the ballroom. Alec could still hear the music faintly in the background. He sat Eleanor down on the sofa near the fireplace as lanterns flared to life all around the room, the man seeming to be everywhere at once. He was very efficient.

Alec knelt before the couch and reached for her leg. She flinched backwards and hissed in a pained breath.

"What are you doing?"

"I'm examining your ankle."

"Why?"

"Well, that is typically what a physician does when someone is injured," he said blandly. Her mouth popped open but before she could speak, Alec turned to the butler. "Would you fetch some water, some strips of cloth, and whisky?" he asked, just as Lady MacTavish came into the room.

"Elle!" she exclaimed. "What happened? Someone said you fainted!" Alec's lips quirked. The gossip had spread even faster than he would have guessed.

"I didn't faint," she said, rolling her eyes. "I just fell."

"Fell?"

"The Stepping Lawn," Alec supplied helpfully.

"Oh my heavens," Jocy said, hand flying worriedly to her mouth, "I should have thought to warn you." Her brow furrowed. "But why were you out there in the dark in the first place?"

"Storming off in a huff, I believe," he said dryly. Eleanor shot him a glare and Jocy gave him one of those calculating looks of hers, her lips curling ever so slightly as she seemed to figure out that Eleanor's annoyance at him had been the root cause of the fall.

"Are you alright, dear?" Jocy asked, brushing the wayward lock of hair from Eleanor's face. It was such a motherly gesture and Alec could see plainly how much Jocy loved the girl.

"It's just my ankle," she said, giving Jocy a pained half-smile.

"Alec, is she truly alright?"

"I won't be sure until she allows me to examine her," he said, looking pointedly at Elle. He'd grown to like the shortened version of her name, and though he'd been trying to use her proper name, even in his head, he finally gave in. Elle met his gaze and rolled her eyes, but nodded, making his lips quirk.

He gently gripped her slippered foot and raised her leg upward. He inched her skirt up to inspect her leg and he barely stifled a gasp, his heart beating rapidly: she was wearing no stockings. He glanced up at the women, brow raised in question, but Elle pulled her lips inward and Jocelyn looked to be fighting a smile, half exasperated, half amused.

"I'm just so forgetful sometimes," Elle said innocently, knowing exactly what he was asking. He knew it was a lie, somehow knew that she had chosen not to wear them and that intrigued him on far too many levels. He fought a smile as he turned his gaze back to her leg. Her *bare* leg. He didn't know why his pulse was racing. It wasn't as if he'd never seen a woman's bare leg before. Not only was he a trained physician, but he had been with countless women in his life, seeing every inch of them bare. So why was seeing Elle's leg making his stomach knot? Why was his mouth dry, his heart thundering as images flashed in his mind that no gentleman or physician should be thinking about?

He eased one hand up from her foot, keeping his touch gentle, but he froze, eyes widening in surprise. Her skin was soft and completely *smooth*. He swallowed hard, the feel and sight making him unbalanced. She gasped quietly as he continued to run his fingers over her skin and he wasn't sure if it was from pain or...pleasure? He forced himself not to look upward, only concentrating on his work, reminding himself that he was here to check her injury and nothing more. But he was so fascinated, so...aroused, that he could barely think.

"So, you're a doctor," she said, sounding a bit breathless...or was that merely his imagination?

"I used to be, yes," he replied, forcing himself to focus. He had been a physician, and a damn good one. He needed to be that again now and stop acting so ridiculous. He examined her ankle, gently probing the skin just above the joint.

"Used to be?"

His shoulders stiffened. The reasons he'd given up his chosen profession came flooding back and he did his best to push them away, to bite back the acid in the back of his throat.

"Yes," he answered simply, but added, "Not to worry: I assure you my knowledge is still firmly intact." He finally glanced up and forced a wry smile. He gently moved her foot this way and that and she inhaled quietly, body going tense. He nodded to himself and eased her foot back to the floor, feeling bereft the second he lost contact with her skin.

"The good news is that I don't believe the bone is broken. It is going to be quite sore for a few days, most likely it will bruise badly, and you'll need to keep your weight off of it so that it may heal properly. You'll be fine in a week or so."

The butler arrived with the items he'd requested, and Rose rushed into the room behind him.

"Oh, Elle!"

Alec indicated that the butler should give Elle the water, and Alec downed the glass of whisky in one quick gulp, enjoying the burn as it slid down his throat before using the cloths to wrap Elle's ankle tightly.

"I'm alright," Elle sighed, clearly already tired of being worried over. Alec found that he liked that. Most ladies he knew adored being worried over, would even go so far as to *pretend* to be ill or injured in order to be fawned over. Elle looked uncomfortable with the attention, embarrassed even.

"Is she truly alright, Alec?" Rose asked him, her eyes shining with worry, her skin flushed.

Elle rolled her eyes. "Why does everyone keep asking *him* that?" she grumbled, though without much conviction.

Alec chuckled. "Yes, she's fine. Should probably get home and rest, though."

"Of course! I'll have da call for the carriage," she said, the brogue she'd inherited from Callum coming out a bit more than usual, as it often did when her emotions were running high. Remembering all the times she'd been spitting mad at him as children, the Scot in her coming out full force, made his lips curl upwards at the corners.

Percival entered the room then, coming to check on Rose and Elle. Rose's eyes lit up and he knew that the two of them would be married soon enough. Percy was a good man, came from a good family, and Alec was glad that he would be the one taking Rose's hand.

"Miss Montgomery, are you alright?"

"I'm fine, thank you Mister Delvington."

"Lord Kentworth, is she—"

"Yes, she's quite alright," Alec interrupted, trying to hide his amusement knowing Elle was fuming at yet another person seeking his assurance over her own.

"She's been hurt, Percy. We have to leave," Rose explained. Percival deflated slightly and Alec could see Rose's look of reluctance when she realized she'd have to lose an evening with him. Elle seemed to notice it too.

"No, you stay. I don't want you to leave on my account. I'll be ok on my own," she insisted, straightening herself on the couch.

"I can escort Miss Montgomery home," Alec offered. "I'm sure one of the staff can accompany us."

Rose's eyes lit with excitement and hope, and she cut them to Elle, clearly silently asking the question. Eleanor's shoulders tensed, but it seemed as if she were not immune to Rose's charms. Alec was convinced that no one was.

"Yes, that sounds wonderful," Elle said with a tight smile, though it sounded like the words had been pulled from her throat by fishing hooks, and that the sensation was not at all pleasant. After some low conversations and strategic planning, Alec and a butler named Collins managed to get Elle into a carriage with most of the revelers in the ballroom being none the wiser. Alec knew that they would all be waiting to pounce on Elle the moment she entered the room again, so it was better that they slipped away unnoticed.

Alec settled in on the bench next to Collins and across from Elle, but the moment the door closed, Alec was keenly aware of just how close they were, just how small the space really was. She seemed to notice as well, her breathing going slightly uneven and her throat bobbing as she swallowed. Was that in irritation or...something else?

Without thinking, he reached down and pulled her leg upward to rest on his lap. She gasped quietly, eyes going wide.

"Elevating the foot should help the injury," he said, keeping his voice even and—he hoped—clinical.

She nodded, but he could see the pulse jumping at her throat as his fingers skimmed the soft skin of her ankle just above the wrapping each time the carriage jostled them as it meandered over the cobblestones. He tried and failed to ignore the sensation, clenching his jaw tightly and looking about the inside of the carriage as if he were bored. He'd always been able to mask his feelings and emotions, and hoped to God that he was doing so now. He wasn't quite sure why he was reacting so strongly tonight, but he didn't want Elle to see it.

"So," Elle finally said softly, having to clear her throat before continuing. "You said you *were* a physician. What happened?"

Alec cut his eyes to her, already prepared to slice her down with a snide remark, but at her expression, he held his tongue. For the first time since they'd met, she didn't look agitated with him, didn't look as if she were hiding contempt just below the surface. She looked interested, and something inside him relaxed for the first time in recent memory.

"I...I couldn't save someone," he said, voice low and a bit rough. "A child," he amended, surprising himself. He rarely talked about this with anyone. He felt weak every time he thought of it. He knew that he would lose patients when he decided to become a surgeon, but told himself over and over that all the good he would do would outweigh the bad. And it had, for a time.

But that little girl had been different. It had broken him in ways he couldn't understand, in ways he didn't know how to repair.

Elle inhaled softly, and though the light within the carriage was dim from the two small lamps mounted on each wall, he could see the sorrow and sympathy that flashed in her eyes.

"I'm sorry," she said softly, and he found himself telling her everything, the words tumbling off his tongue in a rush for reasons he couldn't understand. It was like a part of him had been desperate to talk about it, and now he could barely hold it back.

"She was an orphan that lived near my home at the time. She was seven, maybe eight, and had taken a particular interest in me.

She was shy at first, darting away as soon as I looked her way or tried to speak to her, but I began to leave food for her on the stoop. I know it sounds as if she were a stray cat, but it was all I could think of to get her to trust me—and she was skin and bones." He cleared his throat and Elle's lips quirked up on one side.

"Eventually, she became comfortable enough to linger while she ate, letting me sit nearby, watching me with wide, chocolate-colored eyes. She didn't speak a single word for the longest time, but I didn't mind the silence, welcomed it sometimes even. I'd talk to her though, one-sided conversations where I'd tell her of my day or about patients, about the things I missed from home or gossip my father had shared in his letters. After many meals and many months and many solitary conversations, she finally told me her name—Colette. That was all I got the first day, that single word, with a shy smile, and then she ran off like a shot." He huffed out a laugh at the memory.

"She came around quickly after that. I gave her clothes and coin, and she would often come and sit in my surgery while I did research or made notes in my medical journals. She even assisted me during exams—handing me items or fetching things from cabinets, that sort of thing. We formed a kinship of sorts. She needed a father and, well, I'm not sure what I needed. A little sister maybe. I did miss Rose, so perhaps I saw a bit of her in Colette." *A daughter,* he whispered in his mind. He rarely let himself think the words, but he had seen a future for the two of them, had felt the pull to her, to protect her and raise her and give her the life that she deserved. He'd never thought much about a family or children before Colette, but she made him believe it was something he wanted. "I made her a small cot in the surgery, and she began to stay there most nights. We were well on our way to becoming a little family of sorts. I'd even begun looking into what would be necessary for her to become my ward." He swallowed hard, needing to settle himself for a moment before continuing, the bile already rising in his throat at what was to come. Elle didn't push, just waited in the silence.

"But...she was attacked," he said, averting his eyes and staring out the window. He pleaded with his own mind to keep the memories at bay, but they came upon him, swift and searing: her frail body lying in a heap just outside his back door, as if she'd tried to crawl to him, to somewhere she felt safe; the blood covering her chest and running down her thighs; the slashes across her palms as if she'd tried to protect herself as the knife fell upon her; the deep wounds in her chest and throat showing that she failed. He'd been at the damned pub when it had happened, a woman in his lap and a drink in his hand, having a jolly time. Guilt threatened to swallow him, as it always did. Guilt and disgust. If he had been home, if he hadn't been...No. He stopped the thoughts, knowing that nothing but more pain lay down that way of thinking.

"Her injuries were...severe," he finally went on. "They—they *brutalized* her," he said, voice cracking.

"Oh my God," Elle whispered.

Tears stung the back of Alec's eyes and his throat burned with acid, stomach churning. *So much for my mask*, he thought bitterly.

"I tried to save her, but there was nothing I could do. I was too late." He jolted when a hand grasped his. He pulled himself from the memories and looked down to find that Elle had leaned across the small space between them and had laid her hand upon his, squeezing gently. He raised his gaze to hers, surprised and confused by the caring gesture she was offering.

"I'm so sorry, Alec," she said softly, not even seeming to realize that she'd just addressed him so informally, using his Christian name. He didn't mind, enjoying the sound of his name on her lips too much. But then he remembered that they were not the only ones in the carriage. He cleared his throat and shifted his eyes towards Collins, and Elle quickly withdrew her hand, settling back against the bench. Collins did not seem to be paying them much attention, looking out of the other window studiously. Or perhaps he was just very well trained by Lord Yorkshire, and knew that if he saw something, he never actually *saw* anything.

Alec cleared his throat and forced his voice to come out cool and even. "After that, I gave up medicine. I know it's weakness, but—"

"Of course it isn't weakness," she said sternly, surprising him yet again. "I can't imagine dealing with something like that. Just because you decided to step away from being in that position again doesn't mean you were weak." He blinked several times before clearing his throat.

"Well, that is kind of you to say," he replied, "I don't know that it is truth, but it is kind." Their gazes locked and that feeling unfurled inside his chest again, the one that felt as if a fire were about to consume them both, the tiniest strike of flint sure to send them up in flames. She wet her lips and he realized his fingers were still lightly grazing her skin, moving slowly farther up her leg beneath the hem of her skirt. He shook himself. What in God's name was he doing?

He quickly withdrew his hand completely and gestured towards the window.

"We're here."

She pulled her leg back, and he couldn't tell if he was imagining the flush in her cheeks or if it were just a trick of the light. He and Collins exited the carriage first, with the butler quickly explaining to the waiting footman what had happened and sending him to fetch Lottie immediately. Elle insisted on trying to leave the carriage herself, but when she nearly fell, Alec scooped her up once more, rolling his eyes at her determination to avoid help at all costs.

"I could have done it," she protested weakly.

"You could have cracked your skull on the cobblestone and created even more work for me this evening," he replied with a hint of a smirk as he carried her up the stairs and through the front doors. He could see her biting back a response and he laughed silently.

"Oh my heavens!" Lottie cried as they entered. She quickly barked orders at the rest of the staff and they scurried off in various directions to obey. Alec grinned. Lottie was young but had she not been a woman, she would have made an excellent general in the King's army. It was quite impressive, actually.

"Are you alright, miss?" Lottie asked, fretting as Alec strode forward.

"I'm fine—and for the love of God, do not ask *him* if that's true."

Alec couldn't help but laugh, shaking Elle lightly in his arms as his chest rumbled. She cut her eyes towards him, and though they were slitted in irritation, he believed she was fighting her own smile, her lips curling ever so slightly at the corners. Turning her attention back to Lottie, she said, "My ankle is just a bit sore is all. I promise I'm alright, just tired."

"Of course, of course. William, come take Miss Montgomery from Lord Kentworth."

"It's alright, I've already got her," he said too quickly, not ready to have her leave his arms.

"Oh, if you're sure you don't mind, my Lord. This way." Lottie led them up the stairs and down the long hallway to Elle's bedroom. He set her gently on the edge of the bed, and he may have lingered for the briefest moment, admittedly not wanting to separate from her. Their faces were entirely too close, so close he could see how her pupils expanded, so close he could feel the soft exhalation of her breath on his lips. He fought the urge to lean forward, to press his lips to hers, to tangle his hands in her hair. He shook himself and straightened, stepping hastily away and balling his hands into fists. *What is wrong with me?*

"Thank you," Elle said, sounding a bit dazed, voice breathy.

"Of course, Miss Montgomery." Alec bowed and turned to Lottie. "Place a pillow or two beneath her foot for the evening." He turned back to look at Elle, whose face was pinched and pale with pain. Her ankle had already begun to bruise and swell, and he knew how painful it must be. "A strong glass of brandy or two as well," he added, "and I'll come and check on her tomorrow."

He nodded to Lottie, again at Elle, and then left the house as fast as his feet would carry him.

Chapter 10

The good thing about twisting her ankle was that Elle now had an excellent excuse not to entertain any potential suitors for the next week or so. Of course, the downside was the lack of Advil or ice packs, and having to be carried around like a child. Callum didn't seem to mind, but Elle felt terrible about the whole thing.

"There we are now," he said, setting her gently on one of the sofas in the drawing room.

"Thanks, Callum. I'm sorry—" He cut her off with a raised hand.

"Ack, no apologies. You feel as if I'm lifting a feather pillow, and it's nice tae feel useful."

"You're always useful, dear," Jocy scolded before giving him a quick kiss. He grinned, eyes crinkling around the corners in a way that made him even more handsome. He pulled her in tight against his body, kissing her again, harder, and she giggled. Elle smiled and looked away, loving how hard they loved, and being insanely jealous of it at the same time.

Callum said his goodbyes and headed out for the afternoon. Jocy handed Elle a stack of paper and some pencils.

"I thought you might get bored sitting here all day."

Elle took them eagerly. "Bless you."

"How are you feeling? Not just your ankle. I know yesterday was a hard day."

"I'm...alright, I think. Mostly. It just hit me harder yesterday that this is all...real, ya know? That this is my life now. That everything *then* is just...gone, and then the whole extra layer of my epic failed relationship slapping me in the face..." Her eyes watered, and she shook her head. "It was just...a lot to deal with," she finished with a shuddering breath. "Then to sprain my stupid ankle on top of everything was just the icing on the cake," she said with a laugh, trying to make light.

"Adjusting to this change is hard. Sometimes, a bad day will strike out of nowhere. It happens to me, even now. No matter how happy I am with everything I gained, there is still a part of me that mourns what I lost." Elle nodded, understanding what she meant all too well. "But I'm here to help you with your bad days, anytime you need me."

Elle squeezed Jocy's arm in thanks and Rose bounded into the room.

"Cousin! How are you?" she fretted, coming to sit beside Elle on the couch.

"I'm alright, really. Just a little sore and I don't think I'll be dancing much for the next few days, but I'm ok, I promise." She gave Rose a reassuring smile and the girl finally seemed to accept that Elle was really alright.

"And how was the rest of your evening with a certain gentleman...?"

Rose beamed, blushing slightly, and the two talked for almost an hour about everything and nothing. It was nice chatting with Rose, and she again wondered why she'd been so eager to let Rosie and the rest of them into her heart. But no matter the reason—fate or loneliness or whatever it may have been—the MacTavishs were her family now. Maybe not by blood, but they were her family in her heart.

Percival came to call and Elle passed the rest of the morning sketching while the two love birds sat on another couch, chatting and having tea. Eventually she began drawing Alec as he'd looked the night before in the carriage, staring out the window, lost in what Elle could only imagine were terrible memories of Colette's death. His face had been stark but striking, the lamps within the carriage casting his features in a calming, golden light. She lost herself in the drawing, fingers flying over the page as if she couldn't capture him quickly enough.

"—gomery?"

Elle yanked her head up, only to find Alec standing a few feet away, staring at her in a way that made it clear he'd said her name more than once. She hastily turned the page over and sat it on the table, straightening.

"Al—Lord Kentworth," Elle quickly corrected herself, inclining her head. "I suppose you'll forgive me for not standing to greet you and won't insult my upbringing and manners?"

"I suppose I can look past it this once," he agreed, a hint of a smile on his lips. He eased onto the couch beside her and began inspecting her ankle where it had been propped on top of a pile of pillows. Shivers skated up her spine as his fingers traced gently across her skin. Again, she wore no stockings beneath her dress. She despised them and that was the one thing she refused to accept about this time. When Alec had noticed last night, she would have sworn she saw raw desire flash in his eyes, but his mask settled over his features so quickly, she thought she might have imagined it. He probably thought it one more reason why she was not a lady up to his standards, but she didn't care. She remembered the way he'd gently stroked her skin the night before, without even seeming to realize it, and how that simple touch had sent fire through her veins, made her want him like she'd never wanted anyone else.

She knew how stupid it was, but even now, she barely even noticed the pain, just the feather-light touch of his fingers. He seemed to enjoy the feel of her skin too, touching her more than she thought was strictly necessary from a medical standpoint. She didn't mind. *Maybe I didn't imagine the desire last night?* Their conversation in the carriage had caused something to shift between them. Or at the very least, made her less irritated with him and more intrigued. He'd been so open and honest, so vulnerable, she longed to know what other parts of himself he was keeping hidden from the world. She'd seen beneath the mask and she felt her initial hatred of him fading away.

"How are you feeling today?" he asked as he continued his examination.

"Alright...Sore," she amended when he gave her a pointed look.

"Well, the swelling isn't too terrible. A few days of rest and you'll be perfectly capable of storming away from me again." His eyes danced with amusement when they met hers. He wasn't even trying to put the mask back on now. Whatever shift she'd felt after the previous night, he seemed to feel it too. *Interesting.*

She found herself smiling. "That is good to know."

He remained after his examination, accepting a drink from Lottie and speaking with Percy, Rose, and Jocy. Elle studied him as he interacted with the others. He smiled and laughed, even blushing slightly when Rose told stories of their childhood. Was it because he didn't feel as if he had to play a part here among the

MacTavish family? An extension of his own family by all counts, really. He caught her staring and straightened, clearing his throat.

"Well, I should be going. I'll be back to check on your ankle in a few days."

"Oh, really it's fine you don't have to—"

"You are my patient and I will see to your full recovery," he said, cutting her off politely but firmly. A few days ago, that may have annoyed her, but now, it only made her roll her eyes in exasperation.

A week later, Elle was up and walking again. Her ankle was still a little sore, but the bruising was mostly gone and she was completely over being an invalid. So, with a stubbornness that would have made her mother proud, she mind-over-mattered the hell out of the situation and joined Rose, Jocy, and Callum at the park. To her dismay, the vultures were waiting to pounce the second they saw her. Several men rushed over, making sure she received their flowers and chocolates and well-wishes while she'd been laid up on the couch. She did her duty, smiling and giving thanks for their gracious gestures, but inside she wanted to scream. She was tired of playing this game, tired of feeling like a trophy that these men were desperate to win.

Elle was actually relieved when Alec approached, making the others scatter like stray cats shooed away from the stoop. Henry Astley was the only one who didn't immediately leave. Instead, he lingered, eyeing Alec with thinly veiled contempt. Alec gave him a haughty smile in return before turning his attention to Elle.

"Miss Montgomery. I thought I should check your injury before you take your turn around the park."

Elle glanced at Henry quickly, noting the flare of annoyance in his eyes, before returning her gaze to Alec.

"Of course, thank you."

"In private," Alec added in that tone of his that held authority and reminded everyone around him who he was. Henry clenched his jaw but nodded.

"I have some business to attend to as it were. Miss Montgomery, I look forward to calling on you tomorrow now that you are well enough for visitors once more." He cut his eyes to Alec, as if the statement were really for him instead of Elle. *Fucking boys,* she thought with an inward roll of her eyes.

She barely stopped herself from shooting off a sarcastic "can't wait!" with two obnoxious thumbs up. Instead, she merely inclined her head and allowed Alec to lead her to a stone bench just off the path.

"My ankle is fine. Really."

"I have no doubts," Alec said, leaning down to examine her foot. Again, the brush of his fingers over her ankle made her stomach flutter. *This is getting ridiculous.* "But I do so love thwarting Astley." He glanced up and gave her a rakish smile. She huffed out a laugh and he released her foot, smoothing her skirt back down her leg. "I don't suppose you'd like to assist me in making him truly peevish by walking with me?"

"I would love nothing more," Elle said with a grin, taking his hand and rising from the bench. She found that it was actually quite easy to like Alec once he decided he let a bit of the mask fall away. They walked, though Elle was limping a bit, catching attention from far too many people. Elle sighed. "I can already hear the gossip spreading like wildfire."

"What gossip is that?" Alec asked as they approached the same small bridge where they'd stood during her first promenade. That time she'd wanted nothing more than to shove him over the edge and into the water. Her lips quirked. Ok, so that would still be funny, but now she didn't want to cause him bodily harm in the process. Well, not *much* anyway.

"The gossip that you're courting me."

He leaned against the stone, eyes raking over the lawn, taking in all of the people covertly glancing their way—and the ones who were openly staring, like Matilda Wilshire. He turned his gaze back to Elle and there was a calculating look in his eyes.

"And what if it were more than mere gossip?"

Elle blinked. Would it be so bad to be courted by Alec? The Alec she'd seen over the last week, the one who had told her about Colette? The one who had laughed and blushed in the drawing room? The one who had been so gentle and kind with her injured ankle? To her surprise, the answer was no, it really wouldn't be. But it wouldn't be right to allow him to court her without knowing the truth—well, *part* of the truth anyway.

"Al—Lord Kentworth," she caught herself. "I owe you the truth."

"By all means," he said, gesturing for her to continue, looking amused and intrigued.

"I do not plan to accept any proposal of marriage that may come from this season. I only agreed to participate at all because if I hadn't, it would have negatively affected Rose. It wouldn't be fair to you if I let you spend your time with me, when it could be spent courting someone who might actually marry you." His lips quirked, as if this news made him *happy*. Elle was...confused.

"Can I be honest with you as well?" Elle nodded, not really sure where this might be going. He leaned a bit closer to her and whispered almost conspiratorially, "I have no intention of offering a marriage proposal to anyone. I am only here because my father asked me to be. I do not plan to actually find a bride at the end of all of this, but I must play a part, just as you have agreed to do."

Elle blinked in surprise. "Oh. Oh, well, that's—"

"I have a proposal for you, however. Not of marriage," he added when she cocked her head and gave him a narrowed look. "You have no desire to have anyone else courting you for the next few months, is that correct?"

"Correct." She shuddered at the thought of having to spend another day with Henry Astley.

"And I have no desire to feign a courtship with any of these other ladies. It would not be gentlemanly of me to lie to them, to give them false hope and keep them from other potential, true suitors, but it would be expected of me to call on at least some of them during the season..."

"So...we help each other," Elle said, figuring out where this was going.

"If I make it clear that I have my eye set on you, every other man will accept that and move on to other prospects. That will save you from having to deal with any of them."

"And you won't have to pretend to be interested in any of the other women—or waste their time, either."

"Just so," he said with a nod. Elle rolled it over in her head. She had to admit, it was actually an attractive offer. She eyed him critically.

"You know this would mean that you'd still have to spend time with *me*? Lots of time, if we're going to be believed." Alec's face turned solemn, and he put his hand over his heart.

"It is a grave duty, but I am willing to undertake it, yes." Elle laughed, lips curling into a smile before she could stop them. He smiled back, a hint of the genuine smile she'd glimpsed only once or twice.

"Alright."

"Alright?" he echoed, eyes wide.

"Yes, let's do it."

"You know you'll have to appear as though you actually enjoy my company."

"I shall do my best to hide my suffering." Now he chuckled.

"This will be great fun, I have no doubt."

Well, hell. Maybe it could be.

And so, they started their official courtship, much to the dismay of every other single man and woman in the Ton, apparently. Jocelyn said that the other ladies were sick with jealousy and that many of the men wished they could fight Alec, but of course, they couldn't. Technically, the men could still come to call—there wasn't a dibs situation in play or anything—but they all just knew that if Alec were in the game, they wouldn't win, so why waste their time and energy. If Elle were actually looking for a husband, of course Alec would be the logical choice.

Henry was the only one who didn't let up, still coming to call, though not as often, still asking her to dance at every ball, and still watching her from across the room at every other event. It was an obvious pissing match between the two men and somehow

Elle had become the judge. But overall, the plan was working perfectly, so Elle could handle dealing with Henry.

Being around Alec was nice, actually. He was still a bit haughty of course, but he was also charming and funny, someone she could actually be friends with.

She found herself wishing she could tell him more about her life. Her *real* life, not the half-truths or flat out lies they'd concocted. But even so, she began to find in him a sort of friendship, someone she could let her guard down with, at least a bit. Since she wasn't worried about him thinking badly of her if her etiquette wasn't perfect, she was able to relax. He, too, seemed to be a bit more lax on all the formalities and manners, and she was glad for it.

"So, we're really going to a *boxing match*?" Elle asked, excited for the outing. Everything had been a bit repetitive thus far: sit and talk in the drawing room, walk through the park, have tea or dinner, go to a dance or a play or the ballet—over and over and over.

"We are," Jocy said as they exited the carriage.

"And this is something *ladies* do?" Elle asked, a skeptical brow arched.

"Yes, they do...though many are a bit squeamish of the blood," she added thoughtfully.

Alec was waiting for them and gestured towards a row of seats in the front, shaking hands with Callum as he passed. Rose seemed enthralled with the large space, taking it all in with wide eyes, shining with interest. The building was constructed like a small stadium, with each row sitting slightly higher than the one in front of it, high ceilings with skylights letting in bright sunlight, and a ring in the middle of it all. Rose waved Percy over and soon everyone was seated in a neat row, Elle tucked in between Jocy and Alec.

"Have you ever been to a boxing match?" he asked her. She bit her lip. Oh to see his face if she tried to explain that she'd been a ring girl at a handful of UFC fights in her day, walking around in a barely-there bikini and six-inch heels, carrying a big numbered sign.

"A time or two," she said instead with a sly grin, and he seemed intrigued.

"Well, I've got my money on Tristan there in the black trousers."

He pointed to a shirtless man with light brown skin, black hair, and muscles for days. Elle's eyes widened appreciatively as she took him in. She'd never thought of men in this time as being ripped, but Tristan certainly was.

Alec leaned in close and said in a low voice, "Now, now, Miss Montgomery. It is rather unladylike to stare..."

"Not when he looks like *that*," she breathed out, not taking her eyes off of Tristan. "I'm quite sure it would be far more unladylike *not* to stare. A proper lady should appreciate artwork, after all..." She felt Alec laugh beside her.

Tristan was lean and cut, and in the twenty-first century, he probably would have been a middleweight division fighter, not a heavyweight like his opponent obviously would be. The other man was older, with a thick white beard and a scar running down the left side of his pale torso. He wasn't fat, but he was more thickly muscled than Tristan, built like a barrel. Tristan would be faster, but the other guy sure would pack a punch.

They waited for the match to begin and she could hear Callum and Percy explaining a bit about boxing to Rosie. Elle began tapping her feet in a bored rhythm, but soon it transformed into something else. Her lips curled as she stomped twice before tapping her hand on her knee once. Over and over. *Stomp, stomp, tap. Stomp, stomp, tap.*

Jocelyn turned to look at her, smiling and fighting laughter. To Elle's delight, Jocy joined her, and soon they were both humming *We Will Rock You.* Alec tilted his head at them, and she and Jocy broke off into quiet peals of laughter.

"I don't think I'll ever properly understand women," he muttered under his breath, making Elle and Jocy laugh even harder.

The match finally began, and it was thrilling. The crowd roared and cheered, Callum bellowing what Elle was ninety-percent sure were curses and insults in Gaelic with the way Jocy looked both amused and scandalized. Elle had been right: Tristan was indeed faster than the other man, quick and sure on his feet, but The Bearded Wonder was much stronger and seemed to know a bit more about fighting. Tristan lasted for a while before his speed wasn't enough and he began taking too many hits.

Alec winced as a particularly brutal blow caught Tristan in the jaw, but Elle's eyes lit up. She placed a hand on Alec's thigh without thinking and his entire body tensed. *Oh, right. No touchy between boys and girls.* She quickly pulled it back, but leaned towards him so he could hear her over the crowd.

"The bearded guy,"

"Portsmouth," he supplied.

"Portsmouth. He telegraphs his punches." He turned to stare at her, brow furrowed. "Just trust me. Tell Tristan to watch Portsmouth's right shoulder. He nudges it right before an uppercut every time. He can dodge and catch Portsmouth off guard and off balance." Not only had Elle been a ring girl, she'd dated a fighter semi-seriously for a few months before she'd met Ashton. She'd studied footage of his opponents with him so he could prepare for fights by learning their strengths and weaknesses. She remembered a thing or two.

Alec looked somewhere between impressed and suspicious, but nodded and made his way to the edge of the ring where Tristan was getting water during the short break. He spoke low to the man, who nodded and looked confident and determined.

Alec settled back in beside her, perhaps a little closer than before, their arms brushing. The fighters circled each other again, and Elle held her breath when Portsmouth's shoulder nudged. Alec tensed. Tristan dodged the uppercut and landed a few quick, punishing blows to Portsmouth's kidneys. The bigger man doubled over, and Tristan went to town on his face, his head snapping back with each punch like a rag doll. The crowd went wild, cheering and erupting in screams and applause when Tristan landed the final knockout punch.

Alec turned to stare at a grinning Elle, mouth open in astonishment.

She wiggled her eye brows. "Do I get a cut of your winnings, then?"

"You are truly the most intriguing creature, Miss Montgomery."

She smiled, taking it as a compliment.

Chapter 11

Spending time with Elle was unexpectedly pleasant. Not that Alec expected time with her to be completely torturous, of course, but he hadn't expected to find her so amusing and companionable. She laughed freely with him now that she didn't seem to despise him, true mirth coming out in an infectious giggle that he found himself missing when he was away from her. Most ladies he'd been around had perfected their demur, quiet laughter, were taught the proper times to perform it around gentlemen. They were like clockwork dolls, everything designed and delivered properly without fail so long as the gears continued to turn.

Elle was so alive, so uninhibited despite the very inhibiting circumstances of being a lady in the Ton, so truly unorthodox in so many ways, truth be told, but he enjoyed his time with her all the more for it.

They were several weeks into their "courtship" and things were going perfectly to plan. He was fairly sure that Henry Astley wanted to do him serious physical harm for courting Eleanor, but Alec couldn't seem to make himself care too much about that. In all actuality, it made him grin. Astley could sod off. He was still coming to call on Elle, which was an annoyance, but Alec's presence had deterred all of the other men, so he still felt as if he were holding up his end of the bargain.

Now, they strolled together through a small park near his home. It was mostly deserted with the exception of himself and Elle, Rose and Percival, and Jocelyn and Callum. They'd had a picnic lunch and now each of the couples had fractured off. Percy was pointing to different flowers in the manicured beds lining the pathway, apparently telling Rose fascinating information about them based on her wide smile and bright eyes. Callum sat with Jocelyn on the blanket where they'd eaten, Jocelyn leaning back against Callum's chest. They were having some kind of low conversation that had both of their lips curling. Alec had a brief stab of longing. To have that kind of connection with someone, to feel that kind of utter contentment that was plain on both of their faces, in every line of their bodies...

He shook himself and skipped a rock over the smooth surface of the small pond where he and Elle had strolled.

"Well, that was quite pathetic, Lord Kentworth" she said, looking unimpressed. He stared at her incredulously as she took up her own stone and took a turn, hers admittedly skipping much farther than his own and in a much more graceful progression. She winged her brows several times in quick succession in challenge and triumph, and he wasn't even sure how to respond.

"You know, you are completely unlike any other woman I've ever known," he said honestly.

"How do you mean?"

"Well, you don't seem quite as..." He searched for the right term.

"Proper?" Elle supplied, adding "boring?" under her breath.

"Yes, both of those things," he said with a laugh. "It is almost as if I were around another man." She gave him a look and he hastened to explain. "Not that you are like a man, of course, I didn't mean that."

She smirked at him, clearly having a bit of fun at his expense. He didn't mind, truth be told. He liked the way they pushed and pulled each other, their easy banter and teasing barbs.

"Alec, have you never had a friend who was a woman?" Since their courtship was a farce, they had silently agreed that etiquette could be a bit less formal between them when others weren't nearby. Now, she usually only used his title in a mocking manner which usually made him laugh. He secretly loved when she called him Alec, the name coming off of her tongue making his pulse jump. He tried not to look at that too closely.

"Well…" He pursed his lips, thinking. "Well, no, I suppose not. Rose, of course, but I look at her like a sister." Then a thought occurred to him. "Do you have many friends who are men? Is that common in America?"

"I do and it is." She skipped another rock before turning to face him with a wide smile, the corners of her eyes crinkling slightly. He sighed inwardly. God, she really was beautiful. The late afternoon made her hair sparkle like spun gold and the darker flecks of blue in her eyes glitter brightly. His gaze briefly traveled downward, along the delicate column of her throat, over the swells of her breasts, down her body and the curve of her hips. Something he'd been wondering about for weeks sprang to mind, and he figured they were far enough into this strange friendship that he could ask. Elle didn't seem the type to be offended by much. So, he decided to take his chances. Alec glanced around before voicing the question that had plagued him.

"Well, as a…friend—and physician," he added quickly, "—may I ask you a question?" She waved a hand towards him in a gesture that indicated he should proceed. "When I was examining your ankle, I noticed that your skin was...ah, quite smooth there." His throat bobbed as he swallowed, remembering the touch. He suddenly felt the need to loosen his collar around his throat. She blinked, a look of surprise crossing her face. She clearly hadn't been expecting that to be his question. But the surprise quickly transformed into a look of mischief. He went on hastily, "I've read about some medical conditions which inhibit, uh, hair growth..."

"Nothing medical, Alec. It is quite common where I'm from for women to remove the hair from their bodies," she confirmed. She stepped forward to walk past him, but stopped as their shoulders met, leaning close. "From *all over* their bodies," she said in a soft, sultry voice, communicating...something with her eyes before moving by him. He jolted. *No. She couldn't mean...*

He whirled to stare after her as she strolled away. She glanced over her shoulder and the look on her face confirmed his suspicions. *God in heaven.* The images her words conjured made his pulse jump and his cock harden. He surreptitiously adjusted himself, quickly glancing around to be sure no one had seen, and caught up to Elle.

He had no idea how to respond, so he didn't, merely walked beside her stiffly while she seemed to be holding back laughter, a secretive smile on her face. Did she know what she'd done? What he would be thinking of for the better part of the evening...possibly the rest of his life? He could scarcely imagine what it might be like, but his mind was running wild, the idea of it so foreign and erotic.

He cleared his throat and she chuckled low. Oh yes, she was well aware of what she'd done to his mind this afternoon. He glanced at her and she gave him a look of pure innocence that he didn't believe for a moment, but that made his lips curl. Her blue eyes sparkled with...something. Amusement, yes, but something more. Something sensual and alluring.

Suddenly, the images in his mind shifted. It wasn't just any woman in his mind now, it was Elle. *Her* skin, smooth and bare to him as he ran his fingers softly over every inch of her...*No.* He firmly shoved the images away. It would do no good to think such things when nothing could come from the thoughts. Though they allowed themselves to be less formal than what was ordinary, she was still a lady and he was still a gentleman, a future viscount. Unless he married her—which, of course, was out of the question and the reason for this entire farce to begin with—he could never *touch* her, not in any real way. Not in the way he was suddenly craving like a starving man craves a heel of bread.

"Oh Alec, the things I could teach you," she said, so quietly he thought he may have even imagined it.

"I hear you are courting Jocelyn's niece," Alec's father said with a grin over his glass of brandy.

Alec felt a tiny stab of guilt at his father's obvious excitement. He'd never lied to his father before, not in any serious way, and now he felt as if he were somehow rising a dying man's hopes only for them to be crushed. *He's not dying yet*, Alec reminded himself firmly.

"I am," he said, casting his eyes away from his father's stare, rising to wander to the window. He looked out onto the small garden, missing the grand one at their country manor with a pang. It had been his mother's pride and joy. She tended it herself, with the help of the staff, of course, as it was too large for any one person to maintain, but she had always loved spending hours out among the flowers, nurturing the soil, coaxing the blooms to life. Alec had always associated the smell of dirt and flowers with her, always smelling them on her as she wrapped him tightly in a hug.

She was a bit like Elle, he realized then, doing things differently than what was expected of her. Most viscountesses didn't dig around in the mud for hours each day, or walk around with dirt smudging their noses, he supposed. Though they were very much a part of the Ton by virtue of their family name and title, the Kentworths, like the MacTavishs, had always mostly kept away from it. Alec suddenly longed for the home he'd grown up in with a fierceness he didn't quite understand. Thankfully, they would be returning there, at least for a time, in a matter of weeks.

The MacTavishs held a lavish ball at Chestwick Hall each season, and this year's was sure to outdo all the rest with Rose and Elle both being out in society now. Alec was looking forward to being out of the heart of London for a while, back out in the country where he could breathe. Perhaps Eleanor would enjoy a tour of his ancestral home. He could show her his mother's beloved gardens, and imagining her there among the flowers made him smile. He turned back to his father, leaning against the windowsill.

"Tell me about her, then," Jonathan said, gesturing impatiently.

"She is lovely," he said automatically, the expected gentlemanly response. "Plays piano forte beautifully, is well read. She was brought up in America, so that is a bit odd of course, and her direct family holds no titles, though being connected to the MacTavish family is helpful and Callum has promised a sizeable dowry."

His father waved all of that away. "Come, Alec. *Tell* me about her." Alec sighed, knowing that his father wouldn't stand for the practiced, proper responses he knew he should give, the things he should care about when courting a lady. His father had never cared much about all of that. It was one of the many reasons he and Callum MacTavish had gotten on so well. They both could take or leave all of the pompous pageantry of the Ton. They were both all too happy to hunt and fish out in the country, to get their hands dirty and ride through the woods on horses that were meant to run free, not pull carriages down cobble-stoned streets.

So, Alec tried again.

"She's smart, with a cunning intellect in her eyes, like she is always studying and calculating and learning. She's kind. You know how the ladies of the Ton can be, fighting like cats in an alley, but Elle isn't like that at all. She compliments the other ladies—*genuinely*—fixes fallen curls and missed buttons. She seems to know just what to do or say to make someone feel more at ease. She's an artist, a truly skilled one at that. You should see the sketch she did of Rosie playing her harp, father. It's *stunning*, as if she somehow took Rose right out of the world and placed her directly into the page. It's remarkable. And she's got a wit about her that rivals your own." His father chuckled at that.

"And her looks?"

"God in heaven, she's *beautiful.* Probably the most beautiful woman I've ever seen. Her hair is like spun gold, her eyes like sapphires that burn as if a candle rests behind them when she's excited or contemplating mischief—or vexed with me." He smiled at the memories of how he could still irritate her like it seemed no one else could. "She—" He stopped himself before he went on about her admittedly enticing chest or the sensual sway of her hips as she walked and danced. "Yes, she's beautiful," he said again instead.

His father studied him, a knowing smile on his face. Alec wasn't sure what that smile meant, but the guilt flared again. His father looked as if Alec was going to propose to Elle any day now. *How am I going to explain a lack of one to him?*

"She sounds lovely. I should like to meet her, and I haven't seen Rosie since she officially came out. I'd be remiss if I didn't congratulate her properly—do you think Callum would kick me if I purchased her another pony?" Alec chuckled. Jonathan loved Alec fiercely, but had always longed for a daughter. He put all of that unused love and affection towards Rose instead, showering her with gifts and being the cherished uncle-type figure in her life. Callum always chided Jonathan about the gifts and letting Rosie get away with murder more times than not, but he always did it with a smile, and Alec knew that Callum didn't truly mind. "We will send an invitation for dinner immediately."

Though the courtship was just a game, Elle was actually a little nervous to meet Jonathan Kentworth. She wasn't sure why exactly—she'd heard nothing but good things about the man. Glowing actually. If the term bromance existed here, that would be the exact way to describe the relationship between Jonathan and Callum, the brotherly affection clear in the Scotsman's voice when he spoke of Jonathan—but she still had those jittery butterflies in her stomach as she made her way to the oversized front door of the Kentworth manor. It was basically a castle, dwarfing even the MacTavish's London house.

But her nerves eased the second Jonathan greeted her in the foyer, Alec standing by his side wearing the easy smile he only let show around a select few.

"Miss Montgomery, it is a pleasure to meet you, my dear!" Jonathan exclaimed as he took Elle's hands and kissed the backs like a knight, making Elle giggle quietly. He turned back to his son and quirked a brow, looking so like Alec for a moment that Elle did a double take. Alec was almost the spitting image of his father, and though Jonathan had more laugh lines and gray in his black hair, the two could be brothers.

"You said she was a rare beauty, but I don't think you truly did her justice, my boy."

"Father," Alec muttered under his breath, exasperated and incredulous. Elle glanced his way and found a slight blush creeping along his cheeks and she grinned. Alexander Kentworth *embarrassed?* Now this was a sight.

"A rare beauty?" Elle echoed, a shit-eating grin on her face as she eyed Alec.

He looked to the ceiling, as if he were praying for help, or maybe asking God why he was being punished. Jonathan chuckled at that, a deep, hearty laugh that made Elle's chest warm. Something about the man just made the room brighter, any nerves or awkwardness vanishing in an instant. He didn't hold himself the way she figured some fancy-titled Englishman would, the way so many others in the Ton did, and it immediately made her like him.

Jonathan offered her his arm and she slid hers around it. He patted her hand as he turned them and strode down a hallway towards what she assumed was the dining room.

"Now, would you like to begin with the expected pleasantries, or should we dive right into embarrassing stories of Alec from his childhood?" He winked at Elle and his green eyes, so like his son's, were full of mischief.

"Father!" Alec called from behind them, somewhere between amusement and outrage.

Elle laughed loudly and a familiar, bittersweet feeling swept through her chest. Elle and her own father had been thick as thieves, partners in crime and mischief twins to the extreme. Her mom had called them *The Hellions.* The two of them had gotten shirts made with that scrawled across the front like a team name, wearing them with pride when they got up to hijinks, like when she was sixteen and they'd run off and gone skydiving instead of to the grocery store like they'd claimed. They were always getting up to things, playing jokes or sneaking ice cream, sharing secret. And somehow, within only a few minutes, Elle felt that same connection and relationship bloom inside her with Jonathan. It was startling and painful and so beautiful it made the backs of her eyes burn with sudden tears. She hadn't ever thought she'd feel that way again, believing that anything even close to what she shared with her dad was gone forever. But here it was, blossoming unexpectedly like a winter rose pushing its way through the frost.

"Oh embarrassing stories, of course," Elle answered with a wide smile.

Alec caught up to them quickly. "This is very unbecoming of a viscount, father," he chastised, *"very* unbecoming." She and Jonathan both broke into laughter, and though he was pretending to be irritated with the two of them, Elle could see the joy in Alec's eyes, the...relief? For whatever reason, it brought Alec happiness to see her and his father getting along so well, and, she realized then, that whatever made Alec happy, made her happy too.

"Nonsense," Jonathan scoffed, "I am the epitome of viscount grace and proprieties...now," he said with a conspiratorial smile, "shall I begin with the time he ate all the biscuits and blamed a wild goose?"

Chapter 12

"And he had an absolutely massive cock," Lord Churchill said to the group sitting on the terrace. A large gathering of the Ton was there, some having tea, others playing games on the expansive lawn. Alec was seated across the table and a few seats away from Jocelyn and Elle, the women politely listening to Lord Churchill regale everyone with stories of his recent travels.

Elle snorted and choked on her tea, quickly covering it all with a cough. Jocelyn gave her a stern look and Alec would have bet a kick under the table, and Elle pulled her lips in—trying to hide a smile? Alec watched their exchange with curiosity from his spot. Elle briefly met his eyes, but cut them away quickly. Did she...did she understand what the term *cock* could mean? His eyes widened, but he swiftly schooled his features, smiling blandly at Lord Churchill but looking at Elle out of the corner of his eye. Most ladies didn't even know basic knowledge about their own bodies, let alone about a man's or the various terms for such things.

"Are you alright, Miss Montgomery?" Lord Churchill asked gently.

"Yes, yes, of course. Apologies Lord Churchill." She cleared her throat delicately and then asked, "How was it that you came to have knowledge of Mister Rutherford's...cock?" Her lips twitched at the corners and Jocy looked skyward, as if praying for patience, though there was a trace of amusement there as well.

"Oh, well, he had it out for all to see, of course. Right there in his front garden, if you can believe it." Elle's face turned red with the effort to keep herself from laughing, and even Jocy looked to be on the verge of tears. Oh yes, Elle knew *exactly* what that word meant. *She surprises me at every turn.* The meeting between her and his father had been perfect, though he and his childhood follies and mishaps seemed to be the crux of their conversation and endless laughter. He smiled at the memories. Though the courting was a farce, he had wanted his father to like Eleanor, for her to enjoy Jonathan's company, and he couldn't put his finger on why precisely. It didn't truly matter if they actually liked each other, in the end...but for some reason to him, it *did.*

Since that first dinner, they had become thick as thieves, Elle coming to see Jonathan almost every day, and the two of them talking for hours about everything and nothing it seemed. More than once, just as dessert had been served, Jonathan would need Alec to fetch something for him, only to come back to his plate empty and Jonathan and Eleanor looking innocent as cherubs with chocolate on their fingers. Alec always pinned them with narrowed, accusing looks, but that only made the two of them break into fits of laughter and, admittedly, made him smile more often than not.

Elle seemed inexplicably at ease with Jonathan, the two of them having some strange connection that Alec couldn't understand. He asked Elle about it and she simply shrugged and smiled, saying that Jonathan reminded her of her own father. There had been a sad edge to the smile then, but Alec didn't press. It was clear that she had loved her father and missed him, and if spending time with Jonathan eased whatever ache she felt in his absence, then Alec would be the whipping boy to a hundred embarrassing tales from when he was a lad, a thousand. Anything. He frowned inwardly, not wanting to examine that particular thought too closely, and pulled himself back to the conversation at hand.

"How *interesting*," Elle said, voice shaking subtly. "And did you stroke his cock?"

Now Alec coughed into his fist and Jocelyn quickly cut in at Lord Churchill's confused look.

"Elle, why don't you go explore the gardens? Lord Churchill has some of the most beautiful gardens in all of London," she said with an indulgent smile towards the old man.

"Oh, yes, I would like that very much, if that's alright with you, Lord Churchill." She inclined her head, giving him that brilliant smile of hers that seemed to melt even the coldest of hearts. As expected, Lord Churchill's confusion ebbed, giving way to beaming pride.

"Yes, yes, of course, my dear, of course."

"I shall accompany you," Alec said quickly, standing from the table. This earned him a few knowing looks, a handful of smiles, and one or two barely veiled scowls.

He escorted Elle across the lawn, avoiding a lively game of croquet, and towards a white gazebo near the garden, crawling ivy and small pink flowers winding their way around the columns and roof, their perfume enveloping them as they stepped within the space. Elle leaned her arms on the railing, looking out over the gathering.

"So," he said, leaning beside her. "You find cocks funny?" She snorted out a laugh, but this time, didn't try to hide it. He eyed her. "Now I know for sure that you understand that particular term." She hiked one shoulder. "It isn't something a lady would typically be aware of," he added, urging her to answer his unasked question, the one burning his tongue in its desperation to escape: *How do you know?* Were Americans in the habit of saying such things in front of ladies? Had she heard it somewhere else? His mind flitted to a secret gaming hall he liked to frequent, where the rules of society didn't exist. Men and women mingled and gambled and drank and danced, free of the strangling etiquette that was constantly surrounding him. Could...could Elle have been to such a place? Would she *want* to go? He imagined taking her to Puck's and found that he rather liked the idea.

"I told you the first night we met that I never claimed to be a lady." She grinned and returned her gaze to the lawn and garden surrounding them. "You know," she said thoughtfully, "most of them don't have the foggiest idea about sex, have no idea what to expect on their wedding night."

"Well, of course not," he said dryly, "God forbid a woman understand how she become with child." As a physician, Alec had always disliked how little women were told about all manner of things, but especially sex and childbirth. Why shouldn't they be told of such things? It wasn't only a natural part of life, but for most women, it was considered their *duty* to produce heirs, sometimes as young as sixteen or seventeen. They should be prepared, should be made to understand what would happen to them, to understand how their own bodies worked for God's sake. But, for whatever reason, the rest of society didn't agree with him on that front. *Shocking,* he thought with an inward roll of his eyes.

Elle glanced sidelong at him, and that calculating look blazed in her eyes, the one that made his pulse race, though he had no idea why. Nonchalantly she said, "Most of them may even go their entire lives without knowing what an orgasm even *is*, let alone experiencing one."

Alec's mouth gaped and his elbow slid off of the railing, sending him flailing like a duck.

"Or-orgasm?" he repeated, hoarsely, the word coming out as a question. His mind was whirling. He'd never heard a lady say the word, had never in his wildest imaginings envisioned having a conversation that involved this topic with anyone, especially not Elle.

She turned to face him, her smile mischievous. "Climax? Completion?" she said innocently. "Perhaps you use a different term here." *God in heaven.* Believing that women should be educated in the ways of sex and reproduction, and hearing Elle talk about...about *climaxing* were two very different things. Why was this so...arousing to him? Why was his throat so dry he could barely swallow, his heart beating so fast he feared she might be able to hear the thunder of it within his chest, his cock suddenly throbbing so insistently it was painful?

He swallowed hard and cleared his throat. "Eleanor. Have you...have you been with a man?" He couldn't stop himself from asking, though he knew he shouldn't. Despite how casual they'd become with each other, it wasn't a proper thing for him to even think about, let alone actually ask. But the words had left his lips before he could stop them. He braced, prepared for her to be outraged at his behavior, but her grin only widened.

"Would it make you think less of me if I had, Alec?" There was amusement in her tone, as if the question were humorous for a reason he couldn't understand.

His mouth opened to respond, but no words came out. The part of him that had been raised in high society said that *of course* he would. She was unmarried and being with a man would mean that she was...tainted.

But the part of him that was imaging her in the throes of passion, her golden hair spread across the pillow, her lips parted on a cry of ecstasy as he rose above her...absolutely would *not*.

Before he could say anything, she turned and held his gaze, leaning towards him ever so slightly.

"But come now, Alec. You know that a woman can find release without a man...don't you?" Her voice was pitched low, a velvety sultriness to it that he'd never heard before but he knew would replay over and over in his mind for far too long to come.

He watched raptly as she slowly trailed her fingers down the bodice of her sky-blue gown, over her stomach, lower still...His breath caught as thoughts filled his mind. Terrible thoughts. Brilliant thoughts. Thoughts that made his cock pulse and his pulse race. Thoughts of Eleanor alone in her bed, fingers drifting downward beneath the covers, stroking and teasing before slipping inside—*Dear God.*

She pulled her hand away, resting it on the railing again. His wide eyes met hers and they were filled with amusement. Amusement and something else. Before either of them could say or do anything more, Rosie called for them to come join the croquet game. Elle held his gaze for a moment longer, something burning there that he longed to explore, but she quickly shut it away, as if a blanket had been thrown over a fire, smothering the flames. She smiled and gestured towards the lawn, as if they'd just been discussing the weather and not things that were unacceptable and ungentlemanly and wholly erotic.

"Shall we?" she asked sweetly.

Elle had made a grave mistake. She'd wanted to mess with Alec in the gazebo, push the limits of their newfound friendship and the freedom that came with it. But the way he'd stared at her as she hinted at things, running her fingers down her body, the way his tongue had absently darted over his bottom lip, the way his eyes had flared with desire…Well, her plan had backfired. Big time.

A small ember had flared to life as their gazes held, as her mind ran wild with images of kissing him, of showing him just how much she knew about sex and pleasure. Now, it burned in her chest and she couldn't snuff it out. She laid in her bed, staring at the ceiling, and as her thoughts wandered yet again, the ember grew hotter and hotter. She kicked the blankets off, the room suddenly stifling. She knew that the thoughts weren't going to go away on their own, that the fire was only going to burn and burn until it consumed her wholly—or until she did something about it.

She trailed her fingers downward, under the edge of her nightgown. It had been a while since she'd done this with everything else going on. Time travel and being told you're stuck two hundred years in the past kind of puts being horny on the back-burner, after all.

Now, the slightest touch had her gasping and arching her hips upward, as if she hadn't been touched in years instead of months. She didn't try to keep Alec from her thoughts. Their relationship was fake, their courtship merely a mutually beneficial friendship in disguise, but she couldn't deny that she was attracted to him. Why *shouldn't* she fantasize about him? What harm could it do? *Not a damn bit.*

So she did fantasize about him. She let herself imagine ripping the shirt from his broad chest, running her hands over the sculpted muscles she could tell were hiding just beneath the fabric. She let herself imagine kissing him, wondered if his lips would be as soft as they looked, wondered if he would kiss her gently or like he'd die without it, slamming his lips to hers until they were breathless. She imagined his hands on her body as she delved her fingers, slowly thrusting, rolling her hips. A soft moan left her lips as she imagined him dipping his head to her breast, latching his lips around a tightened nipple, her fingers digging into his hair to hold him there. She imagined him groaning against her skin, his fingers trailing downward...

All too soon, it was too much and she plummeted over the edge of bliss, barely stifling a scream. She lay panting afterwards, surprised by the force of her climax. She hadn't come that hard in...well, too long to remember, honestly. Was it just because it had been a while, or was it the thoughts of Alec? No. She couldn't let herself start really getting into him, or worse, actually falling. This wasn't serious, this was just a game. At the end of the season, they would part ways. She'd go back to Chestwick Hall and try to find a way back home, or, if that proved impossible, try to figure out what kind of life she could have here. He would go back to doing whatever it was he wanted to do, she guessed.

A pang sliced through her chest at the thought of not seeing him, of not walking through the park or having tea or smiling as Callum told stories of Alec and Rosie as children; of not watching his cheeks heat or him roar in laughter while Jonathan told Elle tales about him over lunch in the garden; of not having him in her life.

"Shit, shit, shit," she groaned, throwing her arms over her face. She wasn't just friends with him, not anymore. Once the mask had fallen away and she'd seen the real him, she'd connected with him in a way that she hadn't connected with someone in a long time. Even without being able to share her true past with him, she somehow felt more like herself around him than she had in years. She couldn't even explain it, other than to admit that she had feelings for him. Her stomach knotted, knowing that they were feelings that didn't matter, *couldn't* matter. It wasn't like they could just date in this time. It was all or nothing here, so her answer had to be nothing.

Didn't it?

As soon as she saw Alec the next afternoon, her cheeks flushed. The night before came flooding back, the things she'd thought, the release she'd found with his face flashing behind her eyes. He looked at her curiously, and she quickly teased him about his hair being a mess before he could somehow read her every thought. She forced herself to get her shit under control before that evening, when yet another dance would mean low whispers and their bodies being agonizingly close, but not nearly close enough. *Doesn't matter. We're just friends. And unfortunately, friends with benefits isn't exactly a thing yet.*

She managed to keep her thoughts mostly PG-13 rated throughout the day, but when she saw him at the ball, they veered into NC-17 with squealing tires and burning rubber. He looked far too handsome tonight. Black coat, deep cerulean waistcoat and cravat, everything just had to fit him like a fucking glove, didn't it? She scowled inwardly, sighing at the same time. Life just really wasn't fair.

When he smiled over the rim of his glass at her, or gave her a surreptitious wink at some inside joke, her pulse beat wildly, her skin flushing. She needed to get a grip, but she couldn't quite manage it. She was going to blame the lack of physical contact for her overstimulated state, for the fact that a single sidelong glance or the merest press of their palms could make her shudder.

In between their usual banter and teasing gossip about the other party-goers, Alec seemed to be holding something back. He would study her, open his mouth to speak, hesitate, and then say something that Elle knew for a fact wasn't what he'd originally planned.

"Will you please tell me what's been on your mind all evening?" she finally snapped at him in irritation. They circled each other and she quirked a brow at him in challenge.

"What makes you think—"

"Alec," she said in a low voice when he circled behind her, his body so close that she could feel his heat warming her back. She momentarily wanted to melt into him, wanted so desperately to ignore all the rules and just turn and wrap herself around him, feel him in her arms, feel his heart beating against hers. She shook herself.

"I know you well enough by now to know. So, just say it already."

A lead weight suddenly settled in her stomach. Was he going to call off their deal? Was there someone else he had his eye on for real? Why did that thought bother her so much? It was his right, his duty some would say, to find a wife and end this little charade. But that didn't mean she was going to like it. She held her breath as she waited for his response.

"The first night we met, you told me that you weren't a lady."

She blinked, confused. "Yes...?"

"And you've reminded me of that fact several times since then."

"Uh huh..." she confirmed as they slowly circled each other again, palm to palm.

"Would you say that that is still an accurate statement?" His lips were curling upwards slightly and the knot of unease in her belly unfurled. Whatever he wanted to say, it wasn't anything she should be worried about. No, it was clearly something he was excited about, which only piqued her interest.

Her own lips tilted upward on one side. "I would say that is fairly accurate, wouldn't you?"

He chuckled. "Well, I did not want to offend you by assuming." They joined hands as they revolved in a slow circle, their gazes locked. "Meet me tomorrow night," he said in a low voice.

Her brows flew upward. "What?"

"Meet me outside the door to the kitchens at ten o'clock. There is somewhere I want to take you. Somewhere I think you'll enjoy, but it's very...Well, few proper ladies would be found there. Proper gentlemen either, mind you, but if you recall, I never claimed to be such a thing." He gave her a rueful smirk that made her stomach flip. God, why did he have to be so damned good looking?

"That sounds...interesting." She eyed him carefully. "And you aren't concerned about...being alone with me?" The idea sent a jolt through her. Anticipation. Excitement. Lust. A hearty mix of all three. "I mean, if we're caught, won't it be quite the scandal?"

He eyed her. "I suppose we should take care not to get caught then, shall we?"

Well, if he was willing to risk it, she was officially intrigued.

She nodded. "Alright then."

Now his brows rose, as if he hadn't been sure what her answer would be. Then he smiled, a wide, full smile that made her breath hitch.

Fuck, I'm screwed.

Elle excused herself to use the restroom and headed out into the night. She needed some air to clear her head and get a grip on herself. She wandered away from the house and into one of the many extensive gardens. It was rectangular, with large hedges acting as high walls around the entire thing. Four matching fountains sat near each corner and a larger, towering one occupied the middle of the space. Covered paths ran in between the corner fountains, ivy forming a living roof over each walkway, flowers trailing downward over the edges, and there were lanterns burning brightly atop white marble pedestals throughout the space. It was beautiful and deserted. The perfect place to take a time out from everything happening inside.

Elle left the cover of the pathway she was on and made her way to the fountain in the middle. She sat on the edge and trailed her fingers over the cool water. She wondered where Alec planned to take her, and couldn't tamp down the spark of excitement that shot through her. She was eager for something new, something different, something *fun*. She was getting restless with the endless balls and teas and promenades at the park, but she was also nervous. Elle knew herself and she could only hold back for so long. Being alone with Alec might just be too much for her to handle. What would happen if she slipped? She really didn't think he would be scandalized, but what would he think? Would he—

"And what are you doing all alone out here?" a cool voice asked from behind her.

She whirled, springing from the edge of the fountain as if it had been electrified. Henry fucking Astley stood a few feet away, half in shadow. Her pulse raced. He'd followed her out here into the darkness and seclusion of the garden. Whatever he wanted, it couldn't be good.

"Mister Astley," she said stiffly.

"Miss Montgomery," he replied, voice smooth as velvet, but something about it, about *him* tonight, made the hairs on the back of her neck stand on end. He eased forward a step, out of the shadow, and she took a half step back. Elle had taken self-defense classes, and forced herself to relax and recall what she'd learned. *Hands loose and open at my sides, feet shoulder-width apart, left foot slightly in front of my right, weight back.*

"I wondered if I'd ever get you away from Kentworth." His lip curled in clear disdain, and Elle couldn't tell if it was because he truly hated Alec, or just hated that Alec had gotten in his way with her. She figured it was a bit of both. He moved closer to the fountain, seemingly admiring the sculpture in the center—a beautiful, weeping angel—and she shifted to keep him in front of her.

"It's a lovely evening," he drawled, sounding drunk, "I can hardly hear myself think in the ballroom." He cocked his head to the side. "Can't hear the music out here, though, can we?" His eyes glittered in the dim light and Elle ground her teeth, instincts flaring that the prick had a plan, and she wasn't going to like it. Then she realized the situation they were in: she was out here, alone with a man. *Rule Number One. Fuck.*

"I should go. We shouldn't be out here..."

Henry's lips curled into a wicked grin and he wobbled ever so slightly. Definitely drunk.

"Ah, you're right. It wouldn't be proper of a lady to be found acting...unbecoming out in the darkness alone with a man."

Elle stiffened and narrowed her eyes. "Unbecoming?"

Henry slinked forward a step. Elle braced herself but didn't retreat this time. *Fuck him. If he wants to start this, I'll finish it. Reputation be damned.* Rose was pretty much already engaged to Percy and she didn't think that Percy would change his mind just because of Elle's bad behavior. Hopefully. She wouldn't do anything unless she absolutely *had* to, but she sure as shit would if he forced her hand. She waited, ready.

"Throwing yourself at me like a common whore," he said simply. Elle's nostrils flared as she inhaled sharply. *This fucking asshole.* "Now, we both know that no one would believe your word over mine, so you denying it will do absolutely no good. But as I am a gentleman, I will happily agree to marry you and avoid the gossip of your...misdeeds spreading throughout the Ton. It would be such a blemish on the MacTavish family, after all." He sounded just like Matilda. Hell, maybe the bitch had put this idea in his head to leave Alec open for one of her daughters. No, surely she wasn't capable of such manipulation? Elle really had no idea what people in this damn place were capable of. Marriage arrangements were far more cutthroat than she could have ever imagined, so...she wouldn't put it out of the realm of possibilities.

She ground her teeth as Henry grinned, turning his attention from the fountain and meeting her eyes. He looked triumphant and Elle's decision was made for her. *Not fucking today.*

She took a step towards Henry, and he blinked in surprise.

"I would quite literally rather fuck a cactus than marry you, Henry Astley."

She wasn't sure if he quite understood the full meaning of her words—did fuck even mean *fuck* here?—but as fury flashed over his face, she knew he understood the insult of it at least. She moved to step past him, but he grabbed her wrist, gripping tight, his eyes blazing. Henry had been an annoyance before now, the guy at the bar that keeps trying to dance with you no matter how many times you shimmy away, but overall harmless. She had never gotten the vibes that he would turn into the kind of guy that took things a step too far no matter how firmly you told him no—until now. She would blame it on the booze and the pressures of the season and whatever the weird pissing match between Henry and Alec was that she somehow wound up in the middle of—but that didn't mean she would accept it. Not by a fucking long shot.

He wasn't hurting her wrist, but he didn't look as if he meant to let this go, to let *her* go. Elle merely looked pointedly at his hand and then back at his face, one brow arched in challenge.

"I'm going to give you eight seconds to remove your hand from my body, Mister Astley."

"Have you seen El—Miss Montgomery?" Alec asked Daniel. She'd left the ballroom after their last dance and he hadn't seen her since.

"No, actually," Daniel said, sipping his drink. "Last I saw, she was dancing with you." He shook his head. "I still can't quite believe that you're actually courting her." Alec quirked a brow in question. "You're a lucky bastard," Daniel clarified.

Alec grinned and clapped his friend on the shoulder with a wink before striding off to find Elle. He snagged a glass of brandy and wound his way through the crowd. He didn't see Eleanor, but he did see that prick Astley ducking out of the ballroom and out into the night. Alec was intrigued—and nosey.

He made his way outside and, for a moment, didn't see Astley.

"Where in the devil..." He glimpsed Astley's back as he strode purposefully across the lawn and towards the gardens. Duke Billingsly's hedge mazes and gardens were famed, but Astley didn't strike Alec as the type to admire such things. "What are you doing out here?" Alec muttered as he followed, keeping to the shadows as much as possible. He felt a bit like a spy in one of the silly stories he used to read as a boy, but he couldn't quite bring himself to care. He hoped he found Astley doing something embarrassing, something he could mock the bastard with, or at the very least, laugh about with Elle. Thinking of Elle made Alec's blood heat and his cock suddenly quite interested in the conversation.

"Not now, you bastard," he said sternly to his crotch, shifting uncomfortably. This was getting out of hand. He could barely think about Elle these days without his thoughts spiraling to places it should never go. Improper places. Dangerous places. Delicious places he would give anything to explore.

Astley had disappeared into the fountain garden a few moments ago, and Alec crept along, still wondering what Astley could possibly be doing out here. Taking a piss, maybe? Seemed quite a long walk for that. Or perhaps he was having clandestine meetings under the cloak of darkness? Alec's intrigued was definitely piqued at the thought, wondering what unlucky lady he might have somehow fooled into thinking he was worth throwing her reputation away for.

Alec eased his way through the opening in the hedges and ducked behind one of the large pillars that stood on either side of the path, holding up the trellises that made the roof of ivy and flowers. He glanced around the edge, doing his best to remain hidden, and his blood went cold.

Elle.

Alec couldn't believe what he was seeing. Astley was out here meeting with *Elle?* No. No, no, no, this wasn't right. It couldn't be. Alec shook himself, trying to clear away the roaring in his ears and the light haze from the brandy. What were they saying? He needed to hear. Rage boiled hot and swift in his chest when he realized that Astley had his hand on Elle's wrist, but before Alec could react, Elle spoke.

"I'm going to give you eight seconds to remove your hand from my body, Mister Astley," she said calmly, though her voice was cold as ice. Only her demeanor stopped Alec from storming forward and beating Astley for all he was worth. She was unconcerned with the predicament, speaking to Astley as if he were an errant child.

"How dare you," Astley seethed. "How dare you speak to me like—"

Quick as lightning, Elle struck out at him. Alec stood, mouth agape and frozen in shock. He'd never in his life expected to see something like this. She slammed the heel of her hand into his nose, and even from this far away, Alec heard the crack as cartilage snapped. Astley released his grip on her, his hands flying to his nose as he grunted in pain, cursing loudly. Elle reached out and grabbed one of his wrists, pulling him towards her as she twisted around behind him, bringing his arm with her and yanking it upward behind his body at an unnatural angle. He all but screamed and Elle kicked out at the back of his leg, taking him to his knees. His arm shot up higher behind his back and he cried out again, a whimpering sound slightly muffled by the blood streaming down his face and dripping to the stone.

Alec continued to stand frozen in place, eyes wide, trying to take in what he was seeing. He'd never seen a woman move like that, so in control of her body and knowing just how to defend herself. He'd surely never seen one do it and attack a man in the process. It was...impressive. And strangely, attractive?

"Now," Elle said calmly from behind him, "I don't think that you want to go and tell a ballroom full of people that a *woman* made you bleed and cry like a little girl. So, I'll keep your secret and you keep mine. You know, the one about me being a harlot out in the garden and all that?" she spit, sarcasm thick in her voice. Is that what the bastard had said to her? Was that his plan? To force her into marrying him by threatening to tell people that she'd been in a compromising situation with him out here alone in the darkness? The anger from before flared again, hotter. *Oh, when I get my hands on him...*

"Does that sound like a good plan, Mister Astley?" Elle pulled up on his arm and he tried desperately to hold back his bellow of pain behind clenched teeth.

"Alright! Alright! I won't..." he sobbed, "I won't tell anyone."

"Wonderful," Elle said with a smile, stepping back to let Astley crumple to the ground. "We'll just pretend this never happened then, shall we?" She brushed a bit of dirt from her dress and Alec quickly slinked back out of the garden. He melted into the shadows of the tall hedge wall just outside and waited for her to emerge. Part of him wanted to go in and beat Astley bloody— or blood*ier*, he supposed—but he thought Elle had sufficiently handled that problem for today. He and Astley would row about this one day, but today was not that day. If Alec stormed in now, he honestly couldn't be sure that he wouldn't kill the bastard. Plus, Astley was just petty and crazy enough to press the issue if he knew that someone had witnessed his disgrace, and Alec didn't want anything to possibly come back on Elle or the MacTavish family for this. So, for now, he waited until Elle made it back to the house and then followed, leaving Astley alone and crying in the garden.

The next day passed both in a blur and so agonizingly slowly that Elle wanted to rip her hair out. Alec had given her no details about the evening's plan and she could tell that he was loving her annoyance at not knowing. She'd asked him at least twenty times while they walked in the park and he had merely smirked in response, making her want to scream.

After dinner and a bath and false calls of goodnight to everyone, Elle waited impatiently in her room, pacing and fiddling with the black lace on the bodice of her scarlet gown. It wasn't a formal dress, but it wasn't quite a house dress either. She supposed it would do for a secret, covert operation.

At five minutes until ten, she silently slipped from her room, quickly scooting down the hallway and ducking into a small alcove just before the stairs beside a bust of some long-dead Mac-Tavish with a stern expression on his face.

"Don't you judge me," she muttered to the statue. She stayed there for a few minutes, listening intently for voices or the sounds of footsteps. When she heard nothing, she exhaled softly and bolted quietly down the stairs. She didn't encounter any of the staff and quickly made it outside, the cool night air kissing her face as she closed the door behind her, leaning back against it in relief, her heart pounding. She felt like a teenager again, sneaking out of the house to meet Tommy Hastings down by the river. Of course getting caught then meant being grounded and her dad putting the fear of God into Tommy until he pissed himself. Getting caught now meant being branded a dirty tramp and possibly being forced to marry someone just to save face. *Oh what a time to be alive.*

The small courtyard outside the kitchen was mostly dark, moonlight filtering through the sprawling limbs of a towering tree and throwing erratic pools of light and shadow dancing around as the wind blew. Elle squinted into the darkness, willing her eyes to adjust.

"Alec?" she whispered. She took a few cautious steps forward. "Alec?"

Suddenly a hand was over her mouth, stifling her scream of surprise. She instinctively fought, kicking backwards with a booted foot and shoving her elbow into a taut stomach. Alec grunted quietly in her ear. She relaxed as her fight-or-flight chilled out, and he released his grip. She whirled and smacked his chest.

"Ouch," he whispered, amused, rubbing the spot.

"You scared the sh—you scared me," she corrected herself, hissing at him quietly. He chuckled again and she felt his hand on her wrist, tugging her forward and around the house. She forgave him for scaring her almost immediately and grinned as they darted from shadow to shadow, giddy with excitement. They silently made their way to the street, down the lane, and finally into the waiting carriage.

They were both laughing by the time they leapt inside, Alec slamming the door behind them and rapping on the roof. A second later, the carriage lurched into motion.

"That was quite fun," he said, running a hand through his hair. Disheveled as always, but gorgeous. She was glad to find that he wasn't in finery this evening either, just a simple white shirt, black coat, and trousers. Nice, of course, like everything he owned, but not as if they were dressed to go to a ball.

"Very cloak and dagger," she grinned, and then waved his confused expression away. "Won't the driver find it odd that you're gallivanting around town in the middle of the night with a lady in your midst?"

"Matthew has been sworn to secrecy, not to worry. Plus, it wouldn't be the worst thing he's been an accomplice to in my life," he added with a grin.

Elle laughed at that, wondering what stories Matthew could tell her about Alec. She glanced out the window, trying to figure out where they were headed.

"So, are you going to tell me where we're going?"

"No," he said simply, grinning and leaning his head back against the seat, chest rising and falling quickly from their escape. She rolled her eyes but leaned back as well, catching her breath. After a few minutes, it finally hit her that this was the first time she'd ever been alone with Alec, *truly* alone with him, and she jolted upright against the bench. The carriage suddenly felt very small and very hot and, as Alec seemed to come to the same realization, his eyes snapping open, very, very tense. Their gazes met and held. Elle had the almost overwhelming urge to launch herself across the small space between them, to settle herself over his lap and wrap her arms around his neck, to finally know what it felt like to kiss him, to feel him beneath her as she straddled him, to hear him whisper sweet and dirty things in her ear. She balled her hands into fists and he swallowed hard, glancing away to look out the window.

Without looking back, he said, "you look beautiful tonight."

"Thank you," she said, hoping she didn't sound quite as nervous as she suddenly felt for some odd reason. It was *Alec*, for God's sake. They'd spent countless hours together over the past weeks, and it wasn't like she hadn't actually been alone with a man before. It was fine. Everything was fine. She was perfectly capable of being in a dark, confined space with the most attractive man she'd ever met, a man she may or may not be falling for, and not making a move.

Probably.

She shoved her hands under her thighs just to be sure they didn't reach for him without her permission and he eyed them, but didn't comment. They rode in silence after that, but the tension didn't ease. If anything, it got worse, and she wasn't sure how much more she could take.

Elle blew out a relieved breath when the carriage slowed and Alec exited, giving her his hand to help her down. The street was dark, but Elle could make out what appeared to be a row of warehouses, large and square. Nondescript and, in the darkness, not very attractive. She could hear the sound of water lapping against a shore nearby. The Thames? They seemed to be right on the cusp of that invisible line where the good side of town turned into the bad side of town. Thoughts of Jack the Ripper came to mind and she shivered ever so slightly, glancing around nervously as she tried desperately to remember when, exactly, he had rocked London with his killings.

Alec led her along a narrow sidewalk and then down a darkened alley.

"You know, if you planned to murder me, you could have done it in the carriage," she said quietly. He laughed as he steered her, his hand hovering just behind her.

"No murders planned tonight, I promise."

"Another night then," she quipped.

"Here we are," he said, a smile in his voice. He gestured to a dark, plain door that looked like it had seen better days. The paint was weathered and stained, the wood slightly warped and dented towards the bottom as if it had been kicked. She glanced at Alec with skepticism, but he merely held up a finger, telling her to wait. Where in the hell was he taking her?

He knocked twice in quick succession, waited a second, knocked once more, then half a second, and two more knocks.

"A secret knock? *Seriously?*" she hissed. He gave her one of those cocky grins that she secretly loved, and a few moments later, the door swung open. A burly man with a thick black mustache looked at Alec with recognition and the hint of a smile. He shifted his gaze to Elle, bushy brows rising. He looked back to Alec.

"Never brought a guest before, Alexander," the man said suspiciously in a thick Cockney accent.

"She won't cause trouble, I promise, Jackson."

"Maybe a *bit* of trouble," Elle amended sweetly, and the man—Jackson—smiled widely, big shoulders shaking as he laughed. Several of his teeth gleamed silver in the moonlight.

"Oh, I like her," he said, stepping aside to allow them to enter. Alec gently placed his hand on the small of her back as they walked inside.

"This way," Alec said, steering her to the left when she automatically turned right. "I do believe you charmed old Jackson."

"I am quite the charmer, Alexander," she quipped and he chuckled, low and husky. They walked down a long, narrow corridor with crumbling plaster and piles of trash here and there. It smelled like fish and ash and body odor. At the end of the hallway, they went through another doorway that opened to a dark stairwell.

"Sure, go down the dark, deserted stairwell into the basement of the creepy building," she whispered to herself. "Nothing bad has *ever* happened in that scenario before."

"What was that?" Alec asked as he took a lantern from the wall and led her downward.

"Nothing," she muttered, placing a hand on one of his shoulders to keep herself from falling. He stiffened slightly, but didn't rebuff her. As they descended, she heard faint music and the smell got distinctly better. At the foot of the stairs, they went down another smaller hallway, the music louder now. Lanterns had been hung along the wall, illuminating the corridor. This one was much cleaner than the last, the wallpaper a deep red with black vines curling and stretching along it, like black snakes. At the end stood a large door, the same crimson as the walls.

"Welcome," Alec said with a mysterious grin as he pushed the door open, "to Puck's Lair."

Chapter 13

Elle felt as if she'd stepped through a portal somehow. Er, another portal, she supposed. The last one had sent her two hundred years into the past, this one to another world. The room beyond the red door was large, clean, and lavishly decorated. Brass lamps sat on the various tables and were mounted onto the dark blue walls, and several large chandeliers hung above, crystals hanging down like icicles. The scent in the air was a mix of cigar smoke, whisky, and perfume, but somehow, wasn't unpleasant. A faint blanket of smoke hung around the space, but it wasn't suffocating.

Several tables were scattered throughout the room and people looked to be playing cards. *Poker? Is that a thing yet?* Lounging areas were set up along the walls, with oversized chairs and comfortable looking couches in shadowy alcoves. Waitresses bustled through the space with large trays of drinks, clad in far more daring dresses than Elle had seen at any ball she'd been to, all tight corsets and plunging necklines. A small band played in the corner and people danced in front of them, laughing and twirling and holding each other far closer than what would be considered appropriate. It was Elle's kind of place.

"What do you think?" Alec asked, sounding nervous. He snagged two drinks from a tray and the waitress gave him a sultry smile and a wink.

"It's *amazing*," Elle breathed, turning to grin at him. She could *almost* pretend she was back home, at some sort of themed event in costume. They made their way through the room towards the card tables, and Alec raised his glass here and there in greeting to the other patrons. "How did you find out about this place? It doesn't seem like the kind of spot a gentleman and future viscount should be," she said dubiously.

"Now, how many times must I tell you, Eleanor? I am no true gentleman." He grinned and gestured towards one of the tables. "Do you want to play? I can teach you."

"I would be allowed?" she asked in surprise.

"Of course. The rules out there," he jerked his chin upward, "don't make their way down here."

She felt herself truly relax for the first time since arriving in London. Tonight, she didn't have to worry about saying the right thing or doing the right thing or looking the right way. Tonight, she could just *breathe*. They approached a table with an empty chair and Alec gave her an inquiring look.

"You play. I'll watch."

He settled in, shaking hands with the three men across the table, and nodding at the woman on his left. The woman was beautiful, with hair black as night, lips red as blood, skin a beautiful deep brown, and to call her voluptuous would be the understatement of the century. She smiled at Alec and then glanced at Elle, her smile widening and her dark eyes glittering.

"And who have you brought with you tonight, Alexander?" she purred, never taking her eyes off of Elle. Her accent was exotic, but Elle wasn't sure where she hailed from. It called to mind sun and sand and spices. It was lovely.

She flicked a finger into the air and a moment later, a man bustled up with another chair for Elle, setting it on Alec's right.

"Behave, Isadora," Alec scolded. "I plan to take Eleanor with me when I leave this evening."

Isadora pouted, but winked at Elle. "Well, if you should change your mind, I am more than happy to take her off your hands." Elle's brows rose in pleasant surprise. "And call me Isa, dear," she said to Elle.

Elle smiled back at Isa. "Well, Alec, it seems like you had best show me a good time or I may be trading you in by the end of the night."

Isa threw her head back and laughed, the others at the table joining in. Except for Alec, who, of course, narrowed his eyes at her, his lips tilting upward in a relaxed, crooked smile.

"I shall endeavor to hold your favor then," he said with a wink.

Elle giggled and everyone turned their attention to the game. To her surprise and delight, they were playing blackjack. Elle was a novice card counter—another mischievous pastime she and her dad had gotten into together—and she figured if she could manage it in some of the smaller casinos back home, she could probably do just fine at an underground club in London in the 1800s.

Alec leaned toward her. "It's called vingt-et-un. The object is to have all of one's cards add up to—"

"Twenty-one?" Elle finished with a sardonic look.

"Well, yes. I suppose that was rather obvious from the name, wasn't it?" He smiled, and Elle was amazed how at ease he seemed, like maybe he finally felt as if he could just breathe too. "There are a few caveats, but it is fairly easy to understand once you see a few rounds." Elle nodded, feigning ignorance, and the game began. Elle studied each card, her mind cataloging and calculating.

After a bit, she leaned into Alec, lips inches from his ear. He stiffened, but remained still.

"I'm going to help you win. You're abysmal at this," she whispered. He turned his head to whisper back and she barely stifled a shiver as his breath tickled her ear.

"I am most certainly *not* abysmal!" he said, sounding slightly offended, but quickly added, "but how can you help me?"

"You're going to have to trust me, can you do that?" He pulled back enough to meet her gaze. Hers was a mix of challenge and pleading, and his was full of curiosity. He gave her one slow nod in agreement and she smiled, leaning back in to whisper again. "If I tap your leg, hit. Er, get another card."

"Do you two need a moment alone?" Isa teased in a sultry voice.

Elle pulled away, smiling sheepishly to the table. "Apologies."

Isa waved her away. "None of that, dear. When he looks as he does, and you look as you do—well, it's no surprise neither of you can concentrate. If I were you, I wouldn't even bother getting dressed at all. I would simply stay in bed all day, doing all manner of unholy things—"

"Enough, Isa," Alec cut her off. "Let's get back to the game, shall we? I do believe I was about to take all of Phillip's money."

The first time Elle tapped Alec's leg, he surreptitiously gave her a look that clearly said *are you crazy?* She gave him one back that said *just fucking do it.* He sighed as if exasperated but motioned for another card.

"Bold of you, Kentworth," Phillip said with a deep chuckle, but it quickly faded into stunned gaping when Alec hit twenty-one.

"What was it you were saying, Phillip? Ah, yes, was it that you were happy to hand your money over?"

And so the evening went. They drank and they laughed and they ran the fucking table.

"Would you like to dance?" Alec asked after a while, "I could use a break from taking all of Phillip's money. The poor man is only a Duke, after all. I would hate to take his entire fortune in one evening." Alec grinned and winked at Elle.

"Please, go dance, I beg of you," Phillip groaned, taking Alec's friendly barb about his title in stride.

Elle laughed but nodded. Alec tossed back what was left of his drink and led Elle to the corner near the band. It was different than the music at the balls, the dancing different to match, but the rhythm of it filled her veins with excitement and her body began to move instinctively to the beat. To her surprise, Alec pulled her in close, wrapping an arm around her back. She gasped quietly and he smirked.

"How on earth did you know how to win so easily?"

"A lady never reveals her secrets," she teased. He pulled her even tighter against him and leaned down so that his lips were beside her ear.

"I promise not to tell," he whispered, making her shiver. "I'm an excellent keeper of secrets, Eleanor." She swallowed hard, achingly aware of how close their bodies were, how easy it would be to wrap her hands around his neck and draw his mouth to hers. *Or to find a darkened alcove and do much more than kiss.*

She shook herself but her hand slid across his shoulder and slowly up his neck, fingers lightly trailing along his skin and playing with the edges of his hair. Did she imagine the way his breath hitched? The way his fingers tightened on her? Elle pulled back to look at him, and she saw her thoughts mirrored in his eyes. He wanted just as much as she did. Just as she was about to do something incredibly stupid, Isa interrupted.

"May I cut in?"

Alec forced an easy smile, chasing the moment of crystal-clear desire away. "Are you asking me or Elle?"

Isa pursed her lips. "Hmm, either will do."

"I need a drink," Elle said, "You can borrow Alec." She stepped away, feeling cold and empty without Alec's arms around her. *Stupid, stupid, stupid.* Alec bowed low before taking Isa's hand, making the woman laugh airily. As Elle walked away, she called over her shoulder, "I'll want him back intact, Isa!"

"I make no promises, Eleanor!"

Elle got a drink and smiled as she watched Alec spin Isa around the floor dramatically. The two had obviously danced many, many times before, their bodies knowing exactly how to move together. *What else have they done together?* She wasn't jealous, exactly, but she did wonder if they were still doing whatever it was. When he left Elle for the evening, did he come here and see Isa? The feeling in the pit of her stomach that *wasn't* jealousy suddenly felt like a lead weight.

Elle wandered back to the table where they'd played cards earlier. Phillip groaned and Elle chuckled.

"How about a new game? It's one we play often in America. It's called quart—er, uh, *coins.*"

Alec couldn't keep his gaze from flitting to Elle as he danced with Isa. Bringing her had been an excellent idea. Quite possibly the best he'd ever had. He'd never seen her so relaxed, so carefree and like her true self. It was as if she was breathing for the first time in a long time and the thought hit him like a punch. He hadn't realized until that moment how trapped she must feel in all of this. The season, the Ton, the expectations—all of it. She hadn't been born into this, never would have expected to be thrust into the middle of it by a twist of tragedy and fate. Alec understood all too well the feeling of being trapped, of suffocating from the weight of it all, and seeing her relax with him here, one of the few places he could feel like himself as well, made him think...well, things that didn't matter.

"She's quite stunning," Isa said with a knowing smile, following his gaze. "Who is she?"

"She's a...friend," Alec replied. It was true enough, though the things Alec wanted to do with Elle, *to* Elle, were far from things he should want to do with a friend. Being alone with her in the carriage had been a special kind of hell and he'd nearly lost all control, had nearly pulled her to him and crashed his lips to hers, settled her over his lap and wrenched her down, kissed her throat like he'd been longing to do for weeks until she was begging for more. And he would have given it. He would have given her anything and everything that she wanted in that moment, consequences and reputations be damned.

Isa made a bemused and suspicious "hmm" before she spun away from him and then back again. "Well, she is lovely and you should bring her back as often as possible." She followed Alec's gaze and raised her brows. "What is she doing now?" A large group had gathered around the table and shouts and laughs and groans were rising up from them in waves.

"Taking more of Phillip's money I suspect," he chuckled.

"Oh goodie. Let's go watch!" Isa grinned.

When they made their way to the table, Alec saw that they were playing some kind of game involving coins. A game that Elle was especially adept at by the looks of it. She effortlessly bounced a coin off of the wooden table and into a glass, making half the table cheer and Phillip groan as he took a long gulp of his drink and slid a small stack of money towards Elle. Her cheeks were flushed and she was grinning widely. She met his gaze and winked. He was hit in that moment with a feeling so strong that it startled him.

He...God, did he *love* her? Was this what love felt like? He hadn't the foggiest idea as he had never really given much thought to romantic love before now, but he couldn't find the words to explain the feeling any other way. When she looked at him like that, it was like his entire world tilted, finding the proper axis finally, after all this time. Everything suddenly made sense, everything was suddenly clear and focused. Everything suddenly felt *right*.

Someone hurried up to Isa, talking in low, urgent whispers. The band stopped playing at some unseen signal and Isa raised her voice.

"Time to go!"

Everyone knew exactly what it meant and what they needed to do. Everyone except for Elle, of course. She stared around in confusion as everyone rose from the table, scattering in all directions while muttering quick goodbyes and amused cries of "good luck!"

Alec was beside her in an instant and she rose, blinking at him in surprise. He quickly pocketed her winnings for her as he watched the commotion.

"What's going on?"

"We are about to be raided, I'm afraid," he said, jaw clenched. He hadn't meant for Elle to be caught up in this. If they were found here, Alec could talk his way out of it with ease, but Elle's name could be ruined. Several hidden doors opened in the walls and people began to pour through each of them.

"Get her out of here, Alec," Isa said, pointing towards the wall where the band had been playing moments ago. "Eleanor, it was lovely to meet you. I hope to see you again. Now, go on. Hurry, dear."

Elle muttered a quick "nice to meet you too" as Alec pulled her along.

"Raided?" Elle asked as they neared the door.

"Puck's isn't precisely legal, technically speaking. Sometimes the constables poke in to shake things up, but Isa always pays them off and smooths things over and they leave her alone for a few more weeks. But it wouldn't do well for you to be caught up in the mess." They'd nearly reached the wall when the front door burst open and yells went up, some of anger, some of alarm, some even of amusement. Alec tensed, worried that Elle would be afraid or angry with him for putting her in this situation to begin with, but when she met his gaze, she...*grinned.*

Alec couldn't help but smile back, gripping her hand in his and flinging them through the hidden door. They ran, winding their way through shadowed hallways, Elle giggling in wild abandon as they did and soon he was laughing too. He could only imagine what the pair of them must have looked like, running like thieves and laughing like loons. Eventually, they hurtled up a flight of rickety stairs and flung a door open into a small alley, a different one than they'd come through earlier. They hurtled down the narrow space between the two buildings, splashing in God only knew what, but Elle didn't seem to care. She ran in front of him, still holding his hand in hers. She reached the mouth of the alley and skittered to a stop, nearly making him crash right into her when she stepped quickly back from the street.

Alec heard the shouting, the constables yelling for people to stop running. Elle turned, meeting his gaze for a heartbeat, before closing the distance between them in a few quick steps.

She whispered, "trust me," just before she gripped the front of his jacket and pulled him down to her, her lips slamming to his. His eyes flew wide and he was frozen in place for what seemed like an eternity. Was this truly happening? Was he truly kissing Eleanor? They shifted so that she was against the wall, half in shadow, the cold bricks pressed firmly into her back, and his body covered hers.

She moved her lips against his and it was utter ecstasy. They were soft and warm, and when he slid a hand up the side of her neck, gently cradling her cheek, she parted them on a soft gasp. He didn't hesitate, despite part of his mind screaming at him to stop, telling him that this was a mistake, that it wasn't proper, that there was no way she could want this. He delved his tongue into her mouth, gently thrusting it against hers. She moaned quietly, the sound sending chills of desperate need cascading over his entire body. He gripped her waist with the other hand, and to his utter shock, she hiked her thigh upward, hitching it over his hip. Instinctively, he moved his hand to grip her thigh, sliding her skirt upward and holding her tight, fingers skating over smooth, bare skin. *Christ.*

His blood was roaring in his ears but he somehow heard the shouting getting closer, the sound of beating footsteps as someone ran past the alley.

"You there," a slightly out-of-breath voice said from a few feet away. Alec jerked his head up but Elle nuzzled his neck, moving to whisper in his ear.

"Pretend you paid for me. They don't know we were inside." Then he understood. It was a ruse. She wasn't kissing him like this because she couldn't stop herself, she was kissing him like this to keep them both out of trouble. The bitter sting of disappointment felt like acid in his veins.

But he had to admit, it was a good plan.

Alec pulled himself up to his full height, squaring his shoulders and letting the proud, future viscount shine through. He'd learned long ago that it wasn't his name that made people take note or cower, it was the way he held himself, the absolute authority that he exuded.

In his most haughty tone, he said to the constable, "I'm *quite* busy at the moment, and I didn't pay to be interrupted." Elle ran the lobe of his ear through her teeth and Alec's eyes slid shut for a moment, hips subtly arching forward. Her hands tightened in his jacket and...did her own hips thrust against him now?

The man—no, he was a boy really—the *boy's* bushy brows shot upward in understanding and even in the dim light from the streetlamp, Alec could see his cheeks redden. He must be brand new. *He had better get used to this kind of thing if he plans to stay in this profession long*, Alec thought. He would be seeing far, far worse than this soon enough.

"I...uh, carry on, sir," he said, swallowing audibly. Elle licked Alec's neck before planting a kiss there, just above the spot where his pulse was thundering, and his fingers dug into her thigh. How did she know exactly how to drive him mad? Exactly where and how to kiss and lick and touch?

"I plan to," Alec said in a dismissive voice. He turned his head back and forced Elle's face back to his, pressing his lips to hers again, quickly slanting his head to deepen the kiss. He thrust his tongue against hers, knowing it was a farce, but also knowing it may be the only chance he'd have to kiss her. So, he kissed her for all that he was worth. He wanted her to remember this, to think of him any time she kissed another man for as long as she lived. He wanted to sear himself into her mind and body and soul somehow, wanted to brand her as surely as she was branding him. *I'm ruined,* he thought, *I'm ruined for anyone but her for the rest of my life.*

With that thought echoing in his mind, he kissed her with more vigor, nearly desperate. He tangled one hand in her hair, the pins holding it up pulling free and the tumbling strands slipping through his fingers like silk. She clutched at his coat and she moaned quietly against his lips. He inched his other hand up her thigh and he didn't have to question if she thrust her hips against him this time. She lightly bit at his lower lip and an unearthly noise rumbled from his throat, his cock hard as steel and throbbing painfully. *Christ almighty.* He kissed across her jaw and down the delicate column of her throat, licking and grazing his teeth as she tangled one hand in his hair. He trailed his lips across her collar bone, lower still.

"Alec," she breathed, making him shudder, his hand inching further up her thigh, trailing nearly to her hip, the tips of his fingers trailing over the curve of her backside. *No.* He had to stop this. He had to pull away. If he didn't, he would take her right here in this alley and that was *not* something he would allow to happen, no matter how badly they both seemed to want it in that moment.

He somehow forced himself to calm, moving back to kiss her once more. He finally pulled away, only to press his lips softly to hers once, twice, a final time before leaning his forehead against hers. His heart had never beat so fast, had never felt as if it might fly right out of his chest. Her chest was rising and falling in quick, shallow bursts, and she didn't release her grip on his coat. They stayed that way for what felt like an eternity. Maybe it was. He couldn't be sure, couldn't think of anything except Elle, of the way her body felt against his, the way her heart thundered in time with his own...of how right she felt in his arms. Finally, he found the strength to speak.

"That was..." He cleared his throat. "That was quick thinking, Miss Montgomery."

He realized that he was still gripping her thigh, still lightly grazing his fingers over her skin. He released her, gently lowering her leg to the ground. She released her grip on him and he stepped away. Her skin was flushed, her eyes wide and luminous in the darkness.

She smiled, smoothing her hands down the front of her dress before trying to fix the mess he'd made of her hair. Did she need a moment to collect herself before she could speak? Was she as affected as he was? She cleared her throat quietly.

"Well, I am nothing if not a quick thinker, Lord Kentworth."

He felt the moment between them slip away into the night like smoke on the wind. It made his heart clench, but he was exceptionally skilled at hiding his true thoughts and feelings, so he merely gave her a wry smile back and held out his hand.

"We should get you home."

The ride back to the MacTavish house was a quiet one, both of them seemingly lost in their own thoughts. Alec's mind was whirling, his thoughts a tempest of confusion and nonsense. He kept telling himself that it had just been a ruse, it wasn't real. It didn't mean anything.

Except, that it did. It meant...everything.

"That was quite the evening," Elle said as she exited the carriage.

"One could never accuse me of being boring."

"Thank you. It almost felt like I was back..." She trailed off and her smile was oddly sad. Was she thinking about her home? He imagined she must miss it. "It was the most fun I've had in a long time," she finished.

"You are quite welcome. Good night, Eleanor," Alec said quietly.

She nodded and turned to walk away. She stopped after a few steps, made as if she were going to turn back, but shook herself and hurried on. He watched her go, his chest twisting painfully. Alec had kissed plenty of women in his life—a fact that he wasn't exactly proud of, but it was a fact nonetheless—but the one he'd shared with Elle in that alley had made him forget nearly every other one. It had been fire and passion and he wanted more, wanted to spend the rest of eternity kissing Elle, tasting the sweetness of her lips, feeling her skin beneath his fingertips.

But it hadn't been real.

Chapter 14

"When are you going to propose, son?" Jonathan asked as he and Alec rode back to the manor house. Alec's father had wanted to leave the city early and spend the next two weeks before the MacTavish ball at their home instead of in London. Alec would have to go back to London in a few days for some standing appointments, but he had decided to accompany his father anyway. He honestly needed a break from, well, everything really. He and Elle had both acted perfectly normal after that night at Puck's, but he couldn't stop thinking about the kiss, couldn't stop replaying every little detail in his mind over and over and over until he thought he might go mad.

So, yes, a break from everything was in order. The MacTavish family would arrive closer to time for the ball, so until then, Alec would have a chance to examine his feelings away from Elle. He found that it was hard for him to think logically when she was nearby. When they were together, he couldn't quite seem to remember why being with her in truth was a bad idea, or why expressing his feelings would be wrong. The kiss had to have meant *something* to her. He'd caught her staring longingly at him more than once since that night, her gaze often drifting to his lips, her cheeks flushing ever so slightly. He knew that she hadn't wanted to be courted at the beginning of the season, but things had changed now, hadn't they? Would she truly still be opposed to a marriage proposal if it came from *him*?

He scrubbed a hand over his face. Was he really thinking about marriage?

"Come now, Alec. She's surely expecting it. It isn't gentlemanly to keep her waiting. Are you unsure of her?" Jonathan pushed.

"You only want me to propose because you like her better than me," Alec responded, forcing a rueful smile. It was half true. His father truly adored Elle.

Jonathan laughed but soon a coughing fit seized him. He waved Alec off when he worriedly moved to help his father. "I'm alright, I'm alright. But yes, you are correct. I want to spend all the time I have left with my new daughter. So stop dragging your feet, my boy!"

Alec couldn't help but chuckle, but made no promises. Instead, he stared out of the window, feeling himself relax with every rotation of the carriage wheels. The city eventually gave way to country, brick buildings melting into gently rolling hills and thick woods. He breathed in deeply, the clean air making the knot in his chest loosen ever so slightly. He let his mind wander, trying to sort out what was happening.

He could easily admit that he did have feelings for Elle, but did he love her? Is that what this really was? He felt like himself with her in a way he rarely did with anyone else. She was smart and cunning and beautiful. God knew he wanted her physically so badly he could hardly stand it. He'd had to stop himself from reaching for her too many times to count since that night, had relived that kiss in his mind over and over.

But more than all that, he could see himself having a life with her, a *real* life, not just surviving and going through the expected motions and milestones until one of them finally died. The kind of life his father and mother had once had together, the kind Jocelyn and Callum had. One of love and happiness, which was so rarely the case in marriages.

But they'd agreed that this was all just a charade. Would it be fair of him to turn it into something more? Would she even accept him if he did?

He ran his fingers through his hair, having no earthly idea what to do, but the thought of their relationship coming to an end in just a few short weeks was...intolerable. He pushed the thoughts away, determined to enjoy the time away from the city, to enjoy what little time he may have left with his father.

"I have a surprise for you," Jocelyn said over breakfast. Elle arched her brows in question as she stirred the porridge around the bowl. What she wouldn't give for a breakfast burrito right about now. "I know all of this has been a lot for you to deal with—and you've handled it all beautifully, might I add—but I thought you could use a bit of a break."

"A break?"

Jocy nodded, barely suppressing her grin.

"I thought you and I could go back to Chestwick early, just the two of us. For a few days, all members of the staff will be sent away to make preparations for the ball. We will be all alone in the house. We could...be ourselves for a bit," she said quietly, giving Elle a meaningful look. It took her a moment to realize what Jocy was saying: they could be *themselves*. As in, Elle could act like the twenty-six-year-old graphic artist from 2020. No etiquette, no rules, no false identities, no pretend backstories. Just her.

"Oh my God, yes. When can we leave?"

"As soon as you finish breakfast and get dressed."

Elle sprang from the table, flung her arms around Jocy, kissing her temple, and sprinted from the room like a bat out of hell. Alec was spending some time with his father, so she wouldn't be seeing him much over the next couple of weeks anyway, and, to be honest, a little time away from him was probably a good idea. Things were getting *complicated*, to put it mildly.

She'd known that she felt more than friendly affection for him, but after that night at Puck's she'd been on the verge of falling. Hard. And don't even get her started on the kiss. It had been reckless and insane, but *dear God* had it been the best idea she'd ever had. His lips had been soft but firm, unyielding and demanding, and he'd tasted like smoke and whisky and something spicy she couldn't name. His tongue had been hot against hers, making her bones melt and her body ache. His fingers had left trails of fire across her skin and she didn't think she'd ever wanted anyone as badly as she'd wanted him. She would have happily let him fuck her right then, right there, up against a wall in a dark, dirty alley. *That's* how out of her mind with lust she'd been for him. Kissing Alec was like a drug and she was addicted after one hit. Kissing him had felt so right, had made her shudder in pleasure, had made her crave so much more.

But she couldn't have more. She just couldn't, no matter how much she might want it.

Chestwick Hall was so quiet with only the two of them that it was a little jarring at first.

"We're really alone?" Elle asked as they dropped their bags in the foyer.

"We're the only souls here other than the horses," Jocy confirmed.

Elle grinned. "Mother fucker!" she yelled at the top of her lungs. Jocelyn's mouth fell open in shock, and then she burst into laughter.

"Asshole!" Jocy called out after a few seconds. It was so freeing, like they'd popped the strangling bubble around them and Elle felt herself relax fully for the first time since that fateful day in the woods that brought her here. The two of them stood there and yelled as many obscenities as they could think of to the empty halls, everything eventually just becoming absolute nonsense.

"What, exactly, is a twat burglar?" Jocy asked, breathless.

"I have no idea, but it was fun to say." Elle shrugged and grinned.

"That felt *good*," Jocy said with a wide smile.

"Oh, that's just the tip of the iceberg, Jocelyn MacTavish. There are no proper English ladies allowed in this house for the next two days."

They both sprinted to get out of their dresses and into something comfy, and then spent the rest of the day just...*being*. No pretenses, no lies, no restraints. It felt so damned good Elle nearly cried. Elle fired up her tablet and pulled up *Supernatural*, glad that she'd downloaded the entire series so she always had something to watch on flights if the Wi-Fi was sketchy.

"Who. Is. That?" Jocy asked, openly gawking at Dean Winchester.

"That, my friend, is my future husband."

"Can I borrow him? Just on weekends and holidays?"

Elle snorted and agreed they could share custody. Then they did yoga on top of the ridiculously huge dining table, because why the hell not, giggling nonstop as Elle tried to show Jocy different moves and she toppled over more than once. Afterwards, they laid in the sun on the back lawn and talked about their lives, not having to be careful with their words or worry that someone may be listening.

"Oh! I have a good one—hot showers," Elle said. They'd been playing a game of *What Do I Miss About The Twenty-First Century* for the last half hour.

Jocy groaned. "I would kill for a hot shower. Quite literally. I'd take Matilda out in a heartbeat if it meant standing under a steaming hot stream of water in my old bathroom." Elle threw her head back and laughed, imagining Jocy committing crimes against humanity for a shower. Jocy rolled over onto her stomach and looked at Elle.

"So, how are you doing? Really?"

Elle let out a long exhale. "I'm...alright, mostly. Some days are harder than others. I miss my life and indoor plumbing," she said with a grin, "but I *am* happy here, believe it or not. The customs and etiquette and all of that bullshit is still hard to swallow, but I'm learning to just grit my teeth and revel in the knowledge that this won't last forever. And I love you and Callum and Rose, you've really become my family. I haven't had that in so long..."

Jocy reached out and squeezed Elle's hand, giving her a warm smile.

"You're our family too, Elle. I hope you know that." Elle nodded and forced the lump in her throat away. After a heartbeat,

Jocy added nonchalantly, "And what about a certain rakish gentleman that has been spending nearly every waking moment with you as of late?"

Elle rolled her eyes. "You know it's all just pretend so neither of us has to deal with this stupid courting thing." Elle had come clean to Jocy soon after she and Alec had made their little deal.

Jocy gave her a very motherly look. "Are you sure about that? I've seen the way you've been looking at him lately...and the way he's been looking at you," she added thoughtfully.

"I..." *Was* she sure? No. Not at all. She shook herself. "It doesn't matter. Even if I do have feelings—which I'm not admitting that I do—it doesn't matter. I can't be with someone that I have to lie to about practically everything."

"You could tell him," she offered.

Elle shook her head. "He isn't like Callum, Jocy. He won't believe me. He'll think I'm insane or a witch or who knows what. Either way, it ends the same: him walking away."

Jocy seemed to think it through, and Elle appreciated her not automatically saying *oh of course he'll believe that you're a time traveler! But you'll still live happily ever after!* Elle was a realist and she appreciated not being given lip service.

"He might surprise you," she finally said. "You have to remember, he grew up with the stories of those woods too. His mother believed in the tales...maybe Alec does too." Elle wanted to give in to the hope trying to rise in her chest. She wished she could be honest with Alec, to share her true self with him finally, but she couldn't. Jocy added, "Just...think it over. And remember: he might not know the whole truth about where you came from, but he does know who you are, Elle, I'm sure of that."

Elle gave Jocy a watery smile, letting her words sink through the doubts and warm her a bit. But that was enough of that. They only had a few days to be themselves, so there was no time to waste on moping or worrying.

Elle shook herself. "Ok, enough of the heavy." She jumped up and exclaimed, "We need wine!"

After a bit more Supernatural and a quick dinner, Elle changed into sleep shorts and a cami, and tossed Jocy some leggings and a t-shirt.

Elle jumped onto the bed, phone in hand. Thanks to her solar charger, it was juiced up and ready to go.

"And now," she announced drunkenly, "allow me to introduce you to our queen and savior, Taylor Swift."

Jonathan asked Alec to drop off some paperwork and a bottle of choice brandy at the MacTavish house. They were still in London, but Alec knew he could leave it with the staff and they'd give it to Callum when they arrived later in the week. Plus, Alec hadn't taken Apollo for an evening ride in ages. They navigated the worn trail through the thick woods between the Kentworth property and the MacTavish's easily, even with only the moonlight to guide them. Alec and Apollo had made this trip too many times to count.

When the woods gave way to open fields, Alec spurred Apollo into a gallop, the wind whipping in his hair as they flew through the night, the breeze cooling his flushed skin. His thoughts drifted to Elle, wondering if she'd enjoy riding like this with him, and he knew in his gut that she would. He could picture her now, riding beside him, her golden hair blowing out behind her like a cape of sunlight. Her blue eyes would glitter with joy and mischief, and his heart would stutter at the sight.

"Damn this," he growled to the night, urging Apollo faster and faster until the world blurred around him. They slowed when they approached the house, and Alec frowned. There were no lanterns lit outside and no lights shining from the windows within. Curious, he dismounted and patted the horse on the neck.

"Stay here, old fellow."

Alec approached one of the windows and peered inside. He didn't spy any signs of life from within, no movement, no lights, no sounds of maids scurrying about. There was always *someone* here, even when the family was elsewhere. He pursed his lips and eased his way around the house. As he neared the back, he heard laughter. His brow furrowed as he followed the sound.

He froze for a moment when he finally emerged on the back lawn and gazed upward. Soft light streamed from the open doors to the balcony of one of the rooms, and Elle was there, swaying gently to some type of music Alec could only barely hear. It was strange, with a pulsing beat from an instrument he couldn't name, but he could barely spare that a moment's thought. All he could do was stare, awestruck.

Her hair was in a braid on one side of her head, strands of gold whispering against her temples. Her eyes were closed and a soft smile sat on her lips. Lips he was aching to kiss again so badly he felt as if he might die if he didn't. He clenched his fists at his sides as he continued to watch, throat going dry: she was *barely* clothed. She wore what looked like a short silk chemise, one thin strap sliding down her shoulder and the lace dipping between her breasts in a low V shape. His eyes drifted downward and he suddenly couldn't breathe, couldn't think, could barely stand. Her legs were *completely* bare, some type of silk short-pants covering her rump, but only just so. He could actually see the bottom curve of her pert backside from beneath them and he had to widen his stance at his sudden raging cockstand.

"God almighty," he whispered, scrubbing a hand over his mouth. He stepped back into the shadows of a nearby statue of a mermaid, his heart thundering within his chest. Though she wasn't exceptionally tall, her legs seemed to go on and on as his eyes slowly traveled the length of them. He swallowed hard, his fingers itching to touch her again, to trace the path his eyes had just traveled...followed by his tongue. Did she have any idea of the things he could do to her? The pleasure she could experience? He knew that she might have some knowledge, more than a typical lady at least, but she couldn't know half of what he could offer her, the things he could make her feel. He shuddered at the mere thought.

She turned and grinned into the room, speaking animatedly to someone within—Jocelyn, surely?—gesturing wildly with her hands and jumping up and down. He ignored the way it jostled her breasts. Mostly. Alright, not at all. His eyes were riveted to each tiny movement like a hawk watching a field mouse.

And then Elle began to move her body in a way he'd never seen before. It reminded him a bit of the burlesque dancers he'd seen in France, but even they had not moved like *this*. She whipped her hips in a sinful rhythm that mesmerized him. She threw her head back and laughed, raising her arms above her head as she moved. She reminded Alec of the stories of fairies, dancing with abandon in the moonlight. It was so sensual, so arousing, he could barely breathe. He felt a twinge of guilt for watching her this way, like some miscreant lurking in the shadows, but he couldn't stop himself. She continued to move her body, rocking her hips and twirling in circles, all the while laughing and smiling and looking more relaxed and more beautiful than he'd ever seen her.

She eventually moved out onto the balcony, fanning herself ·with her hands. She raised her face to the sky as she leaned on the stone railing, eyes sliding closed as she inhaled deeply of the night air. Alec was suddenly reminded of *Romeo and Juliet* and he had the urge to climb the trellis and profess his undying love. *It is my lady. O, it is my love! O, that she knew she were!*

"God, I'm a fool," he muttered. He watched her for a moment longer, something inside his chest twisting and shifting. He'd truly never seen anyone look so beautiful.

And he'd never felt love like this before.

Alec hastened away when she turned back to the room, running for Apollo and mounting the horse in one swift, practiced motion. And then they were flying, tearing through the night like a black blur among blacker shadows. His eyes watered, his heart thundering. He was shaken to his core, knowing without a doubt that he loved Elle, but he was also more aroused than he'd ever been in his life. He urged Apollo on faster, trying not to think of Elle, but it was a losing battle. He made it home and handed the horse off to the waiting groom without a word, running through the house as if the devil himself were on his heels.

A few members of the staff gave him strange looks as he bolted past them, taking stairs two or three at a time, not slowing until he made it to his wing. Alec slammed the door to his room shut behind him, leaning back against it, breaths sawing in and out of his chest. He ran his hands through his hair roughly, images of Elle flashing through his mind. With each one, desire lashed him like a whip.

He felt out of control, mindless. He yanked his coat and shirt off, tossing them roughly away. He collapsed on the bed, closing his eyes and letting Elle fill his mind. He wrestled with the laces of his britches, nearly breaking them in his haste. He slid his hand inside and moaned, hips bucking upward off of the bed, heels digging into the mattress.

Alec had never been so hard, so wanton, so aching. He stroked as he imagined Elle: the way her hips had twisted and writhed, the way her chemise had dipped enticingly between her breasts, the curve of her taut backside...He gritted his teeth as his thoughts shifted from what he had seen, to what he *wanted.* He wanted to kiss her lips until they were red and swollen, wanted to thrust his tongue against hers, wanted to feel her moan into his mouth. Alec imagined what he would do if, by some miracle of heaven, she were here with him.

He would tunnel his fingers into her hair and pull her close, shifting his body fully against hers, every inch of him pressing against every inch of her. He would lay her down beneath him and kiss down her throat, lick the soft indention at the base before traveling downward. She would gasp and arch beneath him when he licked her breasts, whimpering for more, writhing. There was so much he wanted to do, wanted to imagine, but as he continued to stroke, he couldn't stop his mind from spurring onward. He imagined rising above her on straightened arms, moving his hips forward and sliding inside her, long and slow and deep.

"*Christ,*" Alec groaned through gritted teeth as he imagined her wet heat surrounding him, her soft cries of pleasure as he slipped in and out, enjoying every movement, every slick thrust, every gasp and whimper. "Ah, God!" he yelled out as he came in a rush. He dug his heels in harder, his hips arching off of the bed, spend lashing his torso and chest, nearly up to his chin. He lay there for long moments afterwards, breathing heavily, his vision slightly blurry. Had he ever climaxed so hard? No, no he had most certainly not.

"I think I am in a great deal of trouble," he said in a breathless whisper to no one.

Chapter 15

Alec waited three days before returning to actually deliver the items for his father to Chestwick. He had come to the country to take time to examine his feelings and that had become even more important after he'd seen Elle on the balcony and he'd nearly lost his mind. So he'd stayed away.

When he finally did come back, the MacTavish's butler, Embry, answered the door.

"Lord Kentworth," Embry said with a low bow, a smile crinkling the weathered skin around his light blue eyes.

"Hello Embry. It is good to see you."

"It has been too long. Please come in, come in. I'm afraid Lord MacTavish has not arrived from the city as of yet."

"Oh that's alright. My father just asked me to bring a few things for him."

He handed the package over to Embry after they entered the sitting room, the older man nodding and assuring Alec he would make sure that Callum received it as soon as he arrived.

"Embry who—oh Alec, dear!" Jocelyn said, beaming as she walked into the room.

Feigning ignorance, Alec said, "Oh, Lady Mac—Jocy," he corrected when she gave him a pointed look. He'd missed the relaxed freedom he felt here, away from the rest of the world. Where he could just be Alec and she could just be Jocy and things were so much easier. "I didn't know that you had already arrived."

"Oh, yes, Elle and I came a few days early while Callum and Rose remained. She didn't want to miss the last dance of the season in the city with Percival, of course. I suspect he is going to propose next week when he and his family stay with us here."

"It is so hard to imagine Rosie married," Alec said with a shake of his head. "I suppose I still see her as the firebrand chasing me with snakes and pushing me into the creek." They both chuckled.

"Yes, it is hard to believe she is soon to be someone's wife," Jocelyn agreed with a wistful sigh. "It all happens in the blink of an eye. You'll understand one day, when you have a family of your own." Alec simply bobbed his head, but Jocelyn studied him in that way of hers, stripping away all of his defenses.

"You love her, don't you?" Jocy asked softly. Alec jerked and cleared his throat, and she laughed lightly. "Don't worry—I think it is only so obvious to me because I've known you practically all your life."

He sighed and ran his hand through his hair, frowning slightly. He hadn't realized quite how unruly it had become.

"I..." he swallowed hard and squared his shoulders, "yes, I do," he admitted, looking to her imploringly, suddenly feeling like a child again needing a mother to fix all the worlds' problems for him with a biscuit and a kiss.

"I know that this courtship was a falsity," Jocy said, surprising him Alec paled slightly. He thought about denying it, but there was no use.

"Are you angry with me?"

"Of course not, dear. If you'd been the only one in on the ruse, leaving Elle to believe you truly did mean to marry her, then I would have Callum tan your hide." She smiled and he relaxed, huffing out a soft laugh.

"And you've known all this time?"

Jocy nodded. "Elle told me soon after the two of you started your scheming." She gave him a look that was half amusement, half chiding. "But no, I wasn't angry about it. Elle has been through so much, had so many things thrust upon her, so many choices taken from her...if she wanted this arrangement with you, then I could never begrudge her that"

A sadness that Alec couldn't understand, but felt like a lead weight in his gut, passed over Jocelyn's features. What did she mean? What had happened to Eleanor? It was true that she never wanted to speak much about her past, always shying away from the subject or giving him only the barest, vaguest details, but he had never been sure why. And it hadn't seemed polite to ask when she so clearly did not wish him to know. Had she suffered some sort of tragedy? Had she been hurt in some way? The thought of someone hurting her made Alec's vision burn red for a moment, his blood boiling in his veins.

"But," Jocy added, giving him a meaningful look, "if your feelings have changed...well, there is a good chance hers have as well." Alec's brows rose and hope flooded his chest like warm embers being stoked to life in a nearly darkened hearth.

"Do you mean...?" Alec held his breath, feeling as if his entire existence was poised on the edge of a razor, waiting for the answer. Could Elle possibly love him the way he loved her? Jocelyn didn't give him one outright, but her smile was answer enough. He exhaled finally, the relief filling his chest and making him feel as if he could fly.

"Elle is drawing in the garden, if you'd like to see her. I'll have Embry bring some tea and sandwiches."

Alec's lips curled and he kissed Jocy on the cheek before making his way to the garden. He inhaled quietly when he saw Elle sitting on a blanket, brow furrowed as the pencil flew over the paper. She was in a simple dress of lilac that fortunately—*or unfortunately?*—covered far more than what she'd been wearing the last time he'd seen her. Images of her on the balcony surfaced: the bare skin of her legs, the pert curve of her backside, the way the strap had slipped down her shoulder and his intense need to place his lips where it had just been. He shook himself, forcing the images away.

She didn't seem to hear him approaching, lost in her art, so he had the opportunity to sneak a look at her drawing. He blinked several times in surprise. It was *him.* In the drawing, his eyes were downcast, but there was a soft, easy smile on his lips that he wasn't sure he wore around anyone but Elle. Something about the fact that she was drawing him made him rub the heel of his hand over his chest, directly over his heart. He took a silent, steadying breath.

"I don't think you captured my obscene handsomeness accurately," he said in a teasing tone. She gasped and turned her eyes up to find him grinning. "Although, to be fair, looks like mine simply cannot be duplicated. Many have tried. All have failed."

Her lips thinned, but he could tell she was fighting a smile.

"And you are *so* humble. I believe that's your best quality."

He scoffed. "Don't be silly, my best quality is obviously my enormous fortune." She giggled, making him grin, and she gestured to the blanket beside her just as Embry brought out the tea and sandwiches.

"I didn't know that you would be here already," he lied, avoiding her gaze and focusing instead on selecting a sandwich from the tray.

"Oh, yes. The city was becoming a bit overwhelming, so Aunt Jocy and I came a little early. I love it here," she said, sighing wistfully and leaning her head back as a breeze blew through the garden, bringing the scent of roses with it.

"I do too. I practically lived here as a boy."

"Oh that's right. I'd forgotten your property abuts this one." Alec nodded and pointed to the west.

"That way, through those trees." He eyed her for a moment before asking, "Would you like to come see it?" He didn't know why he felt so nervous suddenly, but it faded when she smiled widely. God, she really did have a beautiful smile.

"I would love that."

And so, after finishing off the tea and sandwiches, they spent the rest of the afternoon exploring the grounds of Pembroke, the Kentworth family estate, with Embry in tow behind them as to not be improper, of course. The old man, who might as well have been Alec's grandfather, smiled genially as he watched them. There was a look in his eyes that told Alec that he knew exactly how Alec felt. *Christ, does* everyone *know?*

Alec couldn't help stealing glances at Elle as they meandered through the trees. It was truly idyllic, with the birds chirping around them, the scent of flowers in the air, and the sunlight filtering through the canopy, making Elle's hair seem to sparkle. They stowed their horses—after a race to the stable, of course, Elle laughing wildly and Alec calling her a cheater from behind her—and strolled through his mother's gardens.

"She spent hours out here, almost every day. She loved it so much," Alec said around the sudden lump in his throat.

"It's beautiful," Elle said as she trailed her fingers over the blooms. "I'm a terrible gardener. I kill almost everything I touch." She scrunched her nose in an utterly adorable fashion and Alec dramatically threw himself between her and the rose bushes, holding up his hands to thwart her off. She stepped back quickly in surprise, dropping her hand.

"Back! Back you murderer!"

Elle practically snorted with laughter but then wiggled her fingers in the air in his direction, that glint of playful mischief he loved so much glittering in her eyes.

"Hmm, maybe it doesn't only work on plants." She reached towards him and he leapt away nimbly. "Is the great Lord Kentworth *afraid?*" She reached for him again and he backed away down the path.

"Eleanor," he warned, but he was grinning. She raced after him as he ran backwards. "It is really unbecoming of a lady to," he darted to the side as she lunged for him, "chase after a man, you know."

"How many times do I have to remind you that I'm not a lady?"

The path ahead parted and curved around a great stone fountain, a statue of Boudica on a rearing horse in the center. Alec ran to the left and Elle to the right. They stared at each other over the pool between them, both breathing hard, both beaming. Elle made to move to the right, so Alec moved left. She moved left, so Alec moved right.

"Are you afraid of me, Alexander?"

"Terrified," he said, honestly. This woman terrified him in so many ways. Terrified him and thrilled him and tantalized him and challenged him. She laughed at that, but then shifted her gaze over his shoulder, her smile faltering and a look of horror coming over her features.

"Oh my God," she whispered in terror.

Alec's chest tightened and he whirled, wondering what could possibly have frightened Eleanor so badly, the need to protect her flaring inside him.

But he saw nothing.

He heard the splashing and turned back just in time to have water flung into his face by a giggling Eleanor who was now standing in the knee-deep water of the fountain just a few meters away.

"I cannot believe you fell for that!" She put her hands on her hips, looking proud of herself.

"Oh you little wench," he said in a low growl before he leapt over the edge of the fountain and joined her in the pool. She squealed as he kicked up water in her direction, and Alec was fairly sure that Embry probably thought they were insane, but he didn't care. Elle splashed him back and soon they were both drenched and laughing so hard they could barely breathe. He felt like a child again, a lightness radiating down to his soul that he thought was gone forever.

Alec tried to ignore the way her dress clung to her skin, the fabric doing little to hide the curves of her breasts and hips, the flat planes of her stomach. They'd neared each other without even realizing it, now standing so close that their chests almost touched as their breaths sawed in and out of their lungs. Water spiked her lashes and ran in rivulets down her cheeks. He reached out without thinking and brushed a drop away with his thumb.

Her breath hitched and her skin flushed, her eyes burning. Alec didn't drop his hand and she didn't move away.

"Alec," she whispered.

"Yes?" His voice was low and gruff.

She licked her lips once, eyes darting down to his own for a moment. Could she want to kiss him as badly as he wanted to kiss her? No, he didn't think such a thing was possible. He shifted forward ever so slightly. Damn the rules, damn what was proper, damn it all. He needed Elle like he needed air, and he was desperate to *breathe.*

She tilted her face up towards his, her breaths coming fast and shallow.

"Alec, I..." She shook herself and stepped back from him. "I'm glad that I met you," she said in a strangely sad tone. "I never wanted to come here, but...but I'm glad that I did because meeting you has been..." She swallowed hard, as if fighting to get words out—or maybe fighting to hold them back. "I...Alec, I..."

"What on earth is going on out here?"

Elle gasped and they both whirled to find Jonathan Kentworth standing down the path beside Embry, Emmett not far behind, all of them looking utterly amused at the scene before them.

"It, uh, seemed like a good afternoon for a swim," Alec said ruefully, grinning crookedly at his father.

"Children," his father said, shaking his head but chuckling low. "Come on then, have some supper with your father and get out of the damned fountain. Eleanor, it's lovely to see you again, my dear."

Alec and Elle shared a look and, despite the tense moment before, they smiled at each other and made their way out of the fountain and into the house, Emmett complaining good-naturedly about the mess the two of them were making as they were ushered in different directions in search of dry clothes.

Once dressed—Elle was about the same size as his mother and looked beautiful in one of her old rose-colored gowns—they ended their day with dinner and drinks and laughter with Alec's father.

"Oh, I know a good one!" Elle said, taking a long sip of wine. They had been trying to flummox each other with riddles all evening, and Alec had to admit that Eleanor was incredibly adept in solving them—and stumping Alec and Jonathan as well.

"A man rode into town on Friday, stayed for two days, and left on Friday. How did he do it?" She shifted her gaze between the two men, looking smug.

Alec rubbed his chin as he thought through the riddle, and Jonathan repeated it back, slowly.

"Two days?"

Elle nodded. "Two days."

Jonathan steepled his fingers in front of his lips and thought hard, narrowing his eyes at Eleanor, who merely grinned back. She shifted her gaze to Alec and gave him a haughty look. Alec ground his teeth, but after a few minutes, finally threw up his hands. "Oh just tell us already!"

"The horse's name was Friday," Elle said with a satisfied smirk.

"The horse's..." Jonathan repeated before roaring with laughter. Elle joined in and Alec couldn't help but follow suit. It was...perfect. Alec hadn't felt so content, so truly happy in so long. Eventually, the hour grew late and Emmett brought the carriage around for Elle.

"Thank you for visiting with an old man," Jonathan told Elle as he walked her to the door.

She waved his *old man* comment away. "You still look like a spring chicken to me," she said. Alec still wasn't used to some of her stranger turns of phrase, but Jonathan seemed to like this one, grinning widely.

"Will you be coming to the ball?" she asked on the front steps.

"For you my dear, I will make an appearance," Jonathan said, inclining his head and kissing the back of her hand.

"I will see you there, then." She bid them both goodbye, and Alec watched the carriage as it took her farther and farther from him. Jonathan smiled and clapped a hand on Alec's shoulder, squeezing tightly.

"What?" Alec asked as he closed the door.

"You've found someone to show you how to be happy, my boy," his father said with a wink.

Chapter 16

Alec returned to the city two days before the MacTavish's ball. He had several business meetings he had taken on his father's behalf, attended a boxing match, and had drinks with Daniel and a few other acquaintances at one of the popular gentlemen's clubs.

"So, are you going to propose then?" Daniel asked as they walked out into the night. Daniel stumbled slightly and Alec steadied him with a low chuckle. Daniel's own proposal had been accepted earlier in the week and the night had turned into a celebration in his honor.

"I would think it would be above the great Lord Kentworth to propose to whores," a smooth, slightly slurred voice drawled from the shadows. Alec bristled and Daniel whirled around, squinting into the darkness.

"Astley? Oh sod off, what kind of thing is that to say?" Daniel complained, waving his hand wildly.

Alec ground his teeth and stared daggers as Astley waltzed towards them, the red ember of a cigarette shining in the darkness. He flicked it away and spat onto the sidewalk.

"Walk away, Astley," Alec grated, voice cold and hard as ice. Memories of Henry's hands on Elle rose behind his eyes, rage rising in his chest.

"I don't take orders from you, Kentworth," he snapped, peevish and petulant.

"This is one you probably should," Daniel advised, looking worriedly between the two of them.

"He's just a bit jealous of my courting of Miss Montgomery, Daniel, not to worry." Alec said, and then curled his lips in a cruel, knowing smile, holding Astley's gaze. "Why *did* you stop coming to call on her, Astley? Did something happen perhaps? Maybe something a man would be embarrassed for anyone else to know about?"

Henry's eyes blazed with fury, at the reminder of his encounter with Elle, or because Alec knew about it, he wasn't sure. Both, perhaps. Alec smirked and Henry stepped forward, swaying slightly. *Drunk bastard.*

"I just realized I would never want to sully myself with someone like her. I'll bet Eleanor Montgomery has been ridden more than any of the horses in London," Astley laughed coldly.

Alec moved before he'd even made the conscious decision to do it. He punched Astley hard enough that the man's head snapped backward, his entire body spinning from the force of the blow. Alec caught at his jacket and forced him backwards, slamming him against the brick wall of the club. Henry tried to push Alec off, but Alec wrapped a hand around his throat, squeezing.

Alec leaned in close, almost nose-to-nose with Henry. He bared his teeth in a feral, animalistic way that honestly shocked even himself. Daniel squawked in surprise and distress, but knew better than to intervene. Alec squeezed the bastard's throat harder and Astley's eyes went wide with such fear that Alec wondered if he might piss himself. Blood trickled from his lip, dripping over his chin and landing on Alec's sleeve.

"Call Eleanor a whore one more time, Henry. I *dare* you." Astley coughed and clawed at Alec's arm, but it was useless. "I beat you bloody when we were fifteen, again when we were twenty, and I will be happy to do it again now because you're a bastard, but I swear to God in heaven above that if you insult my future wife again, if you even *think* about insulting her, I will end you in ways you can't even imagine." He leaned in even closer and added in a low, menacing voice, "I'm a surgeon, Henry. I know *exactly* where to cut to make the pain last, to keep you alive for *days* while I take you apart piece by bloody piece..."

Utter terror flashed in Astley's eyes, whatever he saw in Alec's face making the man understand that Alec wasn't jesting. Henry's eyes welled with tears and his lip wobbled as he tried to keep them at bay.

"And don't think for one second that I'm bluffing. You can say whatever you like about me, you always have, but you will not say another word about Miss Montgomery. Do. You. Understand?"

Astley somehow bit out a choked, "yes! I-I understand!" and Alec released him, stepping back and letting Henry's body crumple to the ground. He coughed and gasped for breath, and Alec watched with a cold detachment.

"Keep this conversation in mind the next time you think about opening that rubbish bin you call your mouth. And you would do well to apologize to Miss Montgomery for anything untoward you may have said or done to her in the past. Understood?" Astley swiped at his eyes, but nodded. Leaning back heavily against the wall and breathing hard.

"You're bleeding." Alec tossed a handkerchief at him. "Let's go, Daniel."

Alec strode off, not looking back to see if Daniel followed, but a moment later, his friend caught up.

"I've wanted to do that for *years*!" Daniel said, slapping Alec on the back. "Christ, I thought he was going to piss himself!" Daniel laughed and Alec's lips curled upward. He wasn't exactly proud of how he'd just behaved, but he couldn't find it in himself to regret it either. He ran a hand through his hair as they climbed into Alec's waiting carriage.

Daniel settled back into the seat, a slow, drunken grin spreading across his face as he eyed Alec.

"Did you say *your future wife*?"

Elle knew she may be slightly biased, but the MacTavish ball was by far her favorite of the season. The decorations were an elegant mix of English and Scottish, a perfect representation of Jocelyn and Callum and the family they'd created together, the blending of cultures and love. Elle had surprised them with a portrait of the MacTavish family as a gift before the ball, and after gushing over it for a solid hour, Jocy gave it pride of place above the fireplace in the grand ballroom, insisting that it be the centerpiece of the entire shindig. Elle didn't want to seem conceited, but she was proud of her work and could admit that it looked beautiful in the gilded frame Jocy had somehow managed to have made on a day's notice. The woman was a force to be reckoned with, really.

The days leading up to the ball had been a storm of chaos, and Elle had mostly tried to stay out of the way. Every time she offered to help, the staff would politely, but firmly, shoo her away. People arrived in droves, and Elle assisted Jocelyn in greeting each guest warmly before a maid showed them to their rooms. It was a good thing the manor house was so gigantic—Elle would swear at least a hundred guests had arrived and more seemed to be coming every few minutes. Chestwick Hall had been transformed into Chestwick Inn it seemed. The thought made her lips curl into a bittersweet smile. Her parents would have loved the idea of one of these old manor houses being transformed into a Montgomery Hotel.

Elle's stomach soured when Henry Astley arrived. Thankfully, after their little altercation in the fountain garden, he'd stayed away. He'd shifted his sights to a different woman, Caroline Sinclaire, and from what the rumor mill was saying, he'd already been speaking with her father about an arrangement. Elle supposed she shouldn't be surprised that he and Caroline would both attend the MacTavish ball, but she still hadn't been expecting to see him. She plastered a brittle smile on her face as he neared to greet her and Jocy.

"Lady MacTavish. Miss Montgomery." He bowed. Was that a bruise on his cheek? A still-healing split lip? "Thank you for having me." Elle ground her teeth and Henry seemed to be able to feel the tension rolling off of her. "Uh, might I have a quick word with Miss Montgomery? Please," he added, when Elle probably looked like she would rather eat a live worm than go anywhere with him.

"Alright," she said in a tight voice. They moved down the hallway and into the drawing room. Plenty of people were milling about, admiring the space and having lively conversations, but Henry ushered Elle towards one of the windows, slightly away from most of the crowd.

She looked around the room and smiled jovially at everyone before turning back to Henry, the smile gone and fire in her eyes.

"What do you want?" she spit.

"I wanted to apologize."

"Oh, please—"

"No. I mean it. I'm sorry for my behavior. It was...unbecoming and it will not happen again. To you or anyone else. I swear it."

Elle narrowed her eyes at him. He sounded...genuine. "What happened?" she asked, suspicious of this sudden change.

Henry cleared his throat. "I was...shown the error of my ways." He looked over Elle's shoulder and paled. Elle turned and saw Alec standing in the doorway, looking...dangerous. Not outright, not to anyone who didn't know him as well as Elle did, but she could see it. He had on his customary mask of haughty indifference, but just below the surface, something dark was simmering. His jaw was clenched and his eyes were sparking with rage, the green looking like cold, glinting emeralds.

Elle looked back to Henry, who tugged at the collar of his shirt, revealing the hint of a bruise there as well. He looked terrified. Scared shitless, honestly. Had Alec beaten him up? Threatened him? And why? Alec's hands were curled into tight fists at his side as he strolled over.

"Astley," Alec said in greeting, voice cold as ice.

"Kentworth," Henry replied, voice shaking subtly. "I was just leaving. I will see you at the ball." With that, he bolted from the room.

"Are you going to tell me what that was all about?"

"I haven't the foggiest idea what you mean," Alec replied innocently.

"You are full of sh—you're a liar," Elle corrected, catching herself. Alec gave her one of his most rakish smiles.

"How you wound me, Miss Montgomery."

"I mean it," she said, crossing her arms over her chest, "Tell me."

Alec glanced around, smiling and inclining his head in greeting to those walking past the room. He returned his gaze to hers and whatever he saw there must have made him realize she wasn't going to let this go.

He exhaled a little roughly. "Henry Astley is a bastard who gets even more bastard-like when he drinks too much. He needed to be taught manners, that's all."

"Alec," she said in warning. Alec's jaw clenched and his body went tense, as if the memory was enough to make him want to track Astley down and repeat whatever he'd done the last time.

"He was speaking...unfavorably about you within my hearing," he nearly growled. He pinned Elle with a look that was all fire and passion and a fierce protectiveness that made her pulse race and her stomach clench. "And that is not something that I will allow. *Ever.*" His voice was low and rough, an edge to it that she'd never heard before. Call her crazy, but it was...hot. Very, *very* hot.

"Oh," she breathed, unable to think of anything else to say. Later she would get to the bottom of what exactly had been said, what exactly he'd done to Henry, but for now, she let it go because if Alec didn't stop looking at her like that, she was going to jump him right here in front of God and half the Ton. She cleared her throat quietly. "Alright then."

He quirked a brow, but they were interrupted by Lord-Something-or-Another coming to greet Alec. Elle slipped away and tried to regain her equilibrium. Alec had punched Henry at the very least—though she suspected it was more than that—to defend Elle's honor. The look he'd just given her...She shivered at the memory. It said *mine* loud and clear. And fuck if she didn't want to be his. She wanted it so badly she could barely breathe. She hadn't set out for it to happen, had tried her best to stop it once she felt it starting, but it was useless. Just like with Jocy and Callum and Rose, her walls refused to come up when it came to Alec. It was like the part of her that was an expert at keeping people at a distance had gotten lost along the route to the 1800s.

But she couldn't be with him, she just *couldn't*. Not when there were so many lies and secrets between them. It wouldn't be fair to him, and he deserved much better than that. The kicker was that she *wanted* to tell him. She wanted to share everything with him in a way she'd never shared with anyone else before, even Ash. She wanted to crack her soul open and let him see everything, the good, the bad, and the ugly, to see her sharp edges and her fears and insecurities. She wanted him to know her in every way possible, to share her entire life with him.

But she couldn't. He wouldn't understand. He would think she was insane or worse, and would turn away from her.

And Elle was pretty sure that seeing him do that might just break her heart for good.

The ball itself went off without a hitch and as they danced together at the end of the night, Elle could barely remember why she couldn't be with him. She had fallen for him, hard and fast, their brief friendship transforming into something so much more than she could have imagined. She knew it couldn't be, but she let herself pretend, just for tonight, that things were different, that there were no secrets between them and that they were going to be happy and whatever the future held, they would face it together.

She met his gaze and in that moment, she would swear that he knew exactly how she felt. His breath caught, his eyes darkening as something heavy settled over them, more so than ever before.

God she wanted to lean in and kiss him, she wanted to tell him she loved him, she wanted so much more than that.

"Elle," he whispered, the word coming out like a benediction.

"Alec, I..." She swallowed hard as the rest of the room seemed to fall away around them. *Fuck my life, I'm in a romcom.* She wished it could stay that way, that it was real, that were truly alone and the rest of the world didn't exist.

A scream rang out, breaking the bubble around them. Elle quickly pulled away to see what was going on. Alec tensed beside her before sprinting across the room, leaving her standing on the dance floor alone, her blood turning to ice as she realized what had happened.

Jonathan had collapsed.

Chapter 17

The next few weeks passed in a blur, and Alec hardly remembered much of anything. He knew he'd done everything he was supposed to, fulfilled all of his duties, but he'd done it as if he wasn't truly *there*. It was as if someone else had done all those things and he'd merely watched from a distance, numb and unmoving.

Dead.

His father was *dead*. Gone forever. Alec would never again hear his laugh or come to him for comfort and advice. He would never get to admit to his father that he *had* found someone to teach him how to be happy, and that, against the odds, he was fairly certain that she loved him back as fiercely as he loved her. The way she'd looked at him just before...He shuddered, shaking away the memories of seeing his father lying on the floor of the MacTavish ballroom, of squeezing his hand and begging him to hold on, of trying desperately to think of something, anything, to stop this from happening. Elle had fallen to her knees on Jonathan's other side and grabbed his other hand, her face stricken. Jonathan had smiled at her, though there were tears in his eyes, and thanked her softly before turning his gaze back to Alec. He told Alec that he loved him and was proud of him, just before the light left his eyes and death finally took him.

Now, Alec was the viscount. He was the head of the house. He was...empty.

"I'm an orphan," Alec said in a dazed tone one evening as he and Elle walked in the garden with Callum and Jocelyn. They'd all remained in the country to help Alec get all of his affairs in order, even Percy. Alec was fairly certain he'd planned to propose just after the ball, but had refrained out of respect to Alec and the MacTavish family given that they were so close to Jonathan. Alec reminded himself to tell Percival that he should by all means ask Rosie, the sooner the better. Their happiness shouldn't wait just because of him.

They all turned to stare at him.

"Well, I have no mother and no father, so that makes me an orphan now, doesn't it?" He pursed his lips. "Or does that term not apply once you reach a certain age?"

Callum came and clamped a big hand on Alec's shoulder, gripping him tightly and holding his gaze.

"Alexander William Kentworth, your mother and father by blood may have passed on from this world, but you are no' alone. You have a mother and father by choice just here." He gestured to himself and Jocy, whose eyes were shining with tears, a heart-broken look on her face. "You canna tell me you doona know that."

Alec's throat felt thick and his eyes pricked uncomfortably. He gripped Callum's wrist, squeezing it in thanks and giving him a nod.

"Thank you," he said quietly, barely able to force the words out.

Callum and Jocelyn walked ahead, giving Alec and Elle a bit of privacy. They walked in silence for a few minutes, their fingers brushing every so often, making his body jolt.

"I'm an orphan too, you know," Elle said after a bit of time. Alec turned toward her, brows raised. He knew that her parents had died, of course. It was the reason she'd come to live with Jocy in the first place, but they'd never really spoken of it. He wanted to laugh, though there was nothing remotely funny about the situation: they had yet another thing in common now.

"They were killed in an accident." His chest constricted at the quick flash of pain that darkened her beautiful features. "Their...carriage was struck and sent off of a bridge into a river."

He sucked in a shocked breath. "Oh God, Elle. I'm so sorry." He couldn't even imagine. At least he'd had some time to prepare for his parents' deaths, whether or not he'd used that time wisely. To have them both taken so suddenly, with no warning? No chance to say goodbye? He hurt for her, wanted so badly to be able to take her pain or change the past for her.

She shrugged one shoulder. "I was nineteen. It still hurts—some days more than others—but...well, I just wanted you to know that I understand what it's like, and I'm here if you need to talk about it."

"Talk about it," Alec repeated flatly, not even really knowing what he would say. Everything was still so unfocused, like he was trying to see it through a rain-soaked pane of glass: he could see what was outside, knew it was there, but couldn't make out all of the details, just vague shapes and outlines.

"Or cry, or scream, or break things," she added with a soft smile. "I highly suggest the screaming and breaking things first, followed by the crying, and then the talking. Maybe more crying afterwards."

Alec's lips actually curled upward for the first time in what felt like a lifetime.

"Thank you," he said, voice rough.

She gave him a sad smile and hiked a shoulder. "I miss him too," she said softly. "I wish I'd had more time with him."

"And I know that he wished the same. He cared about you very much."

"And he loved you more than anything in the world. And he was so proud of you, Alec. You have to know that."

His chest tightened and he gripped her hand, bringing it to his lips and pressing a soft kiss to her knuckles.

He didn't deserve her. He'd been in a fog since his father had passed, but he did know that Elle had been there. She'd quietly helped him organize papers and make arrangements, despite Bennett insisting she needn't bother herself. Alec vaguely recalled her telling the man that she was happy to help and wanted to be close by, just in case Alec needed her. He hadn't even realized until now how much her presence had soothed him, even in his stupor. Just having her near had kept him from falling into the dark abyss that was calling him when he thought of his loss.

She'd gripped his hand during the funeral, not seeming to care at all what others might think. He'd squeezed it so tightly, he thought for sure he must be hurting her, but couldn't seem to stop, and she hadn't flinched or drawn away. She'd squeezed back, letting him know that she was there. He'd felt like a drowning man at sea, and her hand was a raft, the only thing keeping him from being pulled beneath the waves.

If he hadn't loved her before, he most certainly did then.

Without meaning to, Alec had taken Elle's advice and broken several glasses and a bottle of something, he wasn't even sure what, admittedly having drunk far too much. He screamed until his throat was raw while the broken glass scattered across the floor and the amber liquid trickled down the wall. He wasn't even sure what had happened, really. The bottle had been in his hand one moment, and the next, it was flying across the room. He was having a drink, seemingly fine—or as fine as he could be—and then he thought of the fact that he would never again share a drink with his father. He would never again sit before the fire and sip on brandy and talk about nothing and everything.

But instead of sorrow, it had been *rage* that boiled up inside him. A rage so white and hot and sharp, he was sure that it would somehow destroy him from the inside out. He was furious at the unfairness of it all. His father was a good man, a *truly* good man, so why was he fated to be taken from the world so soon? *It wasn't fair. It wasn't right!*

And the rage exploded.

He'd thrown the bottle with all his might. It sailed across the room and shattered against the wall with a satisfying crash. He screamed as he swiped the rest of the glasses off of the sideboard, sending more glass scattering across the floor. He wasn't even yelling words, just awful bellows of rage and fury. He fell to his knees and let himself break, the rage transforming now into utter agony, a terrible, bottomless abyss of loss. He let the darkness take him under, just for a time. He let his grief surround him and strangle him. He wrapped his arms around himself and cried as he hadn't before, even after his mother's death. Alec had loved his mother, but Jonathan Kentworth had been like the sun. He'd burned so brightly, had been the light that had guided Alec his entire life. How could he be expected to survive without the sun? How could he possibly continue on? He felt as if he could actually feel his heart splintering, a crack forming that would never, ever heal, a part of himself being cut away forever.

Alec didn't know how long he stayed there on his knees, but at some point, the tears stopped coming. He sat back, leaning against his father's desk. He supposed it was his desk now, but in his mind, it would always be Jonathan's. He let out a long, shuddering breath. He felt...better, actually. He huffed out a laugh. Of course Elle had been right. She always was, wasn't she?

Now he could think on everything without the pain tearing him apart. He regretted so much and that guilt clawed at his chest, like an animal trapped within his body, desperate to escape. He should have come home sooner, should have spent more time here with his father once he knew that Jonathan was ill. But after his mother and then Colette, he hadn't been able to bring himself to do it. Alec told himself that if he didn't see it with his own eyes, if he didn't acknowledge it while he stood in front of it, it couldn't be real. Of course, that had been ridiculous and the physician in him knew that his father was dying whether he accepted it or not. Now, he'd wished he'd spent the little time they'd had left together, here in their home. Riding and hunting and talking together in front of the fire deep into the night.

But the bitter tragedy of life is that it was far easier to have clarity when looking back, after it was too late.

He would have to live with his regrets about his father, but he would not have regrets with Eleanor. He loved her, he knew it in a way he couldn't explain or comprehend. It was as if it were something that had been written into history long ago, something that was inevitable, and they had only needed to wait for the right time. What had started as a simple mutually advantageous arrangement, had turned into the most significant relationship in his life. He'd never felt a connection to another person as he did with Elle, had never laughed with another or confided in another as he did with her. God knew he desired no one else the way he desired her.

And surely she felt the same for him. He could feel it, could sense it whenever they were near, knew it from the way she helped him through his grief. He knew it, but that didn't stop him from being riddled with nerves as he slid off of Apollo and walked up the front steps of Chestwick Hall. His heartbeat pounded loudly in his ears, faster than it had ever beat before. His throat felt dry and he was entirely too hot, tugging at the collar of his shirt, suddenly feeling as if it were strangling him.

He eyed the sky warily, the dark clouds swirling overhead making an ominous feeling settle deep in his bones. Was this an ill omen? A sign he shouldn't be doing this? *No. No, this is right.* He gripped the flowers he'd picked from his mother's garden so tightly that he crushed the stems and stained his palm green.

"Bugger," he hissed as he wiped it furiously on the leg of his trousers and waited for the door to open. He gave Lottie a wide smile when she answered, and the girl flushed a deep crimson, as she always did.

"Lord Kentworth," she said with a bow before gesturing for him to enter. "Are you here to call on Miss Montgomery?" Lottie asked with a smile as they walked down the wide hallway to the drawing room.

"I am, as a matter of fact." *For the last time, I hope.*

Jocy, Callum, and Elle were all laughing about something when he entered the room, and he was struck again by Elle's effortless beauty. Her hair was pulled back from her face and pinned loosely at the back of her head with sapphire pins that matched her eyes almost exactly. A few tendrils were pulled free around her face in a way that only Eleanor seemed to be able to make look elegant. Alec practically stumbled forward, not acting at all like the viscount he now was.

She met his gaze, and she looked so damned happy to see him his chest ached. She had to feel the same way he did. She just *had* to. Callum caught his eye, and gave him an encouraging, surreptitious nod. Alec had spoken with him about this already and he had given his enthusiastic blessing. Alec took a deep breath and tried to quiet his obnoxiously loud heart. *Better get to it.*

"Miss Montgomery. I've come to...That is, I'd like to..." Damn it. He'd rehearsed what he was going to say all morning. He'd penned a lovely proposal with all of the expected sentiment, even quoting Shakespeare for God's sake, but now it all suddenly felt far too stiff and formal for his Eleanor. Abandoning what he'd stayed up half the night writing, he instead held her gaze, letting the feeling of belonging wash over him, settle into every inch of his body and soul. *Home*, he thought. *She's my home.*

"Elle," he started again, holding her gaze as he drifted ever closer. Her eyes were wide, her mouth slightly parted, and she seemed to be holding her breath. "I never wanted marriage. At least not the kind of marriage that it seems most in the Ton have, one treated as a business arrangement and nothing more. I knew others could exist, ones based in true love, in two like souls finding each other. I saw it with my mother and father, and with Jocelyn and Callum," he glanced to the pair who were watching on with soft smiles, "but I never imagined that lightning could strike a third time so close to my heart, that I could ever hope to be so lucky." He paused, swallowing hard past the lump in his throat.

"You are the most beautiful person I've ever had the privilege of knowing, Elle. Beautiful not just in body, but down to your very soul. You have become a friend and confidant, a partner in mischief and grief, the sunrise on the horizon of even my darkest nights. You are stubborn and wily and smart and unlike anyone I have ever met. I still find you vexing," she huffed out a soft laugh, eyes shining, "but I thank God that I did not, in fact, stop finding you at all because in you, I have found everything I could ever want, Elle. I have found the other half of my soul." He smiled, squeezing her hands. "All that to say, that I'm afraid that I've gone and fallen madly and inconsolably in love with you."

"Idiot," she whispered, making everyone in the room laugh. Her eyes were shining with tears—ones of joy, he hoped.

"Just so," Alec said with a grin. "I cannot fathom an existence where you are not with me, cannot tolerate even thinking of it. You are truly my dearest friend, and now I am asking you to also be my wife, so that you may call me an idiot for the rest of our lives."

She swallowed hard and squeezed her eyes shut as a single tear spilled down her cheek. A flash of lightning speared through the sky outside, a rumble of thunder not far on its heels. The storm was baring down on them faster than he expected.

"I...I can't," she whispered, face pinched as if she were in pain.

It took a moment for the words to register. Alec's smile faded and his brow furrowed. He felt as if Apollo had kicked him in the chest. She was saying...no? He didn't understand.

"Elle? I don't—"

She rose quickly. "I—I have to go. I'm sorry." She ran from the room as Alec stood motionless, watching her go and struggling to make sense of what had just happened. Had he done something wrong? Had he misunderstood her feelings? No. No, he knew that she loved him too. He *knew* it. So why?

Jocelyn placed a steadying hand on his arm.

"Oh Alec," she said quietly. "Just give her time...she's...things are...complicated," she finished, sounding anxious.

"I thought," Alec shook his head, still staring blankly at the spot where she'd just been sitting, "I thought she felt the same. I thought that she loved me as well." His voice was so low he wasn't even sure they could even hear him.

"We all did, lad," Callum said before he *oompfed* as Jocelyn elbowed his stomach.

"Callum," she scolded in an annoyed hiss. "That isn't helpful."

"What? She looks at him the way I look at you, Jocy. And you said she'd even told you as much. It's why I gave my blessing in the first place."

"*In confidence*," she hissed again, outraged. "I told you that in confidence! And you knew about this? And didn't tell me?"

Callum shrugged, as if he wasn't bothered. "I thought it would be best to keep it a surprise." Jocy narrowed her eyes at him, but Alec needed to know.

"Is it true? Jocelyn, please tell me..."

"Yes," she said on a wary exhale. "Yes, she does love you, Alec. I'm sure of it."

"Then why—" Movement outside the window caught his eye and stole his words. Elle was flying across the lawn on the back of a white mare. Lightning flashed again, spearing towards the ground in the distance and the rumble of thunder came faster now. The storm was almost on top of them. And Elle was riding off into it.

Away from me.

"Go, Alec," Jocy urged him, knowing exactly what he was planning. It was all the permission he needed to go after Elle, even knowing it would put them alone together. Callum and Jocelyn didn't seem to care and it wasn't as if it were the first time they'd been alone together. Not that they knew about Puck's, of course.

Alec sprinted from the room and nearly tripped down the front steps in his haste to reach Apollo. He mounted and then they were off.

"Go, boy, go!" he begged. Apollo shot across the drive like a bullet, tearing across the lawn in the same direction Elle had gone. The mare had been quick, but Apollo was quicker. They would catch up soon enough. "The woman is as vexing as ever," he grated through clenched teeth just as the sky opened, the rain coming down in a thick waterfall all around him. Lightning and thunder filled the dark sky and he urged Apollo faster when he caught a glimpse of Elle in the distance, cutting towards the trees.

"Eleanor!" he yelled, but the wind and rain took the words before they could reach her. "Where in the devil does she think she's going?" he muttered.

Alec leaned low over Apollo's back and squinted against the rain as the two of them flew through the woods, Elle and her mare a light streak against the darkness ahead. When he made it to the clearing around the pond, Elle had already put her horse inside the small barn and was running up the steps to the enclosed gazebo. Apollo whickered loudly, stomping at the already-soaked ground, making Elle turn.

"Elle!" Alec called, rain pelting his face like stinging bites.

"Go away, Alec!" she yelled over the rain. "Just go!"

She didn't wait for a response or to see if he obeyed, just simply ran up the remaining steps and inside, slamming the door behind her.

"That little wench," he gritted out, somewhere between astonishment, annoyance, and, damn him, a bit of amusement. Alec slid off of Apollo and quickly got him settled into the other stall. Lightning illuminated the sky and thunder cracked. Alec ran a hand down the horse's neck. "You're alright, boy."

Alec braced himself against the wind and rain as he ran the short distance to the gazebo. He threw the door open and stood dripping on the threshold, breathing hard and taking in the space. There was a low sofa, a beautifully carved desk of deep red wood, a matching chest, and a large easel, a half-finished portrait on it and others stacked against the walls. *She must come here to paint and draw*, he realized. The portrait on the easel was of him. It was similar to the sketch he'd seen her doing that day in the garden, the day before they'd explored his home and played like fools in the fountain. In this one, he was in profile, looking off in the distance a half-smile on his lips. *How often does she draw me?* he wondered. That had to mean something, didn't it?

He tore his gaze away from the easel and finished taking in the room. There was a thick fur rug in the center, pillows and blankets piled in one corner, and a crystal chandelier hanging from the ceiling. Everything was in shades of blue, some light as ice, some the same deep blue as Eleanor's eyes.

Elle was lighting the last lantern on the wall and whirled to meet his gaze.

"God, you can't follow the simplest instructions, can you?" she snapped. He blinked. *She* was angry with *him*? She was the one who had refused his proposal! She was the one who had ridden out into a storm like a lunatic, putting herself and her horse in danger! And she had the audacity to be angry with *him*?

"What in the bloody hell do you think you're doing?"

"Go. Away," she seethed, but her anger seemed...odd. Like she was trying desperately to be angry, when really she was something else entirely.

"Eleanor, talk to me, damn you." He strode forward and to his relief, she didn't back away. He gripped her upper arms in his hands, her skin slick beneath his fingers from the rain. "Elle, I thought..."

"You thought what?"

"I thought that you felt the same way that I did, that we'd both become...more to each other." He tried to keep the vulnerability from his voice, the pleading, but he felt like his heart were being squeezed by an iron-gloved fist. She held his gaze, the anger—or false anger—seeping away to reveal something that was a cross between adoration and agony. He frowned, not understanding.

"Alec, I..." She squeezed her eyes shut and shook herself, flinging her arms to force him to release his grip on her. Before he could even react, she was rushing back out into the storm.

"*What in the bloody hell?*" he ground out through clenched teeth, eyes turning towards the heavens. He ran after her, catching up to her easily halfway across the grassy area between the gazebo and the tree line. Was she planning to *run* away from him now? Not even bothering with a horse, even in the middle of a storm?

"Elle! Stop this!"

She whirled on him, but whatever she'd planned to say got lost as lightning speared a towering tree limb that stretched over the clearing just above them. Thunder cracked almost immediately, so loudly his ears rang. She screamed as the branch came plummeting down towards them.

"Elle!" he cried out as terror gripped him. He yanked her towards him, stumbling back several steps just as the limb slammed to the ground in the spot she'd just been standing a moment ago, sending bark and splinters flying in all directions. Eyes wide in shock, Elle let him drag her back through the pelting rain into the relative safety of the gazebo. She moved across the room, hugging her arms around herself, shaking. From cold or fear, he had no idea. He ran a hand roughly through his wet hair.

"Would you truly rather get yourself killed out in this storm than talk to me? Than to *marry* me?" he demanded, voice laced with anger and hurt, chest heaving. "God, would it really be so bloody terrible, Elle?!"

"No," she said, so quietly he wasn't sure he'd heard her correctly.

"What?" he barked, confused.

"You think I don't want to marry you, Alec? I do. I want it so fucking badly that it makes me want to scream!" He stared, dumbfounded. "I want to spend every minute of every day of the rest of my life with you. I want to fall asleep with my head on your chest and to wake up wrapped in your arms. I want to do other things that would make that gentlemanly little head of yours spin, things that exceed your wildest dreams." A rush of heat flooded through him at that, and he suddenly realized that they were alone together in the small space, the rain beating a steady rhythm against the roof and closing them off from the rest of the world. "I want to have a family with you, I want to grow old with you, I want...God, I want everything. I love you, Alec. More than you can possibly understand."

Before he could stop himself, before he could wonder why, if all of this was true, she had refused his proposal, he closed the distance between them in two long strides and slammed his lips to hers.

Chapter 18

Alec's hands shook slightly as he cradled her face, lips firm and warm against hers. He pressed them there once, twice, before pulling away enough to speak.

"Elle," he whispered. "I'm sorry, I—"

She cut him off, leaning in to kiss him again, going up on her toes and fisting her hands in the front of his soaked shirt, pulling him closer. She knew she shouldn't, knew that this could only end with both of them being hurt, but the moment his lips brushed against hers, she decided to be selfish. So fucking selfish. She had to know what it felt like to touch him, at least once before everything went to shit. The love she'd seen in his eyes when he'd proposed, and then the hurt...Well, it had damn near broken her. After this, she was going to hurt him all over again, but she couldn't make herself stop. Instead, a terrifying urgency overtook her, like a timer had started to countdown on the brief window of happiness she could have with him today.

Better make it count.

She urged his lips apart with her own and he understood exactly what she wanted, opening his mouth and gently rolling his tongue against hers. She shuddered, moaning at the sensation. He was sure and gentle, but with the promise of unbridled passion just beneath the surface. She shivered at the thought of him releasing the reins.

She quickly undid the double rows of buttons and pushed his jacket off of his shoulders, the thick material landing with a wet thud on the floor. She yanked at his shirt, pulling it free from his pants so that she could tunnel her hands beneath the fabric. She ran them upward over the hard ridges of his stomach, the muscles clenching and jumping at her touch. He groaned and shuddered. His skin was smooth and tight and warm, despite the cold rain having soaked them both.

He ran his hands over her shoulders, down her back, palming her ass and using the grip to pull her harder against him. She gasped when she felt him, hard and ready. She nearly whimpered, needing him to touch her so badly she felt like she was going crazy. She clawed at his shirt in a frenzy, somehow getting it off of him and flinging the sopping material away. She pushed him back, managing to pry herself away long enough to stare at his bare chest.

Dear God.

Elle wasn't really sure what the hell men of this time did to work out, but whatever it was, Alec was a pro. His shoulders were broad and heaving, his chest defined, a scar running across his left peck that she would one day ask about. Her eyes traveled lower, and she bit her lip at the sight of his stomach, taut and flat, the ridges and hollows of his abs contracting as he breathed, the lightest trail of nearly-blonde hair leading downward from his navel. She swallowed when her gaze reached the waist of his pants. They sat low enough that she could see the slight indentions beside his hips that honestly turned her a little feral. She wanted to run her tongue along those ridges, over every single inch of him.

"Elle?" he breathed, voice gone husky. "Elle, we shouldn't...We can't...God, when you look at me like that I can't *think.*" He ran his hands through his rain-soaked hair, and the way it made his muscles bunch and flex made her entire body shudder, her toes curl. There was no stopping this now. It was a runaway train and she was sure they would crash and burn, but she didn't care.

She stepped forward again, leaning in to kiss his chest, just over his heart. He sucked in a ragged breath. She planted another one as her fingers ran along his stomach, making him groan. She couldn't stop touching him, couldn't get enough. She'd been longing to do this for weeks, had been desperate to feel him beneath her fingers, feel his skin against hers. It was like setting a match to a pile of kindling, every inch of her going up in flames with no hope of stopping the spread. She had every intention of making her way downward, sliding to her knees and showing him just what kind of tricks women had learned since this century, but she never got the chance. He gripped her shoulders, turning her suddenly so that her back was to his chest. She gasped.

"Alec, I don't want to stop. I don't care if it isn't proper or any of that. I want you. I *need* you. *Please.*"

"Elle," he said softly, and it sounded like a prayer.

He leaned down to kiss her neck, just below her ear. She moaned and tilted her head, urging him to do it again. He did. He trailed kisses down her throat and lightly over her collarbone. She gripped his thighs behind her, wiggling her ass against him, moaning when she felt his cock hard against her.

"Eleanor, if you don't stop that, this will be over sooner than I'd like," he rasped at her ear, nipping the tiniest bit and making her moan obscenely. God, he was sexy. He stepped away from her and she missed the heat of him. He tugged at the laces on the back of her dress. His fingers were deft, the laces quickly loosening as he worked, leaning down to kiss her shoulder or neck every few seconds, as if he couldn't help himself. She realized with a jolt what he would find in a moment once he got her dress off: she'd worn her own bra and panties today. She did that sometimes when they were safely hidden away at Chestwick, a way to feel more like herself. *Well, we're about to find out what he thinks about twenty-first century lingerie.*

He slid the dress from her shoulders and it fell to the floor around her ankles in a damp heap. She stepped out of her slippers and waited. He fingered the black strap of her bra and she could hear the slight frown in his voice.

"What is...I've never seen...*Christ almighty*," he gasped. Elle turned her head to find his eyes fixed firmly on her ass. He scrubbed a hand over his mouth. She had to admit that the black lace cheeky briefs looked phenomenal on her. He reached out, seemingly unable to stop himself, and ran his big hands over her ass. He kneaded her flesh gently before raising his eyes to hers. He swallowed hard.

"Elle, if you want me to stop, you must tell me now."

In response, she licked her lips and turned to give him the front view. His eyes moved downward and he shuffled his feet apart as he uttered low curses. She was fairly sure he wouldn't know how to unhook her bra, so she did it for him, unclasping the small closure between her breasts and letting the lace slide away.

She tossed it aside and waited, watching him while he watched her.

"*Eleanor*," he rasped. He moved quickly, pulling her hard against him, their bare chests pressing together as he kissed her like he couldn't survive another second without his lips on hers. His tongue delved, thrusting against hers as her breasts slid against his slick chest. Her nipples puckered at the friction, and she needed more. As if he could read her thoughts, he raised his hands, covering her breasts. She gasped, thrusting her chest forward into his palms, begging for more. He moaned into her mouth, thrusting his tongue harder as he massaged and kneaded.

"Christ, you're beautiful," he whispered against her lips before kissing along her jaw and down her throat, over the swells of her chest. Bless him, he didn't make her wait: he immediately laved his tongue around one aching nipple. She cried out in pure bliss, her back bowing as shock waves of pleasure rippled through her body.

"Oh *God*," she moaned as she tunneled her fingers into his hair. He licked, rolling his hot tongue all around before closing his lips over the hardened peak. She bucked forward, digging her nails into his scalp as she held him against her. He groaned against her nipple, flicking his tongue over it again as he ran the pad of his thumb over the other. *Dear God.* It had been so long, she might come from just this.

"So sensitive," he whispered. "So responsive..."

He moved so quickly that she yelped in surprise, making him chuckle, as he lowered her down to the floor beneath him. He laid her on the plush rug in the center of the space and walked on his knees to the pile of pillows and blankets in the corner to tug a few over. He settled a pillow under her head, leaving a few others nearby.

He ducked his head to kiss her breasts again, making her squirm. He began to move lower, kissing and licking down her stomach. He seemed especially intrigued by her belly button ring.

She'd never imagined anyone would be seeing her stomach, so she hadn't seen the harm in leaving it in.

"This is...interesting," he breathed as he planted a kiss just beside her navel. She laughed lightly but it quickly turned into a gasping moan as he kissed lower. Her stomach clenched.

Did...did men here do that?

Dear God, she hoped so because right now, if he didn't, she might die. He made it to the waistband of her panties, kissing lightly along the top, from one hip bone to the other.

"I'd very much like to kiss you, Eleanor," he whispered against her skin, dipping lower to brush his lips ever so softly over the thin material of her panties, making it *very* clear where, exactly, he meant to kiss her. "Is that alright?" His voice with low and smooth, far too seductive to be legal.

Her entire body went taut at his words, at the fact that he was asking her, at the thought of his mouth on her.

"Yes," she breathed. "*Please.*"

He glanced up her body, the look in his eyes purely carnal, making her toes curl and her breaths shallow. He rose to his knees between her thighs and hooked his fingers in the sides of her panties. She would have bet a million dollars that he wasn't breathing as he slowly slid them down her legs. She didn't try to hide, just let her knees fall wide and let him look his fill. She'd never been particularly shy with this kind of stuff, never self-conscious. It wasn't because she thought her body was perfect by any means, but she'd always figured her body was her body, flaws and all, and if someone else didn't like it, then fuck 'em. That was a them problem.

But even if she had been shy when it came to her body or being naked, she could never be with Alec. The way he looked at her, the way he touched her, it was like he was worshiping her. How could you possibly be self-conscious when someone was acting like you were a goddess?

"Christ," he bit out, staring between her legs. He absently tossed her panties aside and reached forward, running a finger over her smooth skin. She'd teased him about this very thing once, and now she was fairly certain he'd been imagining it ever since. She had gotten laser hair removal years ago, mostly because she had sensitive skin and shaving often left her with razor burn which drove her absolutely crazy, but also because she was lazy. It had been the best money she'd ever spent to not have to worry about shaving ever again. His big body shuddered as he brushed his fingers over her, again and again, seeming to marvel at the feel of her.

"God almighty, Elle. I thought you were *jesting*." He shook himself. "Your skin is so smooth, like cream," he said, almost in wonder.

She arched her hips upward, desperate for him to stop trailing his fingers everywhere but where she wanted him, where she *needed* him. He seemed to understand and held her gaze as he finally slid one between her lips before pressing it inside her. She bit her lip and clawed her fingers into the rug beneath her, gasping loudly.

"*Bloody hell.* You're so...tight. So *slick*." He looked as if he were somewhere between pleasure and pain, some blissfully torturous place that looked sexy as hell on him. He leaned down to kiss her as he started to thrust his finger slowly, in and out, in and out, driving her crazy. She bit at his lower lip and he gave an appreciative *mmmm* sound. Elle wrapped a hand around the back of his neck, holding his mouth to hers, digging her fingers in when he added a second finger. She cried out and he caught the sound.

"Oh God, Alec," she breathed against his lips.

"Are you alright?"

"YES," she moaned, slowly losing her mind to the sinful rhythm of his fingers. He kissed along her jaw, chuckling low and raspy against her neck before kissing her there. She was already on the verge, could already feel the familiar tension building. It had been months, almost an entire year at this point, since anyone had touched her like this, and she was on the razor's edge. She'd always likened coming to a roller coaster: first is the slow, steady climb up the hill and then the brief weightless feeling when you crested the arch, just before you careened over the edge. She was already halfway up the hill, the tension building and building— but he pulled his hand away, making her whimper.

She didn't stay upset for long: he settled to his stomach, shoulders between her thighs and when he dipped his head, she held her breath...before crying out in utter ecstasy, her voice barely audible over the pounding rain. The first lap of his tongue was like fire, setting her entire body aflame. Nothing had *ever* felt so good. He made a highly arousing sound that was somewhere between a growl and a moan.

"*Eleanor*," he rasped. A shocked plea and an expletive all wrapped into that one single word. She met his gaze and his eyes blazed like fire. "Your taste...*my God.*"

"More," she begged. "Please please please, Alec." His lips curled at the corners in the sexiest little smirk she'd ever seen. He licked her again, slowly rolling his tongue up her pussy, and she threw her head back. He knew what the hell he was doing, that was for sure. He alternated between long, slow laps of his tongue and deep thrusts, turning her into a mindless puddle of lust. She couldn't stop herself from moving, undulating against his open mouth, wanting it all over her and to never stop.

"Stay still," he scolded, pinning her hip down with one hand and using his other to spread her lips with two fingers. He licked her slowly, like he was savoring every minute. "You taste good, Eleanor," he said in a low voice, a bit hoarse. "So damned good." She shuddered at his words, not expecting them from him, but wanting to hear more. *The dirty talking viscount. Who fucking knew?*

He moved upward, flicking his tongue against her clit and she yelled out.

"*Fuccckkkk!*"

She dug her hands into his hair as he licked and sucked, sliding a finger back inside her. Her eyes flew wide: she was suddenly cresting the hill, that weightless feeling making her stomach flutter before—

"Alec!" she screamed, barely intelligible as she plummeted over the edge, down, down, down in an endless freefall. Lightning flashed brightly behind her eyes and thunder cracked, rattling the windows. Waves of pleasure crashed against her, and her muscles shook from the force of it.

"Elle?" he asked, uncertain. She opened her eyes and met his gaze. He looked too sexy for words with his hair even more tousled than usual from her fingers, sweat and rain making his skin glisten in the lantern light, his eyes burning like green flames. She sat upwards, a hand shooting out to grasp his neck and pull him to her for a searing kiss. He seemed frozen in surprise for a moment, but then quickly recovered, kissing her hard, hands roving all over her body: up her sides, across her back, over her breasts. It was as if he couldn't decide where he wanted to touch first, so he just touched everywhere.

She pushed at his pants, desperate to get them off, and he nearly choked when she gripped his cock in her fist. She moved her hand, up and down, slowly, enjoying the feel of him. Thick. Hard as steel. Skin hot against her palm.

"Christ," he bit out, arching his hips forward as she pumped. He maneuvered while she continued, managing to kick off his boots and lose his pants. She sucked on his bottom lip while she ran her thumb over the crown, spreading the bead of moisture around and around, and making him shudder.

God, she wanted him so badly, she couldn't stand it any longer. She released her hold on him and laid back, beckoning him to join her. He took a minute to let his gaze travel down her body, his lips curling into that sexy, cocky smile of his. He licked his bottom lip before biting down lightly, making her squirm.

"You are beautiful, Eleanor Montgomery. *Beautiful.*"

"You aren't so bad yourself, Lord Kentworth," she teased, breathless, as her own eyes drifted down his sweat-soaked body, over his straining erection. She writhed her hips, wanting him to fuck her so badly she might combust.

"Alec, *please,*" she begged.

He swallowed hard. "Do you know...Do you understand what will happen?"

She arched a brow. "And if I say yes? Will you think less of me?"

"Of course not," he said, reaching out to trail a finger down her stomach. "Nothing you could ever do would make me think less of you, Elle. *Nothing.* I don't care if you've been with a man before. All I care about is the fact that you're here, with me, now."

Talk about fucking swoon. She was so lost for this man it was unreal.

"I know what will happen, Alec. You don't have to worry."

He nodded, studying her for another endless moment.

"And you're sure that you want this?" he asked, dark eyes searching hers.

"I'm sure," she breathed.

He exhaled in what seemed like relief, eyes sliding closed for a brief moment. When he opened them, they were dark and determined. He reached over and grabbed one of the pillows he'd dragged over.

"Up," he commanded simply. Elle frowned in confusion. In a voice so low and husky and sexy it should be outlawed, Alec said, "lift your hips, Eleanor."

She inhaled sharply. *Well, well, well.* She'd sorely underestimated men of this century. She did as he asked, a knowing smirk quirking his lips. He settled the pillow beneath her and then spread his body over hers, holding himself up on one straightened warm. The other bicep flexed as he stroked himself and she wiggled her hips at the sight, desperate for him.

He stared down with an expression she'd never seen before. There was desire there, of course, but there was a look of such love that the word didn't seem remotely adequate. He was looking at her like she suspected a blind man might react to seeing a sunrise for the first time. Her chest constricted and tears pricked her eyes.

He stroked a drying curl away from her face, letting his fingertips trail down her cheek.

"Alec, please," she whispered. She reached down and trailed her hand over his. He released his grip and let her wrap her hand around his cock. She stroked once, twice, before positioning him in just the right spot, pressing the head just inside. He hissed and shuddered, and holding her gaze, he slowly eased his hips forward. They both gasped, the gasps turning into moans of pleasure as he slid inside her in one long, slow thrust.

"*Elle*," Alec bit out, stilling for a moment. "Elle, are you alright?" he asked in a ragged whisper. She wiggled her ass a bit, adjusting and getting him seated even further. She nodded and he leaned down to kiss her as he moved his hips backward before easing forward again. She half moaned, half cried against his lips, digging her fingers into his lower back. He gripped her hip with his free hand, clenching her so tightly, as if he were afraid she would disappear if he didn't hold on for dear life, but she only wanted him to hold her tighter.

He kept up a slow, steady rhythm, but it seemed as if he were holding back, his muscles trembling from the exertion.

"Harder, Alec," she whispered. "You won't hurt me, I promise."

He looked down at her, gauging if she was serious or not. She arched her hips, demanding and desperate, fingers digging into his back, begging. Finally, he began to move, *really* move, and Jesus, Mary, Joseph, and the Great Pumpkin, it was beyond good. He thrust his hips forward, slamming into her over and over and hitting all the right spots. He forced her hands up, pinning them beside her temples, intertwining their fingers. He kissed her hard and she hitched her leg over his hip, urging him to keep going, and squeezing his hands so tightly she thought she might break the bones.

Alec shifted back to his knees, hooking her knees over his elbows. With the pillow beneath her, the angle was sublime. She moaned and writhed as he pounded his hips forward over and over. She grasped her breasts, kneading and pinching her own nipples, the pleasure nearly too much.

"Jesus," Alec rasped, "Elle, you're...My God, don't stop that." He watched raptly as she gladly obeyed, as he continued to thrust and grind his hips. As if he couldn't stand for his lips to be apart from hers for a second longer, he moved again, body long and hard against hers as he kissed her deeply, keeping up his savage rhythm.

"Alec, oh God, harder," she moaned, digging her nails into his back. He obliged, slamming his hips forward until she was nearly mindless. He nipped at her lip and this time she shifted, pushing him away. Confusion was plain on his face for a moment until she followed him up, easing him back so that he was sitting and settling herself over his lap.

"Elle," he whisper-moaned as she slid down onto his cock, wrapping her legs around his waist and her arms around his neck. She kissed him again as she rocked her hips. He reached behind her and pulled the pins from her hair, letting the drying curls fall loosely down her back. He tunneled his hands through it, cupping the back of her head, holding her to him.

"I love you," he whispered against her lips. "I love you, Elle." Her heart sputtered, the words suddenly making the entire world shift, making her feel as if she were exactly where she had always been meant to be. And though she knew it would splinter soon enough, she ignored the coming pain, holding onto the truest thing in her life. Alec. He was hers. He had always been hers, she'd just had to travel two hundred years into the past to find him. Fate really was a crazy, drunk bitch, wasn't she?

He tilted her head back, exposing her throat to him.

"I love you too," she whispered as he kissed down her neck, using his other hand to wrench her hips harder against him. "I love you, I love you, I love you," she repeated.

"You feel so good. I can't...I've never..." He couldn't seem to be able to finish the thought and that was alright because she was nearly beyond hearing. All around them, lightning lit up the sky thunder rumbled, and rain pounded against the roof, drowning out their gasps and cries and moans. Sweat ran down her temples and over his chest, their skin slipping as they moved.

"Right there. Fuck, Alec, I'm going to come." She had no idea if he would even know what that meant—what the hell did they call it nowadays?—but he seemed to understand what she was getting at, his eyes flying wide. He slid his hand between them, and lightly ran his fingers over her clit, massaging with just enough pressure. Oh, he *absolutely* knew what the fuck he was doing.

"Oh God!" She exploded around him, head thrown back as her entire body spasmed and shook. This wasn't a leisurely roller coaster ride. This was being strapped to a rocket being shot out of the stratosphere by NASA. She screamed out in pleasure, fingers digging into his shoulders, hips undulating as she continued to ride him. Stars darted across her vision, heat flooding through every inch of her body.

She'd had good sex in her life, had always been fairly lucky when it came to partners, but this was on a different level. The reason, she knew, was because she'd never felt love like she had with Alec.

And the cruelest irony was that now that she understood, now that she'd *finally* found it, she was going to lose it all.

Chapter 19

"Elle, I can...oh dear God, I can *feel* you."

Alec was fairly certain he'd somehow fallen asleep and this was the sweetest dream he'd ever had. If that was so, he never wanted to wake. Seeing Elle completely unclothed had nearly dropped him to his knees. She was...God, he didn't have a word to describe it properly. Beautiful. Stunning. Perfect. Life-altering. None of them seemed like enough. Every inch of her made his pulse race, his mouth water, his cock throb. He longed to explore her every curve, every hollow, every scar, spend hours worshiping her like the goddess she surely was.

Her undergarments had been strange to say the least, but he supposed fashion varied across the world. Perhaps all women in America wore such things. *Then all men in America are lucky bastards, indeed.*

When he'd tasted her, he thought he might die. And the way she'd reacted? Rolling those luscious hips to his mouth, begging him for more, finding her release on his tongue with wild abandon. It had made him so hard that his cockstand was *painful.* Sinking inside her body had felt like heaven. She was so tight around his cock, it felt like a fist, so slick and hot, he nearly spilled the second he entered her. He'd somehow managed to last, and it was unlike anything he'd ever experienced.

He'd admittedly had plenty of women in his life, but this was so completely different. The way Elle stared at him, the feeling in the depths of her blue eyes, it seared him to his soul. He didn't understand why she'd refused his proposal, but right now, that didn't matter. Nothing outside of this room, this moment, mattered.

The look of pure ecstasy on her face as she found another release, her inner walls clenching him tightly, it was enough to send him over the edge. He felt the familiar tightening at the base of his spine, and as she kissed him and whispered that she loved him, he let himself go. He yelled her name as he climaxed. He pumped deep inside her, over and over, and she moaned, scratching at his back like a cat, writhing her hips as if she...enjoyed it?

When he was done, he buried his face in the crook of her neck, both of their chests heaving. She gently stroked his back as they caught their breath, their hearts slowing over what seemed to be hours. Eventually, he lifted his head and brushed sweat-soaked tendrils of hair from her forehead, leaning in to kiss her softly. She sighed in what seemed to be utter contentment and leaned her forehead against his.

"I love you, Eleanor." He'd never meant anything more in his life. How could three simple words somehow be the most important he would ever utter?

She let out a long exhale, and then whispered again, "I love you, too."

His eyes slid closed as utter bliss washed over him, her words echoing in his head. *I love you, I love you, I love you.* Not said in the throes of passion where anyone might say all manner of things and mean none of them. No, she said it now as if she'd never meant anything more in her life.

He eventually shifted her out of his lap and laid her down on the rug, grabbing the blanket and tossing it over them as he settled down beside her. He wrapped his arm around her, pulling her close, still not completely convinced this could possibly be real. She rested her head on his chest and they simply lay there in contented silence for what seemed like an eternity as the storm raged on outside.

"Was that...alright?" he finally asked.

She shifted so that she could rest her chin on her upturned hand and meet his gaze. She gave him a sensual smile, the hint of mischief that he adored sparking in her eyes.

"It was...adequate, I suppose."

He blinked. Then blinked again.

"*Adequate?*"

She hiked a shoulder and gave him a superior look, one that said *you tried your best, poor boy*. He narrowed his eyes and reached for her, rolling so that she was pinned beneath him. She gasped and giggled.

"I am a viscount, Miss Montgomery. I do not do things *adequately.*" He leaned down and kissed her softly, languidly, teasing her with laps of his tongue and soft nips at her bottom lip. She was panting and squirming beneath him after just a few moments. Christ, he was already hard again, already desperate to get inside her once more, but he continued to torture her, slowly grazing his fingers along her throat, over her collarbone and between her breasts. He trailed one finger over her skin, circling her nipple but never making contact, and her breath hitched, her back bowing and begging him silently to touch her. Instead, he merely moved to the other breast, repeating the same movements. She was quivering by the time he skated his fingers down her stomach, brushing ever so gently over her quim. She bucked and the begging wasn't so silent now.

"Alec," she breathed, half plea, half warning.

"What was it you were saying about *adequate*?" he teased, leaning in and biting at her lower lip, pulling away when she tried to kiss him fully. She groaned in annoyance, but the way she was rolling her hips, the way her nipples puckered and her pupils expanded, the black nearly overtaking the brilliant blue, he knew that she was enjoying herself.

"Prove me wrong," she challenged, voice throaty and entirely too arousing. She bit her lip and let her knees fall wide in clear invitation. He ran a finger along her opening, shuddering at how wet she already was. He quickly delved two fingers inside, and she cried out, arching her hips in time with his thrusts. He kissed her hard and demanding, and when she said his name again, he withdrew his fingers, quickly pushing back to his knees and fisting his cock. He had an idea, but...

"Do you trust me?" he asked as he stroked. Her eyes were riveted to the movements, her tongue darting out to trail lazily along her bottom lip. She...liked watching him touch himself? *Christ, this woman...*

"Yes," she said, voice low and husky. He grinned at her and her breath hitched.

He released his cock, reaching out to grip her hips and lift her easily, turning her so that she was on her hands and knees before him. He groaned, running a hand down her spine and over the curves of her backside. She moaned and shivered, arching her back and shifting her knees farther apart. The view...He bit the inside of his cheek, nearly releasing again just watching her, spread and ready before him, that perfect arse in the air.

He ran the head of his cock across her opening as he palmed her ass and she moaned, begging. He hissed through clenched teeth when he slid inside, the feeling just as intense and incredible as it had been the first time.

He didn't begin slowly this time. He knew that he wouldn't hurt her and that she was ready for whatever he had to give. So, he took her hard, pounding into her, wrenching her hips back as he moved.

"Oh God, yes! Yes, yes, yes," she panted. "Harder. Fuck, Alec. *Harder!*"

The words were like music to his ears and he obeyed her commands, wanting to give her anything and everything she wanted. Always. He loved that she was vocal, that she demanded and pleaded. He pounded into her from behind, her screams of pleasure and the sounds of their bodies slamming together mixing with the rain and thunder.

What felt like hours later, they'd both found release again and they lay sprawled over the rug. The storm had finally ebbed now, only occasional flashes of lighting and the low rumble of thunder in the distance, though the rain still came down in sheets.

Though part of him longed to delay it, to keep this moment as perfect as possible, he had to ask the question that had been plaguing him. The one dark spot on the most amazing day of his entire life.

"Eleanor," he whispered softly against her hair. "Why did you refuse my proposal? Why don't you want to marry me?"

She tensed and moved away from him, sitting up and holding the blanket across her chest.

"I...I just can't, Alec." She rubbed her eyes, and then looked around the room. Their clothing strewn in all corners, the blankets and pillows, the stool on its side—*when the devil had they knocked that over?* That satisfied look of contentment faded, something between regret and sorrow taking its place. He frowned, a sense of unease skittering up his spine. "We shouldn't have...Damn it. I'm sorry."

She leapt up, rummaging around in the discarded piles around the room. Alec was momentarily distracted by the curve of her backside and the enticing view as she bent at the waist. She sighed in annoyance and ended up grabbing his shirt, sliding it over her head. It came to her knees, but the sight of her in it was unbelievably arousing for reasons he couldn't even understand.

"Elle, stop. *Stop,*" he said again, rising to his feet and grabbing her upper arms. "Talk to me," he pleaded. She turned away and he frowned in annoyance, reaching for his pants and stabbing his legs inside. He couldn't very well have this conversation—and they were going to have it, even if he had to stay out here with her all night—naked.

"Elle," he said again, crossing his arms over his chest. Whatever she heard in his tone made her turn back to him. They stared for a moment and then her eyes watered and her shoulders slumped, as if in defeat. She squeezed her eyes shut for a heartbeat, and when she opened them again, it looked almost as if...she were saying goodbye? He moved forward, gripping her arms again gently, needing to hold on to her before whatever was coming tried to pull her away. He wouldn't let that happen. Nothing could take her from him. Nothing.

"I can't marry you if I can't be completely honest with you, Alec. And I can't be completely honest with you."

"Of course you can," he said, confused.

"No, I can't, Alec. Not about this."

Unease settled in his stomach like a heavy ball of ice, the cold slowly spreading outward through the rest of his body.

"You can tell me anything, Elle. Anything." What could she possibly be so afraid to tell him? She looked pained.

"We should go. We need to go." Her gaze drifted around the room, eyes watering and he got the feeling she was avoiding his stare.

"No, we don't," Alec said. "Elle, look at me. Look at me, damn it!" She finally did, pressing her lips into a hard line. "Tell me what in the bloody hell is going on. I don't understand. We spend an afternoon like this together, doing...all the things that we did, you tell me that you love me and I know it was the truth, Elle, I *know* it. So why? Why are you trying to push me away now? Why won't you just tell me what's wrong?"

"I can't," she said again, clenching her jaw.

"God, just tell me, Elle. Talk to me. *Please,*" he begged. "Please just—"

"I'm not from here, Alec!" she blurted, cutting him off.

His brows drew down in utter confusion. It wasn't at all what he'd expected her to say.

"Yes, I know, you're from America," he said slowly.

"No. I mean, yes, I am," she shook her head in frustration, "but that's not what I meant." She let out a long, shuddering breath, and seemed to brace herself for a blow.

"I mean, I'm not from *this time.*"

Chapter 20

Oh God. She'd said the words. She'd said the words out loud. Elle held her breath and kept her gaze locked on Alec's as she waited for him to respond. It felt as if she were waiting for her entire world to collapse, and yet, a tiny flame of hope burned in her chest. *Let him believe me. Let him understand, or at least try to. Please.*

"I don't understand," he said finally.

"I..." She steadied herself, knowing how ridiculous it was going to sound. "I'm from the future."

He blinked at her, confusion clear in his eyes. He released his grip on her arms and took a step back. That tiny step felt like a crevasse opening between them, a split in the ice that they'd never be able to cross back to each other. *No. No, no, no.* The first splinter began to slowly work its way through her heart. *He's walking away from me.*

"The future," he repeated, his voice even, but she could see the tension in his shoulders, lines of stress bracketing his lips.

"I know it sounds crazy, but it's the truth, I promise you."

He took another step backwards. Hurt fluttered across his face before he closed his expression off, the mask sliding back into place, the one she'd hated for those first few weeks. Another crack in her heart.

"If you didn't want to marry me, if you don't truly love me as I thought, you could say that, Eleanor. There's no need for outlandish stories."

"It's not a story," she protested. "I'm from the year 2020. I don't know how I was brought back exactly, but I was."

"2020," he murmured with a humorless laugh.

"Alec, please, just listen."

He took another step back, shaking his head. He was looking at her as if he didn't even know her. The physician in him was looking at her like she was utterly insane, the way he'd probably looked at plenty of patients who were indeed out of touch with reality.

Panic began to claw at Elle's chest, razor sharp and burning. She'd thought she'd been ready for him not to believe her, for him to walk away, but now that it was actually happening, she couldn't bear it. She could barely breathe, her throat feeling thick and her ribs shrinking, closing in around her lungs.

"Wait. Just wait," she begged, flying to the wooden chest. She opened it, tossing out extra paint and brushes, searching for her things. She'd stowed them out here for safe keeping once everyone else had returned from the city. She yanked the zipper of her bag open and grabbed the first thing her fingers touched. A t-shirt. *Damnit...wait.* Her eyes widened in triumph. She whirled and found him staring at her, his mask slipping and something between agony and sorrow settling over his handsome face. He was just finishing shoving his feet into his boots, his coat gripped in a white-knuckled fist. *No. God, he's leaving.* She held up the shirt like it was the holy grail.

"This is clothing from my time."

He backed away, holding up his hands to halt her. "Eleanor, enough. Stop this. You are either lying or you're truly unwell, and I cannot bear either."

"No, I can prove I'm telling the truth! Alec, just look at it." She held the shirt out towards him, desperate to make him see. "The dates—"

"Enough!" he shouted, freezing her in place. Tears stung her eyes and she tried so hard to breathe, but it was impossible. "Enough," he said again, softer. "I will not tell anyone of what happened here, but I...I must go." This was it. He was saying goodbye.

He turned and strode out of the gazebo and into the rain, shrugging his coat on as he went. She rushed out onto the covered porch, watching him go. He didn't even bother with his horse, leaving Apollo in the small barn.

"Alec, please!" she yelled over the downpour. Tears streamed down her face, and she felt a sharp, searing pain in her chest, a pain that somehow hurt everywhere, all at once, sending shards of glass into her blood and making her vision tunnel. He slowed and turned his head, as if he was going to look at her, but he stopped himself, his shoulders tensing, and he continued on.

Elle sank to her knees on the cold, wet wood, still clutching the *Warped Tour* shirt in her numb fingers. She cried like she hadn't cried since her parents' deaths. Great, racking sobs that made her bones hurt from the force of them. She cried, and cried, and cried.

He'd walked away.

Chapter 21

Alec walked through the woods, walked away from the woman he loved more than he ever thought possible. Rain fell heavily upon his head, but he didn't care, could barely even feel it, really. Everything was numb. His body, his mind.

His heart was the only thing that wasn't numb. It was aching as if it had been crushed, and yet it was also screaming at him to turn around, to go back and forget what she had said, to pretend it had never happened.

I'm from the future.

He shook his head at the absurdity. There were only two explanations: one was that she had made up a ridiculous story to avoid marrying him, which honestly...hurt. Or two: she was unwell. He swallowed hard at the lump in his throat at the thought. He'd seen what happened to those who saw things that weren't there, who believed things that couldn't possibly be rooted in reality. He knew where they went and how they were treated.

Alec stopped walking and titled his head back to the sky, bellowing in frustration and pain and confusion and the utter, unbearable feeling of loss. Loss of the woman he loved, loss of the life he had seen in his mind's eye, a life filled with happiness and laughter, a family. He closed the thoughts off, the pain too much. How could it hurt so badly to lose something you never actually had?

He'd told himself not to look back as he walked away, but he hadn't the willpower to manage it, and he'd glanced over his shoulder just before the gazebo was obscured from view. The image of Elle was seared in his memory: crumbled on her knees on the steps of the gazebo, looking so utterly *broken*. The thought of it sent a stab of pain through his chest. He ached seeing her like that, knowing that he was the cause of it.

But he couldn't possibly be expected to remain, to not think her mad. He would be true to his word, he would never speak of what had happened in that gazebo, would never tell a soul of her claims. He wouldn't see her carted off somewhere or have the MacTavish family's name tarnished. He would confide in Jocelyn and Callum only, so that they may handle things quietly and appropriately. He could offer assistance. He still had colleagues he could reach out to for aid who would be discrete.

But...something wasn't quite right—besides the obvious. Something in the back of his mind was screaming that the situation wasn't making proper sense, that he was missing something vital. Alec took several deep breaths, forcing himself to think about this logically. He called on his training and experience as a physician. He'd had to learn to separate his emotions from himself, to look at things critically and logically and scientifically without letting fear or worry or sympathy get in the way.

Alec staggered to a fallen tree slightly off of the path and sat down heavily. The branches above him shielded him slightly from the rain and he exhaled as he cleared his mind. He rested his elbows on his knees and forced his mind to look at everything with a cold detachment.

Elle had never exhibited any signs of her mental faculties being altered in any way. In fact, she was extremely intelligent and was incredibly adept at adapting to situations. Her behavior was odd at times, of course, and she seemed more...forward thinking than most women, it was true, but that was hardly proof that she...that she was from...He couldn't even force himself to think the ridiculous words!

She had obviously created the ridiculous lie in order to avoid marrying him, but that didn't make plausible sense, did it? She could simply have said no, could have made hundreds of other excuses if he pressed for a reason: she hated him, she had no desire to marry, she couldn't give him heirs, she had murdered someone and was a fugitive from the gallows, she was secretly in love with Isa and they planned to run off to the islands together. Any of them made far more sense.

So, why *this* particular lie? What was the point?

And, further, if she was lying simply to push him away, why had she been so desperate for him to believe her? She'd looked so panicked, her eyes wide and almost unseeing, her breaths quick and shallow, as if she couldn't get air into her lungs properly. She had clung to the garment like it was the only thing keeping her from drowning, like it was the absolute proof that she needed if he would just look at it.

But he hadn't. Of course he hadn't. And a part of him felt as if that refusal was a betrayal. He forced that thought away, not wanting to look at it too closely.

So, the idea that it had been a lie didn't make any sense, which meant that the only explanation was that she was ill. A profound sadness settled into his bones. To see the woman he loved struggling with such a thing...

But then a tiny voice whispered across the back of his mind, like the softest caress: *What if there is a third option?*

He pressed the heels of his hands into his eyes, pressing hard until stars burst across the darkness. *Proof.* The word stuck in his mind like a carriage wheel stuck in mud. All physicians were at their hearts scientists, and scientists sought out truths by finding *proof.* And she felt as if she had it. She'd told him she could prove to him that she was telling the truth...He pinched the bridge of his nose, halting the thoughts.

"No, this is lunacy, I can't even entertain the idea..."

And yet a small ember of hope began to glow in the center of his chest, an ember he couldn't explain and refused to give any credence to, but it was there all the same. Even if she believed something so...insane, could he not love her anyway? Love her through anything and everything? Isn't that what being in love truly meant?

He opened his eyes and stared at the trees, but not really seeing them. No, he was seeing Elle.

Elle spilling his drink on him the first night they met. Elle utterly annoyed by his presence when every other lady would be flattered and think themselves blessed. Elle challenging him at every turn, that look of quiet defiance in her eyes. Elle laughing and scheming with his father. Elle dancing with him, the way her body moved like smoke. Elle kissing him. Elle touching him. Elle wrapping her arms around his neck as their bodies were closer than any two people had ever been. Elle saying that she loved him with such reverence. Elle. Elle. Elle.

She was all he could see.

She was all he wanted.

And then, he was up and running back towards the clearing, his father's voice echoing in his mind: *you've found someone to teach you how.*

Elle had taught him how to be happy, how to love, how to truly feel again.

Perhaps, she could teach him to believe the unbelievable as well.

Elle didn't know how long she sat there. Long enough that the rain had seeped into her bones, that the cold had made her fingers and toes numb. And still, she sat, clutching the t-shirt and trying to breathe around the ache in her chest, the utter brokenness she felt. Hollow. That was it. She felt as if someone had opened her chest and scooped everything out. She was just a shell now, empty and hollow and broken.

She stared at the steps below, barely seeing anything.

Two boots suddenly appeared, and then a hand reached for her. She jerked her head up in shock and confusion.

Alec.

He'd come back.

But she didn't let herself believe, didn't let herself hope.

She eyed him warily. Had he come back to try to take her to some mental institution? A dirty asylum where they would try to lobotomize her or something? Or maybe to tie her to a pyre and burn her like a witch, though he admittedly didn't really strike her as the witch-burning type.

He was soaking wet, damp hair falling into his eyes. He pushed it back and held her gaze. He looked skeptical and confused, but there was also a spark of hope.

"Show me," he said simply, voice gruff. His hand was still there before her, waiting. She reached out and took it, the life raft she so desperately needed. He pulled her up and led her back inside.

He released her and strode across the small space, grabbing the stool that she used when painting—that they had apparently tumbled into and sent flying into the corner at some point—and pulling it to the middle of the room. He sat heavily, crossed his arms, took a deep breath, and looked at her expectantly. She was seventy-eight percent sure she was going to puke. Before, it had been a desperate panic to get him to listen, to stop him from walking away. Now, she could actually think about what she was doing, what she needed to do and say and how to explain, and, yep, she was definitely going to puke.

This is what you wanted, she told herself. *You wanted to explain it to him, wanted to share with him, wanted to make him understand.*

So, she pushed her shoulders back and forced herself to do it. She moved towards him and held up the shirt she'd been clutching all this time. She shook it out, holding it by the sleeves. The familiar yellow arrow and red *Van's* circle was printed in the center.

"Nothing in this time could possibly look like this. We call it a t-shirt. They're made with big machines that haven't been invented yet, and the design is put on by a special printing process. This one is from a concert festival I went to a while back." He simply stared, jaw working. She took a deep breath and turned it around. "Look at the dates," she said quietly.

There, on the back, was a list of cities and dates of shows. Granted, this was from a few tours ago, but still, the dates all began with *20,* so it was as good as anything else she could show him. His brow furrowed. He reached out and took the shirt, studying the back closely. He ran his fingers over the letters, pulling them away and rubbing his thumb and forefinger together, as if trying to figure out what the material was, if it had come off on his hands. He paled slightly but continued staring. She knew he was trying to process, his analytical mind doing its best to make sense of what he was seeing, though it was probably screaming that all of this was impossible. She went to the chest and grabbed her wallet, phone, and tablet. Juggling everything, she turned back, coming to stand in front of him, but leaving space between them, treating him a bit like a wild animal. She fished out her driver's license.

"This is what we use for identification. It has my name and birthdate—1994. And see, the date the card was issued: 2018. Oh and here: money. Look at the dates on the bills." He took everything she handed him, studying it all quietly, his green eyes grave and serious. She waited, not wanting to push too much on him too fast, but her heart was pounding in her ears, her entire body trembling slightly. Could he possibly believe her? Could he accept everything? She decided the tablet and phone may be too much just yet and set them aside. *Baby steps, Elle. He's trying.*

He was quiet for a long, long time. She chewed on her thumbnail and desperately wanted to ask him what he thought, tell him anything and everything he wanted to know, but she forced herself to remain silent. She needed to let him absorb everything, sort through whatever he needed to, on his own. He came back, and for now, that was more than she could have hoped for.

"I...I don't..." He scrubbed a hand over his face. It was shaking slightly. Elle felt a pang. She knew it was too much to put on him, but she was desperate for him to believe her, for him to understand that she wasn't crazy. "I don't understand how this is possible," he said quietly.

"Neither do we," she said quickly, relief that he was still sitting here and even trying to talk to her about this flooding through her like a tidal wave, "not really. There are these trees—"

He jerked his head up. "We?"

Oh shit. Jocy's secret wasn't hers to tell.

"Jocelyn and Callum know the truth," she hedged. "You can talk to them about it if it will help you, uh, come to terms." She swallowed hard. "But no, we don't know why it happened or how. There are two trees deep in the forest on the other side of the property and they're...fuck, they're magic, I guess is the only way to explain it. I stepped through them, passed out, and when I woke up, I was here."

"From...the future," he said, a bit unsure, as if the words felt strange on his tongue. Hell, they probably did. Time travel wasn't a big topic of discussion in this time as far as she knew. Wells hadn't even written *The Time Machine* yet—she'd checked not long after arriving.

"Yes. Alec, I know it sounds absolutely insane, but I swear to you that I'm not crazy. It's the truth. I will show you every shred of evidence I have, will tell you anything you need to hear. I just...I need you not to leave. Please. I need you to believe me. Or believe enough *in* me not to turn away."

He met her gaze and reached out a hand, surprising her. He gently cradled her face, stroking her cheekbone with his thumb. His other hand shot out and gripped her hip, tugging her forward and into the space between his thighs. She went boneless when he pressed his lips to hers. It wasn't the frantic, carnal kisses they'd shared earlier. This was a deep, slow kiss meant to communicate words that couldn't be said. She kissed him back, trying not to cry and failing miserably. He pulled back and rested his forehead against hers, gently wiping her tears away with his thumbs.

"I...believe you," he whispered. "It makes no sense and part of my mind is screaming that I'm mad for even entertaining the thoughts, but the other part has always relied on facts and what you've shown me cannot be explained any other way. "So," he let out a shuddering breath, "the only explanation is that you are telling the truth."

"'When you have eliminated all which is impossible, then whatever remains, however improbable, must be the truth'," Elle recited quietly, pulling back to meet his gaze and brush the hair from his forehead.

"I...well, yes, that's wonderfully put," he said, brow furrowed, but the tiniest hint of a smile curling his lips on one side.

She laughed lightly. "I can't take credit. A beloved detective in a series of books will say it one day."

He shook his head slowly. "That will take quite a bit of getting used to, I imagine." He exhaled roughly and glanced out the window. "We should get back. I'm sure everyone is quite worried...and most likely quite scandalized by our extended absence." He leaned in and kissed her again, and she twined her hands around the back of his neck, fingers playing with the strands of his hair.

"Well, we did do a few very scandalous things out here, Lord Kentworth," she agreed, breathless, remembering in great detail all the scandalous things, wanting to repeat them again all night long. He groaned lightly in the back of his throat and gave her one more quick kiss before pulling away. "Thank you," she said softly. "Thank you for coming back, thank you for trying to believe me."

"I'm not whole without you, Eleanor. If you say you have traveled through time to be here, then I will thank whatever magic brought you back. I cannot imagine my life without you, and while I can't lie and say I understand how this is possible in the slightest, I...don't care." He tucked a lock of hair behind her ear. "I will try to accept everything, but until then, I will trust in you. And that will be enough."

Elle leaned in and kissed him, eyes watery.

"I love you, Alec."

"And I you." He sighed and a hint of a smile curved his lips. "Now, as lovely as I would look in your dress, I believe you should probably give me back my shirt instead."

"Oh, Elle, we were so worried!" Jocy cried when they walked back into the study. She rushed forward and pulled Elle into a fearsome hug before holding her at arms' length, looking at her in that motherly way, searching for any signs that she was hurt. "You're alright?"

"I'm alright, I promise." She glanced between Alec, Jocy, and Callum. "I, uh, told him. About me," she added hastily, "about...where I'm from."

Jocy's eyes flew wide and Callum pinned Alec with a hard stare, waiting to see how he'd responded, Alec imagined. And Alec didn't blame him. He knew that Callum loved Elle and would be ready to defend her and do whatever it took to keep her safe— including tossing Alec out on his arse.

Alec stepped forward and intertwined his fingers with Elle's. She let out a breath. Had she been holding it? Worried that he'd already changed his mind and was ready to run screaming for the hills? He squeezed her hand lightly, trying to reassure her. He didn't understand much of anything that was going on, and could still scarcely believe that he was entertaining the notion that Elle had come from a different *time*, but he knew that he loved her more than his own life and would stand by her no matter what.

Callum nodded, taking this as a sign that Alec could be trusted and allowed to continue breathing air. A smile spread over his face, his eyes crinkling. Jocelyn smiled widely as well, laying a hand on Callum's arm. They shared a look, somehow communicating without saying a single word.

Callum said quietly, "you're sure, mo grá?"

"I am."

Callum crossed to the door and closed it quietly, turning the lock with a loud click that Alec tried not to believe was ominous. Jocy gestured towards the sofa.

"Jocy, you don't have to—" Elle rushed, looking upset.

"I do, Elle. If it will help you, help Alec and you be together, then yes, I do. And I'm happy to."

Alec was confused, but he suspected that would just be his normal state of being for quite a while, so he made his way across the room, Elle in tow, and sat. Jocy sat on one of the chairs and Callum stood behind her, a protective and supportive hand on her shoulder. She smiled up at him, patting his hand, before turning back to Alec.

"Alec, I know all of this must be extremely difficult for you to understand or believe, but I assure you that it's all true." She took one quick, deep breath. "I know that it is because, well, *I'm* not from here either."

Alec blinked. Was she saying...*No.* There was no way...

"Are you saying that...that you, um, *traveled* as well?" Alec cut his eyes to Callum, who nodded. He looked as if he completely trusted and believed in what Jocelyn was saying. Could Alec hope to one day have that kind of surety about all of this?

"Aye, Alec," Callum said with a knowing smile. "I do no' question it. My family has long believed in the tales of magic in those woods," he said, tilting his head towards the window, "and we believe that it was that magic that brought them here, brought them *back*."

Alec inhaled sharply but tried to remain calm. Then his brows drew down.

"My mother, she told me the stories of the woods. Fairies and magic and strange things happening...It's all real?"

"Well, I doona know if it is fairies or no', but there is magic, of that I am certain."

"And," he swallowed hard, shifting his gaze back to Jocy, "*when* did you come from?" Alec asked quietly, feeling incredibly silly and glancing to the door to be sure that no one had heard him ask such a thing.

"It was the year 2000 when I left."

"And you came from the year...2020?" Alec asked, turning to Elle. He could scarcely wrap his mind around that. He'd been so shocked by the idea of time travel and everything else, that he hadn't actually thought about the passage of time itself, of how far in the future Elle—and Jocelyn apparently—had lived. He suddenly wondered what that world might look like, what kind of advancements had been made over the centuries, how everyone lived then.

"Yes," Elle said, squeezing his hand. Jocy and Callum didn't seem to notice or care that he and Elle were being so forward, but he supposed in light of everything else, the two of them holding hands wasn't much of a shock.

And so, they spent hours answering every question Alec had, and giving him time to just be silent and think through everything they'd told him when he needed it. When the sun had long since set, Alec felt...alright. He still had to force himself to accept everything every few minutes it seemed, had to tell his analytical mind that not everything could be explained—Elle said things like "relativity" and "wormholes" and "tachyons," but it was all close to gibberish to him. Even still, he found himself feeling surprisingly ok, all things considered.

"Are you sure you're alright?" Elle asked for what seemed like the hundredth time that day. Alec felt exhausted down to his soul, but as he reached out and cupped her cheek, felt her lean into his touch, he knew it was all worth it. He understood now how much of herself she'd had to hold back from him, how much he still had to learn. How much he still had to love.

"Well, that depends," he said, and her face pinched with worry, paling slightly. Ever since she told him the truth, it seemed as if she'd been holding her breath, just waiting for him to decide it was too much and run from her—again. He almost winced. Of course, no one would possibly blame him for such a reaction, but he still felt a pang of regret and guilt. He'd hurt her when he'd turned away from her, and that was something he would spend the rest of his life making up for.

"On what?" she asked worriedly.

"On if you've changed your answer to my question from this morning." She relaxed, lips curling upward. She feigned a bout of forgetfulness, tapping her chin thoughtfully.

"Hmm, did you ask me something? I forget..."

Alec pulled her to him and pressed his lips to hers, loving the feel of her smile against his mouth, of the way her body melted into his.

"Marry me, Eleanor," he whispered against her lips. "Please."

She pulled away and studied him for a long moment. "Are you sure? I know all of this…Well, I know it can't be easy and if you need time to really think about it, to make sure you're really—"

He cut her off with another kiss. When he pulled away, he brushed a curl from her face before cradling her face and making her hold his gaze, gently stroking her cheekbones with his thumbs.

"Eleanor Montgomery, there are many things that I am going to need time to process fully, things that I will be unsure of for quite some time. But my love for you, the way my soul aches for yours, the fact that a world in which we are not together is not a world I can even imagine, let alone deign to live in—*those* are not among them. Those things are as certain and sure to me as my own name."

Her eyes were glassy and she gave him a smile that made his heart skip a beat inside his chest.

"Well, that was a hell of a speech."

"Of course it was," he said with his customary arrogance that she loved to loathe. "Now," he brushed his lips against hers so softly it was almost the ghost of a kiss, "will you marry me?" he breathed against her mouth.

"Yes. Of course I will, you idiot."

He pulled back and quirked a brow. "I do not think it bodes well if you insult me the very moment we become engaged."

"I'll take my chances," she replied, throwing her arms around his neck and pulling him hard against her, kissing him in a way that stole his breath and scorched him to his soul.

Chapter 22

"It's just up ahead," Elle told Alec as they strolled through the cursed woods. Though she supposed that wasn't really a fair moniker now. The woods hadn't really cursed her after all. They had given her a new family, the love of her life, everything she'd always wanted but had never quite found back home. She was still a little pissed it had taken her from the land of flushing toilets and Pop Tarts, but she figured it was a pretty decent trade off in the end. She smiled at Alec and he caught her glance.

"What are you grinning about?"

"Oh just thinking about the way I woke you up..."

Alec stutter stepped and she laughed loudly, the sound echoing among the trees. They'd formally announced their engagement and Jocy was already well into the planning of ceremonies for both Elle and Alec, and Rose and Percy. They'd be officially married in a few months, but Alec had been all too happy to say fuck etiquette—the two of them had spent almost every night together over the past two weeks. No one at Pembroke seemed to care, and if rumors were spreading about the two of them being together before they were married, well, none of them could really give a fuck less.

Elle's lips curled as she recalled that morning, kissing down his stomach while he dozed, him waking groggily just as she closed her lips around his cock. The adorable sleepy look had disappeared within seconds as she held his gaze, twirling her tongue around the head before sucking him deep.

"Christ, Eleanor!" he'd rasped, arching his hips off the bed, sending him deeper into her throat. She didn't mind, merely moaned in pleasure, and sucked him harder. He tangled a hand in her hair, and she licked and sucked and driven him crazy. When she'd reached downward and began to rub herself, his eyes had bulged. "You aren't...are you..." After that, words had failed him and it was just a stream of groans and grunts until they both came hard, her against her own fingers and him on her tongue. It had been amazing and now, she longed to do it again, had half a mind to drop to her knees right here, but she stopped herself. *Barely.* They were out here for a reason, after all. She needed to behave...for now.

Overall, he had taken the time traveling news better than she could have expected. It was a bit rocky there at the beginning, but really, she hadn't taken it all that well at first either. He would retreat into his thoughts sometimes and she could see his mind working, trying to make facts and science as he understood them make everything make sense, but he would always come back out again, always assure her that he wasn't going anywhere.

And he loved asking her questions about the future, particularly fascinated with the medical and scientific discoveries that would occur over the next couple of centuries. Elle wished she knew more about all of that so she could give him more of what he craved, but he seemed perfectly happy to hear about the state of the world, methods of travel, sports—anything and everything. He loved looking through her photo albums, particularly the ones of her in barely-there bikinis on spring break trips, and they would sit and listen to music together for hours. He was fond of The Beatles, Eric Clapton, and Ed Sheeran.

"Oh of course the Brit is a fan of the Brits," she'd teased, rolling her eyes.

"I cannot help it that we are—and remain, it seems—superior," he'd teased right back.

"Do I need to remind you of how the Revolutionary War turned out, Lord Kentworth? It literally just happened like, yesterday." He'd launched himself at her across the floor of the gazebo then, tickling her until she was breathless and then doing other things that left her equally breathless for entirely different reasons.

He pulled her to him now, yanking her from her thoughts. He pressed his body firmly against hers and curled his fingers into her hips.

"Mmm, I believe I've forgotten what happened. Could you remind me?"

Elle smiled and moved her hand between them, brushing her fingers along his erection, almost purring in delight and desire. They had been all but insatiable since that first day in the gazebo, and she didn't see how that could possibly change anytime soon. She wanted him—desperately—what felt like all day, every day. He moaned quietly and bit at her lower lip just as she began to unlace his pants, deciding that their research expedition could wait after all, but then he stiffened and jerked his head up.

"Do you...do you feel that?" he asked, brows furrowed. He swung his gaze around them.

"Feel what—" She broke off when she felt it too. The rippling static electricity shivering up her spine. "Oh my God," she whispered. She hadn't realized how close to the twisted trees they'd been, but now she could see them just around a small thicket of briars. Alec moved towards them, almost as if he were in a trance.

"This is it, isn't it? This is the place. I feel it, just as you described." His voice was filled with wonder. He reached out towards the carving on one tree and Elle's heart stopped beating. If they were feeling the weird static, then it meant the magic was firmly in the "on" position. What would happen if he...

"Alec, no!" she screamed, flying at him. He grunted when she collided bodily with him, knocking him off balance. She channeled her inner Bobby Boucher and took him to the ground, knowing she'd only been able to do so because she'd taken him by surprise.

"Elle, what the devil is wrong with you?" he demanded as they tumbled through the leaves and underbrush.

"You can't go near it. It'll take you...fuck, I don't know where it'll take you!"

He sat up, that analytical look in his green eyes, nearly the same color as the leaves around them, and she ran her hands through her hair. What in the fuck did this mean? What was going on?

"You said you've come here before, since you arrived?" She nodded. "And Jocelyn and Callum as well. They've visited." Another nod. "And none of you have ever felt this...this strange shocking sensation?"

"No, never. I felt it before I was brought back, but not since then. We assumed it was a one-way door." His eyes widened and he smiled.

"Then you could go back," he said simply. "Elle, you could go home."

You could go home.

Alec's words had echoed through her mind as they made their way out of the woods. She couldn't stop herself from looking over her shoulder, as if the twisted trees would somehow be following them like the villain in a horror movie.

You could go home.

It kept repeating over and over in her head, so loudly she could barely even keep up with the conversation after they rushed into the house and told Jocy and Callum what had happened.

"How is this possible?" Jocelyn asked. All eyes turned on Elle and she realized the question had been directed at her. She shrugged and chewed on her thumbnail. They went around and around, theorizing why it was finally working, wondering what it might mean, arguing over what they should do, but Elle couldn't focus on it. Her mind was a million miles away. A million miles, and about two hundred years.

When she'd first been brought back, all she wanted was to go home. She'd begged for it, bargained for it, prayed for it despite the fact that her praying was admittedly rusty. But now? Now, everything she loved was *here*. Why was she finally being given the chance to go home—possibly anyway, seeing as how they couldn't even be sure when the doorway might spit her out again—now? When things finally felt right after so, so long of everything feeling off.

And yet, a part of her still longed for her own time, for the only life she'd known, the one she should have had. Not the one with Ashton, of course, but the one in the time she was meant to be in, the one where she had her job and her house and Starbucks and the internet.

Why was the doorway suddenly working again, when it had had the *Sorry, We're Closed* sign firmly in place for decades? Was this all some cruel joke? Callum thought that the magic gave them what they needed, took them where they were meant to be. So, did that mean that she wasn't actually meant to be here? *No, no, no.* She knew that being with Alec was so fucking right, she just *knew* it in one of those ways you couldn't explain, something so deeply rooted in your very being that there was no questioning it.

She rubbed her temples, trying to think of everything they'd discussed during her research. They believed the magic had given them each what they'd been asking for, whether outright or in their hearts...

She jerked her head up.

"What were you thinking about?" she asked Alec, clearly interrupting but not caring.

"What do you mean?" he frowned.

"When you felt the shocks, the weird tingling sensation, what were you thinking about?" Her cheeks heated remembering what they had been doing the instant he'd felt it. "Other than the, uh, obvious," she added hastily and giving him a pointed look.

His lips curled into a lazy, crooked smile that looked so damned good on him it should be illegal.

"Other than the obvious..." he echoed, his eyes skating down her body. Callum cleared his throat and Alec shook himself. "Apologies," he said with a sheepish grin. "I was thinking..." his brow furrowed, "well, I was thinking about how badly I wished I could find a way to make the doorway work for you again, so that you could go home."

That must be it! The magic was responding to Alec's need to give Elle what she wanted. Or what he thought she wanted. What she maybe wanted? God, she didn't know and her head was spinning and she wanted nothing more than to drown out all of her whirling thoughts with some really good tequila right about now.

They continued the discussion for what seemed like hours, maybe days, and Elle's mind wandered. She thought of home, wondering what had happened to her house. Had it been sold? Was it still just sitting empty since she was probably listed as a missing person? What about her things? Probably in a storage container somewhere. She thought of all the comforts she'd been missing: cars and power and central heating and air; online shopping and fast food and the overall emphasis on personal hygiene in the world; television and music and her right to vote. She thought of Ashton, of her friends—or acquaintances or whatever they might be, really—of her clients. If she did go back, how would she even explain her absence without sounding like she needed a little T-O in a facility somewhere?

"—nor?"

She looked up to find everyone staring at her again. It clearly wasn't the first time they'd said her name.

"Sorry, what?"

"It's a risk, but is it one you're willing to take?" She knew what they were saying now, they'd been over and over it: it was risky because there was no guarantee that it would take her back to her own time.

"I..." Was she? At the thought of leaving Alec, her heart clenched painfully.

"Elle, it's what you want, isn't it? What you've wanted since you were brought here? You could go back where you belong," Alec said softly, sitting beside her and taking her hands in his.

"Why would you want that?" she asked, yanking her hands away. He'd been talking all day about her leaving, about her going back where she belonged, and she was so exhausted and confused and hungry—ok, hangry, really—that she just snapped. "Why are you so eager to send me away? Are you really totally fine with never seeing me again?" she demanded, standing up as rage burned her chest. He reared back, blinking rapidly.

"Elle, Wh—"

"No. No, this is bullshit, Alec! I thought you loved me, I thought you wanted to marry me. Why are you so ok with me leaving, after everything we've been through?" Beneath the anger, there was pain, and it made her voice break slightly at the end.

Alec...smiled at her. That stupid, perfect, charming, melt-the-panties-right-off-your-ass-cheeks smile that she hated and loved and wanted to smack off of his face.

"Why the fuck are you smiling?!" She actually stamped her foot like a child.

"You really haven't been paying attention to anything we've been saying, have you?" He rose and slid his hands along her cheeks, tunneling his long fingers into her hair. "Eleanor, if you think I could possibly live without you, then I have done an abysmal job of showing you just how much I love you and shall strive to remedy that for the rest of my life."

"Then why—"

"I'm coming with you, of course."

Now Elle blinked, unable to process the words.

"You...you would come with me? You would leave everything?"

"Without a moment's hesitation."

Elle let herself imagine it. Alec with her in 2020, learning to drive a car, watching Netflix, spending hours reading medical journal articles. And she could see it. She could see it all so clearly it took her breath away. Whatever other obstacles there would be if he went back with her—and good lord would there be obstacles—she didn't care. They would figure it out because they would be together and really, that's all that mattered.

"Elle, I love you, in this time or any other. So long as I am where you are, then that is where I am meant to be." He brushed hair away from her face and kissed her.

Pulling back, he smiled at her shell-shocked expression and shook his head ruefully.

"So, when are we leaving, love?"

Chapter 23

Alec laid with his head in Elle's lap as she gently ran her fingers through his hair. He hummed in contented pleasure, adoring when she did that. He adored anything that involved her hands on him, truth be told. Gentle caresses or playful touches, wiping dirt from his cheek after doing *yard work* as she called it, or scratching her nails down his back in the throes of passion, leaving bloody marks that he wore as badges of honor.

They lounged on a quilt, enjoying the warm evening air, light, cool breezes rustling the leaves every so often and washing the scent of Elle's perfume over him. She leaned back on one hand, continuing to run her fingers through his hair with the other, humming quietly. He reached up and grabbed her hand, bringing it to his mouth so that he could kiss her knuckles and then the gold ring that never failed to make his heart leap. His wife. She was his *wife,* and that knowledge still seemed like a dream some days. He didn't know what he'd done to deserve this life, as strange as it was at times—time traveling certainly made their lives far from normal, to be sure—but he thanked God for it every day. He wouldn't change a single thing, would go through everything all over again if he had to if it meant ending up here with Elle in his arms and his heart—and his bed.

His blood heated at the mere thought of her in their bed. *Dear God*, the things the woman could do with her body, the things he'd experienced, the things they'd taught each other. He shifted his hips as his cock stiffened at the mere thought of it all. Images of her from that very morning, hands bound with a silk scarf and secured to their bed posts, her hips rolling and head thrashing, begging him to *"stop teasing and fuck me, damn it!"* His lips curled at the memory even as a tremor of desire ran through his body.

"Are you cold?" she asked.

"No, I'm alright," he promised.

The sun had nearly set, and the sky looked like one of Elle's paintings, streaks of deep pink and orange being chased by the darker purple and blue of true night.

"The moon is beautiful tonight," she said quietly. He shifted his gaze, staring at the orb already beginning to glow a bright grayish gold against the fading light.

"Men really go there?" Alec asked. She'd told him all about the wonders of space travel, but he could scarcely believe it. It was still hard for him to wrap his mind around much of what she'd told him of the future: great wars and terrifying weapons that could decimate entire countries; communication devices that could span oceans; medical miracles that would allow a surgeon to replace one person's failing heart with another healthy one, or to operate on a child while still within its mother's womb. Sometimes, he had to sit with the knowledge quietly for a time, and she always kissed him softly and let him be to work through everything in his own mind. Other times, he wanted nothing but to ask her endless questions, making her laugh.

He stared at the moon once more. Some things from her time, like automobiles and boats large enough to hold thousands upon thousands of people, or what she'd explained were called airplanes, weren't all that hard to imagine. The mechanics and physics of those made sense to him.

But humans traveling out among the stars? Impossible!

She laughed quietly. "Yep. July 16, 1969. The first man will walk on the moon and the entire world will watch with bated breath."

Alec sat up and turned to look at his wife. She looked beautiful, as she always did, with her hair in loose curls flowing down her back, her blue eyes looking brilliant as gemstones even in the fading daylight.

"Come here," he said softly. She didn't hesitate, just crawled into his lap, settling her knees on either side of his hips, her dress rucking up to reveal soft, bare thighs. He ignored the way she felt on top of him, ignored how his cock pulsed and the desperate need to take her right here in the garden. Well, he *mostly* ignored it anyway. He could scarcely keep the images of her twirling about the brass pole she'd had erected in one of the spare rooms in their wing from his mind. When he asked her what on earth the purpose was as he watched the workmen secure the thing in place a fortnight ago, she merely smiled that secretive, seductive smile of hers, the one that made his blood turn to fire in his veins, and told him she'd demonstrate soon.

And *dear God*, had she. He'd barely been able to remain in his chair as he watched her sway and twirl and wrap her body around the damned thing, moving like sin made flesh. Only his promise to sit until she was finished kept him in place, but once she was done, he'd flown to her, slamming his lips to hers before taking her hard against the wall until they were both nearly mindless.

It was his new favorite room in the entire manor.

She wrapped her arms around his neck and leaned in to kiss him softly.

"Are you sure you don't regret your choice?" he asked when she pulled away.

"This again?" she said with an amused smile. "No, Alec. I don't regret it, not at all. Sure, I still miss running water and Amazon Prime, but this is where I'm meant to be. This is where *we're* meant to be."

Alec thought back to the day she'd made the decision that they would remain in the past:

"When do you we leave, love?" he asked her. "I'll need a bit of time to get my affairs in order, to make sure all of my property and wealth transfers to Rosie and Percival for the time being—if that's alright with you, of course," he said to Callum and Jocy.

"Of course, if that's what you want, Alec," Jocy said softly. She looked both happy and heartbroken all at once.

"I can get everything sorted within the week, if that's your desire." He already had thoughts of how, with Callum's help, he could most likely make some of his land and wealth available to them in the future as well. He looked at Elle, waiting for her to speak. She still had that faraway look in her eyes, the one that told him she was only half hearing everything. Or half believing it anyway.

She looked incredulous when she finally focused, shaking her head.

"You've already thought this all through? But it only just happened, only just became a possibility."

Alec shrugged a shoulder. "There isn't anything to think through, not really. You are going, and I will always go where you go. Always. Whether it be across the earth or time. You are my home, Elle. Not a city or continent or even a century. You."

Her eyes watered and then her lips curled into the most beautiful smile he'd ever seen. He smiled back, his chest feeling like it would burst from joy at seeing her so happy.

"So, again I ask, when do you want to go?"

She kissed him hard, not caring that anyone was watching.

"Never," she said, pulling away. "We aren't going. We're staying here, Alec. We're staying with our family," she added, turning to smile at Callum and Jocy.

His brow furrowed. "What on earth are you talking about? Of course we're going. You—"

She slapped her hand over his mouth and his eyes flew wide with shock. No one had ever dared do such a thing.

"Shush," she commanded. "The fact that you were ready to give up everything for me, to change your entire life and leave everything you've ever known without hesitation, just to make me happy...." She shook her head a little and shifted her hand from his mouth to cup his cheek. "This is where we're supposed to be, Alec. I know it. I think the magic was giving us a choice, but I'm choosing to stay here. I'm choosing the life that I never expected, but wouldn't change for anything. I'm choosing the life I was meant to find."

Alec kissed her then, so deeply that Callum finally cleared his throat and he and Elle pulled apart, laughing. He and Jocy were smiling though, and she rushed forward and wrapped Elle in a hug, laughing through tears. Callum clapped Alec on the shoulder.

"Well, I canna say that I'm no' happy that you're staying. I would have felt as if I'd lost a daughter and a son in one fail swoop if you'd gone." Callum's voice was rough with emotion and Alec nodded, pulling him into a tight embrace.

Elle met his gaze over Callum's shoulder and he smiled. Alec would have been happy in the future with her, he had no doubts. He would be happy with her anywhere, in any time, but he was glad that they were remaining. Though he was ready to give up everything if it meant being with Elle and giving her everything she could ever want, he would have missed Callum and Jocelyn and Rosie. Hell, he would have even missed Percy who was fitting into the family effortlessly. Alec was glad to not be leaving his family—not one given to him by blood, but one made by fate.

But there were still matters to settle.

"If you want to stay, I'll stay," Alec said, grinning, "on one condition."

"Just one?" Elle said with a quirk of her brow.

"For now," he amended. "My condition is that you become Lady Kentworth as soon as humanly possible."

"Now that," Elle said before crossing to him, wrapping her arms around his neck and looking at him like he was the most perfect thing she'd ever seen, "I can get on board with."

Elle leaned in now and gently sucked on his bottom lip, pulling him from his memories with a low groan.

"I don't regret choosing this life, Alec. This is where we're meant to be. My life then hadn't felt complete in a long time. I had a beautiful home, a job I loved, and plenty of acquaintances, so I know that I was very lucky and that I couldn't really complain, but still—something was missing. I didn't always want to acknowledge it, but deep down, I was restless, searching for something without even realizing it." She kissed him again. "I was searching for you, Alec. I know that now, deep in my soul. So, no, I don't regret my choice."

His heart clenched. He'd been so worried that she would, that she would resent him in time, but she'd seemed genuinely happy with her choice and had been flourishing. After the MacTavish ball, almost everyone in the Ton had wanted to commission a portrait by Elle, and Alec's chest never failed to bow with pride when he saw one of her creations hanging on a wall somewhere. She'd painted a beautiful piece for Rosie and Percy to hang proudly in their new home, a stately manor on the far side of the MacTavish property. Everything seemed to be falling perfectly into place for everyone he cared about and he had never been happier.

Elle kissed him again and then pulled back to study him. It looked as if she were debating on saying something more. She licked her lips, almost...nervously?

"Though, I might regret staying here in the age before modern marvels like epidurals and teething rings...once the baby comes."

Alec's breath hitched and for a moment he was frozen. Had he heard her properly? Had she really said...

She nibbled her lip and held his gaze, that mischievous glint in her brilliant blue eyes. Then all at once, his chest swelled and his eyes watered and his entire body lit with a joy he never knew could exist. He loved Eleanor, loved her more than his own life, but the love he felt growing inside his chest was something entirely new, something entirely different. It was something he'd always wanted, but in an abstract, intangible way. He'd had a small glimpse of it with Colette, God rest her soul, but now, it was wholly real and wholly beautiful and wholly theirs, together.

Alec had to clear his throat several times before he could speak, and he felt a tear streak down his cheek. Elle's own eyes watered at the sight and she brushed it away with her thumb.

"Are you saying...You're...We're going to have a child?"

She nodded, laughing and crying at the same time.

"Are you...alright with that?"

"Alright? *Alright?* Elle, I..." He had no words. There would never be words to accurately express to her how much this meant to him, how happy he was. So, instead, he slammed his lips to hers, kissing her so deeply, so reverently, that soon they were both gasping for air. He shifted so that she was on her back on the blanket, and she quickly had his laces undone and his cock free. He tore what she'd explained were called panties from her body, pulling her dress up her and over her head in one quick, practiced movement. Neither one of them cared if anyone saw them, and the staff had come to expect to see the two of them *"going at it like rabbits all over the fucking place,"* as Elle had so eloquently put it.

"Alec," she breathed in that way that undid him. Part plea, part prayer, part demand. He wasted no time, moving to cover her body with his and sinking deep inside her with one long thrust of his hips. She cried out and arched up, and he balanced on his forearms as he began to move, deep measured thrusts as he kissed her lips and neck, as he whispered that he loved her, that she was the light of his existence, that she had made him the happiest man ever to live. He shifted, intertwining their fingers and raising their joined hands above her head. She squeezed his hands tightly, raising her hips in time with his thrusts, their bodies in perfect rhythm. They were made to fit together, made to move together, made for each other in all ways.

"I love you," she whispered against his neck. "I love you, I love you, I love you."

What felt like hours later, she came apart beneath him and he followed just after as the moon shone down on them.

They lay tangled together afterwards, staring up at the stars. Alec rested a protective hand on her still very-taut stomach, feeling such a strange, intense, unexplainable connection to the life inside, the one he and Elle had created.

"You know," he said softly, "my father told me that he wanted me to be happy when I first arrived for the season. I told him that I wasn't sure if I knew how to be." His chest clenched thinking of his father, a sudden swift pain at the thought that Jonathan would never meet his grandchild. "And he told me that I simply needed to find someone to teach me."

Elle looked up at him, lips curving in a slow, sweet smile. Alec let out a long, shuddering breath.

"Thank you, Eleanor. Thank you for teaching me how to be happy, how to love and be loved."

She traced her fingertips over his lips, a look of such love in her eyes that he could hardly stand it.

"I love you, Alexander Kentworth."

"And I love you, Eleanor Kentworth," he said with a slow, blissful grin.

She settled her head on his chest.

"If it's a boy, we'll name him Jonathan," she whispered. "I think he'd like that."

Alec's eyes burned and he squeezed her tighter against his side. "I think you're right, he would. Thank you, love."

Not long after that, her breaths became deep and even, her body relaxing against his. She'd fallen asleep in his arms. *Where she belongs*. Not for the first time, and certainly not the last, he was so profoundly grateful for whatever had brought her to him. Call it fate, call it magic, call it fairies. Whatever it was, he owed his entire happiness to it.

"Thank you," he whispered again, pressing his lips to her temple, his own eyes sliding closed. "Thank you, thank you, thank you."

Big shout outs, thank yous, fistbumps, and hugs:

- To my husband, family, and friends for always supporting this strange little hobby that I can't seem to quit.
- To my awesome PA, Laura, who rocks my socks on a daily basis and helps keep me (relatively) sane.
- To Lexie, Kayleigh, and Kala (ha - still funny) for always hyping me up, for always supporting me, for helping me make decisions because I am incapable of making them myself, and for the endless hilarious Book Babes chats. I love y'all so hard and would not be here without you.
- To my Pastry People – I love you all dearly and honestly probably would have given up by now if not for all the love and support y'all show me constantly.

More books by K.D. Miller:

ALL available on Amazon and included for FREE with Kindle Unlimited subscriptions!

New Adult Sci-Fi:

Titan Rising (Outliers Series, Book 1)

Titan Unleashed (Outliers Series, Book 2)

Titan Reckoning (Outliers Series, Book 3)

New Adult Fantasy:

Evansfire

Adult Paranormal Romance:

Dark Burning (Veracity of the Gods, Book 1)

Sweet Tempest (Veracity of the Gods, Book 2)

Red

Adult Contemporary Romance:

Carpe F*cking Diem

Puck the Holidays

Signed paperbacks available on my website!

www.kdmillerbooks.com

www.ingramcontent.com/pod-product-compliance
Lightning Source LLC
Chambersburg PA
CBHW021412010826
48972CB00014B/1775